THE GREATEST COURSE
THAT NEVER WAS

*The Secret of Augusta
National's Lost Course*

THE GREATEST COURSE
THAT NEVER WAS

*The Secret of Augusta
National's Lost Course*

J. MICHAEL VERON

Sleeping Bear Press

Sleeping Bear Press
310 North Main Street
P.O. Box 20
Chelsea, MI 48118
www.sleepingbearpress.com

Printed and bound in the United States.

10 9 8 7 6 5 4 3 2 1

Library of Congress Cataloging-in-Publication Data on file.
Veron, J. Michael
The greatest course that never was : the secret of Augusta National's
lost course / J.
Michael Veron.
p. cm.
ISBN 1-886947-92-9
Augusta National Golf Club—Fiction. 2. Golf courses—Fiction. 3.
California—Fiction. 4. Caddies—Fiction. I. Title
PS3572.E763 G5 1999
813'.6—dc21

2001020716

For Charles A. Murphy III, M.D.
When men have courage, anything is possible.

Preface

When Charley Hunter called me about this story a few months back, I thought he was pulling my leg. After all, solving the greatest golf mystery to come along in years—which he did with the story of Beau Stedman in *The Greatest Player Who Never Lived*—ought to be enough for one person. So I had trouble believing that Charley had wound up in the middle of another great story, particularly one that again involved Bobby Jones and the Augusta National Golf Club.

He finally convinced me, though, that his tale of a secret lost course was no joke. So I signed on again to help him bring this, our second story together, to the rest of the world.

I told Charley, though, that it was time he settled down and got on with the practice of law. For one thing, it appears that he's pretty good at it. Besides, it seems to me that enough is enough. If you want to be a lawyer, be a lawyer. If you want to be a golf historian, you better move to Golf House at the United States Golf Association Headquarters.

I don't know whether he'll listen to me, though. I guess only time will tell. More than anyone I've ever known, Charley seems to have a remarkable talent for finding himself in the middle of some pretty interesting situations.

I am grateful to Charley for involving me once again in his adventures. Working with him on *The Greatest Player Who Never Lived* was a great experience. Although we both knew how important it was to bring Beau Stedman's story to light, neither one of us anticipated the enthusiastic reaction that it has received. We both believe that the story of *The Greatest Course That Never Was* also fills an important gap in the historical record and have looked forward to sharing it with you.

I am also thankful once again for the loving care and support that Charley's latest golf discovery has received from everyone at Sleeping Bear Press, from Brian Lewis on down. They don't just publish books at SBP; it is perhaps more accurate to say that they give birth to them. From the editorial process through production and promotion, their love of what they do is evident and shines through once again, I hope, in the pages that follow. So I am compelled again to thank Brian, Adam Rifenberick, Danny Freels, Lynne Johnson, Jennifer Lundahl, Karmel Bycraft, and other members of the SBP gang too numerous to mention for their wonderful work in documenting Charley's efforts to bring this important part of golf history to light.

My dear friend Bo Links figures just as prominently here as he did with *The Greatest Player Who Never Lived*. A published author in his own right, Bo's unbounded enthusiasm for life in general (and for golf in particular) is very infectious and inspiring. He read the first draft of this book and offered his usual prescient vision of what could make it better. Anyone who has enjoyed Bo's novel, *Follow the Wind*, knows that his gift for storytelling is quite remarkable. Even I'm smart enough to heed whatever advice he gives.

My family plays a big part in this, too, as they always do. I still have my day job, so most of my writing is carved out of time they would otherwise have with me in the evenings and on weekends. But they never complain and remain encouraging at all times. It is a cliché to say that I could not do this without their patience. It is also true.

While I'm on the subject of my day job, I want to express my gratitude to Tammy Garbarino (my paralegal) and Yvonne Hankins (my secretary), who keep me organized so that I can make the best use of my time with Charley. They are better to me than I deserve.

My friend and fellow lawyer, Rick Norman, inspired me when he wrote *Fielder's Choice* a number of years back. In my first book, I failed to acknowledge that the example he set played a big role in my decision to work with Charley Hunter, and I want to correct that oversight here.

I am also grateful to Dave Kaspar, our PGA professional at my home course, the Lake Charles Country Club, for his firsthand knowledge about Byron Nelson. He was able to speak with Mr. Nelson to fill in some details about certain events that Moonlight had described to Charley. In addition, my friend Ron Prichard, who is a talented golf architect, provided me with valuable insight about the nuances of his profession and verified historical details about the lost course that Charley "rediscovered."

I have been and remain especially grateful to the many golf writers around the country who embraced *The Greatest Player Who Never Lived*. Perhaps the biggest thrill in all of this for Charley and me has been the chance to become colleagues of sorts with people whose work we have admired for so long. In championing our work, they have welcomed us into their midst with an openness that is probably unique among professions.

I cannot close without also thanking my good buddy Robert Dampf. He also read the first draft of this book and offered his thoughts and ideas, which I found valuable. More importantly, however, Robert also secures the tee times for our weekend golf games, and I can't risk losing my spot by failing to mention him by name.

Chapter 1

I HAD NOT expected to receive any mail on my first day at work. After all, the start of my career as a new lawyer at Butler & Yates was not exactly the talk of Atlanta. In fact, the firm wouldn't even mark the occasion until later in the summer—after I had presumably passed the bar exam.

Even then, it wouldn't exactly be a media event. Instead, there would be a couple hundred engraved cards mailed to friends of the firm announcing that Charles F. Hunter had become an associate there.

That's why the letter came as such a surprise. Outside of my family and a few close friends, I had no idea who would know—much less care—that I was here.

I also noticed that the postmark was two weeks old. The letter had apparently been lying around for a while. Whoever sent this little missive must have known for some time that I was coming to work at Butler & Yates.

To add to the mystery, it bore no return address. The only clue about its origin was the postmark from Augusta, Georgia, just a hundred miles or so east of Atlanta on Interstate 20.

Aside from its significance as the home of the Augusta National Golf Club and the Masters tournament, I couldn't think of any real connection that I had with Augusta.

I knew the letter wasn't from one of my classmates in law school. Almost all of them preferred E-mail to the U.S. Postal Service.

There wasn't anything distinctive about the envelope. It certainly wasn't Crane's Crest. Instead, it looked to be right out of a box of the cheap kind you could buy at the corner drugstore. Judging from its slightly yellow tint, the box had been on the shelf for a long time, too.

In contrast to the computer-generated addresses usually seen on mail received at a law firm, this envelope was addressed to me in a crude handwriting. That certainly added to my interest.

"Good morning."

My reverie was broken by the sound of a soft female voice. I looked up to see an auburn-haired 40-something secretary standing in my doorway with a cup of coffee in her hands. She had the no-nonsense look of someone who knew a whole lot more about the law business than I did.

"Sorry if I surprised you."

"Oh, no," I assured her.

She smiled at my obvious lie.

"I'm Gloria. I was here when you clerked last summer. I work for Mr. Guidry down the hall. He asked me to give you a hand if you need anything."

I suppose it was her way of letting me know that she hadn't

volunteered for the job. I could imagine that few secretaries relished the notion of transcribing the awkward dictation of a new lawyer, or otherwise nursing him through his early efforts at malpractice.

Nonetheless, I was pleased that Emile Guidry had taken an interest in me. He was one of the stars of the firm. Now in his mid-50s, Guidry was at the top of his game as a trial lawyer.

He had built his reputation by defending chemical companies against suits brought by individuals who claimed to have been poisoned by various kinds of noxious emissions. It was no easy trick convincing a jury that his Fortune 500 clients were the good guys, but he brought in one defense verdict after another. Usually, he was able to persuade the jury either that the plaintiff hadn't been hurt too badly or that his condition had some other cause. No one was better at medical causation than Emile Guidry.

Guidry was originally from New Iberia, a small town in South Louisiana. Perhaps its most noteworthy claim to fame was its close proximity to Avery Island, home of the McIlhenny family plantation where the world-famous Tabasco pepper sauce is produced. Guidry was a genuine Cajun or, as he preferred, "coonass."

When I first heard him use the term, I was a bit surprised. I had heard it used before, while I was in law school in Louisiana at Tulane, but always with somewhat derogatory connotations.

However, I had never been altogether sure what it meant, so I asked. Guidry said that it was a slang word for Cajun. He then explained that, like most colorful references to race or nationality, "coonass" was either a term of endearment or an insult, depending on who said it to whom—and how much alcohol had been consumed at the time. I asked him where the term came from. "You don't want to know," he laughed, and I knew it wouldn't do any good to ask again.

I had first gotten to know Guidry when he asked me to draft a research memorandum for him on the recovery of nonpecuniary damages for breach of contract. I busted my tail on it, and it came out well. It was the high point of my budding professional career when he called me in to compliment me on it.

"This is a good piece of work, Charley. I can see why you made the law review."

Since it was my first research assignment outside of law school, I was thrilled by his approval. Guidry was confirming for the first time that what I had learned in class was transferable to the real world.

He gave me several more research assignments during the course of my clerkship. I must have passed muster as a law clerk, because now he wanted to put me under his wing. Having his secretary check on me was a good sign. He knew better than I that you can only learn so much in law school. I had years of on-the-job training ahead of me before I'd be able to do all the things real lawyers do. An old hand like Gloria could teach me a lot of things my law professors couldn't.

Holding up the mysterious envelope, I said to Gloria, "I've already gotten my first piece of mail."

My ragtag little trophy obviously didn't impress her. "Maybe it's your first big case," she said in a clearly facetious tone.

She then excused herself to finish typing a brief, and I turned my attention once again to the envelope. Tearing it open, I found a clipping of an obituary from the *Augusta Chronicle*. It read:

George "Chico" Carter

George "Chico" Carter passed away yesterday, May 24, at his home in Augusta after a long illness. He was 86.

Mr. Carter was a lifelong resident of Augusta. He retired from the Augusta National Golf Club, where he worked for many years as a caddie master. He was a member of the Knights of St. Peter Claver and the Hip-Hop Social Club. He is survived by five children, eleven grandchildren, and three great-grandchildren.

Funeral arrangements are made through Thompson Funeral Home. There will be a rosary tomorrow at 7:00 P.M. and a funeral mass at Sacred Heart Catholic Church on Friday at 2:00 P.M.

The family has requested that memorial donations be made to the American Cancer Society and the Sacred Heart Altar Fund.

I had no idea why someone would want to send me this obituary. I noticed a small slip of paper that was also in the envelope. I pulled it out and looked at it. It consisted of only two words, written in the same crooked hand as the address on the envelope. The note read: "It's time." It was unsigned.

Time for what? As far as I could tell, I had no connection whatsoever to George "Chico" Carter or his family. Whoever sent this couldn't have expected me to attend the funeral; the clipping was over two weeks old. Someone thought it was important nonetheless to let me know that Mr. Carter had passed on to his great reward.

That made me a little uncomfortable. Getting an obituary in the mail wasn't exactly the bright note on which I had hoped to start my new career. I don't know how long I spent pondering the whole thing when I suddenly noticed Emile Guidry standing in front of me.

"You okay, Charley?"

I must have jumped, because he quickly added, "I didn't mean to startle you. You were looking awfully deep in thought about something."

I quickly pushed the envelope and its meager contents aside. "I'm sorry. I was just…daydreaming."

Guidry seemed placated and changed the subject. "My secretary's name is Gloria. I don't know if you met her last summer, but I've asked her to help you if you need anything at all."

I nodded appreciatively. "Yeah, thanks. She's very efficient; she already came by a little while ago. I can use all the help I can get."

"She's first-rate. I lucked into her when her boss at Marcus and Scofield retired. She can show you around the courthouse and introduce you to the few people in it who are willing to help you when you really need it. In a pinch, that kind of information can save a lawyer's ass."

With that he was out the door. I burst out laughing. Emile Guidry was never one to beat around the bush. It was a great exit line.

Gloria may be good, I thought, but could she help me figure out why someone would send me Chico Carter's obituary? I tucked the envelope into the top drawer of my desk.

Chapter 2

I DIDN'T HAVE a whole lot of time to worry about the mysterious obituary. Before the end of the day, Emile Guidry had dropped a foot-high stack of files on my desk.

"I've been holding onto these for your arrival. They're collection files that First National Bank sent over a couple of weeks ago. Each file has a note that's in default. Your job is to turn them into money."

It must have been obvious from the vacant expression on my face that I had no idea how to go about doing that. Guidry pointed to the top of the stack.

"That top folder is a form file. It's got fill-in-the-blank pleadings, everything from the petition to the judgment debtor examination. Bring me your first one, and I'll look it over. You'll be fine after that."

As he was leaving, he offered one last bit of advice. "Make sure you ask for your attorney's fees. If you don't plead it, you don't get it."

Being a bill collector was not exactly the glamorous start I had in mind. I knew that I had to begin somewhere, though, and I comforted myself with the realization that this would at least force me to learn my way around the courthouse. Besides, the amounts of the various promissory notes indicated that these were just small consumer loans. Whatever mistakes I made while climbing the steep learning curve ahead of me weren't going to hurt my client a whole lot.

Too, I liked the idea that these were *my* files. Although I couldn't sign pleadings until I passed the bar, I would be in charge of each case I filed. I would get to make the decisions about whether to give the defendant a little more time to plead (or to pay), when and how to take a default, and what to do if a defendant failed to show up for a debtor examination. If I showed good judgment about these things, I knew that I would get to move on to bigger and better things.

I worked very hard on my first set of pleadings. So hard, in fact, that it took me several days to complete them. It's kind of embarrassing to think about it now. Any experienced secretary in the firm could have cranked out 20 sets of pleadings in the time it took me to do one, but I didn't care how long it took. I wanted Emile Guidry to be impressed.

If I was expecting high praise for my work, I was sorely disappointed. He took one quick look at my initial pleadings, handed them back, and said, "Good. Go with that."

Heading back to my office, I felt a little embarrassed at having expected more. This was, after all, routine collection work, not a Supreme Court brief.

I spent the next several days calculating the amounts due on each note and plugging the numbers into my form pleadings.

My confidence grew as my first pleadings were accepted by the Clerk of Court, which meant that I had at least satisfied certain minimum requirements of form.

The pace of my work naturally quickened as I grew more comfortable with what I was doing. While most of the cases I filed met with no opposition and proceeded quickly to a default judgment, a few prompted answers that denied the debt. This allowed me to send interrogatories to the other side to learn if there was any basis to contest our claims. To my pleasant surprise, I discovered that engaging the enemy was fun. It made me feel a little more like a real lawyer.

That's when I got the second letter. It arrived on a Wednesday morning, tucked in the middle of the various pleadings, CLE ads, and court notices that otherwise dominate every lawyer's daily mail. Next to all the crisp and neatly addressed business mail, the crude, hand-addressed envelope stood out like a sore thumb.

It appeared to be in the same handwriting as the first letter. Again, there was no return address. Again, the postmark was from Augusta, Georgia.

It was another obituary. This one was even more yellowed. Given how rapidly newsprint ages, that didn't really mean much. I opened it carefully, I suppose out of a lawyer's instinct to preserve the evidence (of what, I had no idea).

Eddie Eumont
Funeral services for Eddie Eumont, 83, will be held at 10:00 A.M. Monday, February 18, at

New Sunlight Baptist Church in Aiken, South Carolina.

The Rev. Isiah Russell will officiate. Burial will be in Gray's Cemetery in Augusta.

Mr. Eumont died recently in a local hospital.

He was a native of Augusta. He was a graduate of Kalb West High School. He spent most of his adult life working at the Augusta National Golf Club. He moved to Aiken when he retired.

Survivors include his wife, Dorothy (Jones) Eumont; three sons, Jay Anthony Eumont of Savannah, Paul Michael Eumont of Dallas, Texas, and Samuel George Eumont of Atlanta. He is also survived by six grandchildren.

Immediately, I noticed that this obituary related to another former employee of Augusta National. Other than that, though, I didn't have a clue what it meant.

Of course the obituary came with another note. It was just as cryptic as the first. All it said was, "He knew about it, too. So did Stedman."

That got my attention. Stedman seemed to refer to Beau Stedman, the great player befriended by Robert T. "Bobby" Jones Jr. As almost every sports fan knows, Bobby Jones was arguably the greatest golfer of all time. Although he was a career amateur, the young man from Georgia with movie star looks dominated the world of golf during the Roaring

Twenties, winning five U.S. Amateurs, four U.S. Opens, three British Opens, and a British Amateur—all in a span of eight years. His greatest triumph, of course, came in 1930, when he won all four of these major championships—what sportswriter Grantland Rice dubbed the "Impregnable Quadrilateral" —in the same competitive season. Sensing that there were no worlds left to conquer, Jones shortly thereafter retired from competition at the ripe old age of 28.

Jones was something of a Renaissance man. In the midst of all his golfing exploits, he also managed to acquire an engineering degree from Georgia Tech and an English degree from Harvard before spending sufficient time studying law at Emory to pass the bar and become a lawyer. He then entered the practice of law at Butler & Yates, where he was a partner for virtually his entire career.

Jones's achievements in the golfing world continued after his retirement from competitive play. In 1932, he began construction on the Augusta National Golf Club. It was a monumental task, coming in the midst of the Great Depression, and only someone of Jones's stature could have pulled it off. Shortly after the club opened, he organized a spring invitational tournament to be played there. The event became known as the Masters and today is recognized as one of the four major modern championships of golf.

This remarkable man's connection with Beau Stedman began when Stedman was a young caddie at East Lake Country Club in Atlanta, where Jones had been a member since childhood. Upon seeing the then-teenaged Stedman's obvious gifts for the game, Jones made him his protégé and began grooming him to be his successor as the next great golf champion.

Unfortunately, not long after venturing out into the world of competitive golf, Stedman was falsely accused of murdering the wife of the manager of a club where he was working. Jones, who knew Stedman to be innocent, eventually arranged for his young friend to play matches against the greatest players of the day under various aliases. Over a period of several decades, Stedman beat all comers, and Jones had carefully recorded his phenomenal string of victories in private files at his law office.

Stedman's story remained tucked away in those files until the summer after my first year of law school at Tulane, when I accidentally discovered them while clerking at Butler & Yates. I had been given what I thought to be a routine task of cataloguing what remained of Jones's old files. Piece by piece, I put together the remarkable story of how Stedman managed to meet and beat virtually every great player in the game over a span of some 30 years without ever being exposed. I then spent the better part of the next two years working to get this unknown champion the recognition he deserved. Through an extraordinary chain of events, we were ultimately able to clear Stedman's name and bring his story to light.

Not surprisingly, my Stedman adventure had created quite a stir in most golf circles. As a consequence, I had gained something of a reputation as a golf historian/sleuth. It was more than I deserved, but it earned me a number of speaking engagements before various golf associations and historical societies. And, of course, it didn't hurt my standing with the firm, either. Anything that celebrated the life and times of Bobby Jones scored lots of points with the powers that be at Butler & Yates. I felt pretty certain that the fanfare surrounding my discovery of Beau Stedman had as much to do with my being invited to join the firm as any of the legal work I had done as a law clerk. That was okay with me; I like to think that what I did with those files showed good lawyering instincts.

All of that aside, I could not fathom what it was that Stedman and Eddie Eumont supposedly knew or how it had anything to do with me. It occurred to me that someone might have just been having a bit of fun with me. It wouldn't have been the first time, and jerking a lawyer's chain probably appealed to lots of folks.

But if this was a practical joke, it was pretty original. And if the idea was to arouse my curiosity, it was working. After a week or so, I had been able to put the first note out of my mind, kind of like the odd piece of junk mail you get every now and then that makes no sense. But the second letter made it clear that the first was no accident. Someone was communicating with me in a deliberate way. And he either gave me a hell of a lot more credit than I deserved for figuring out his message, or he wanted me in the dark. I figured it was the latter.

I didn't have a whole lot of time to give it much more thought than that, though. I was getting a steady flow of new files from the bank, and it was all I could do to keep up with my paperwork. In fact, even though I was arriving early and staying late, it seemed that I was making painfully slow progress in mastering what even Gloria probably thought was pretty routine stuff.

They say the toughest year of marriage is the first. I don't know about that, but it's certainly true about the first year of law practice. So I didn't have the luxury of pondering what these mysterious letters meant because I was too busy trying not to be overwhelmed by my new job.

On top of that, I had to study for the Georgia bar exam, which was coming up in early August. There were various preparation, or "cram" courses offered, and I signed up for the one that Emile Guidry recommended. Classes met for three hours a night from Monday through Thursday for three weeks in July. I usually went straight from the office to class, sometimes eating a sandwich in my car on the way.

It was right toward the end of the course, at this most hectic time of my life, that I found another letter in my morning mail with the unmistakable earmarks of the earlier notes. I suppose I was equal parts irritated and intrigued when I saw the same postmark, same handwriting, and same lack of a return address. I tore it open, wondering what stranger's obituary would be inside.

However, there was no obituary this time. Only a note that said, "I'm the last living soul who knows, and I'm old. Don't let the secret die with me."

I put the note down. What secret? Was someone just teasing me, or was this a genuine plea for me to expose some dark mystery? If I really was supposed to reveal a secret of some kind, why was my correspondent unwilling to reveal his identity?

I didn't share these musings with anyone. I mean, what could I have said about these strange little notes? I didn't know what they meant, who sent them, or why. I just figured it was better not to discuss any of this with people in the office, who were just getting to know me. While I wasn't quite sure what they thought of me, I had managed to make a fairly positive impression based on the way I handled the Stedman affair. I didn't want them thinking I missed the attention and had manufactured a new controversy just to regain the spotlight.

There was one guy that I could talk to about it. Ken Cheatwood. Cheatwood had clerked at Butler & Yates with me the previous two summers. He had received an offer to join the firm as an associate, too, but elected instead to take a clerkship in Miami with Judge Wayne Lee Shoss on the Eleventh Circuit Court of Appeals. My buddy just couldn't turn down a year in South Florida with lots of beaches and lots of golf.

Unfortunately, Cheatwood wasn't supposed to start at the court until September 15, which was still a couple of months off. He would be out of pocket until then, probably hanging out at a golf course somewhere. My buddy had been an All-American in golf at Oklahoma State during his college days and even played the minitours for a couple of years before law school. He wasn't just a good player, either. Cheatwood dearly loved the game's history and traditions, and he had played an important role in helping me with the Beau Stedman story. That's when I discovered that he had great instincts for pulling seemingly unrelated facts together. This was just the kind of challenge he relished.

I needed to talk with him, but it would have to wait until he surfaced. In the meantime, learning how to be a lawyer was enough to occupy my time.

Chapter 3

I HADN'T EXPECTED to be taking any depositions as part of my collection work, but I was glad to get the opportunity when it came. It was in one of my larger cases where the amount involved justified the expense. In answers to interrogatories, a defendant who owed the bank some $45,000 denied that he had signed the promissory note that formed the basis of the suit.

At first I didn't know what to do. No one had ever said that they hadn't signed the note. Like most nonsensical things I encountered for the first time, it stopped me in my tracks.

By this time, I had just gotten the news that I had passed the bar exam. Now that I was considered a real lawyer, I tried to avoid running down the hall to get Emile Guidry's input on every little problem. But I was at a loss about what to do, so I went to see him.

"Why don't you take the guy's deposition? Put a copy of the note in front of him and ask him if that's his signature. If he denies it, ask him if he knows who did sign it. Ask him to name his closest friends and family."

"Why would you ask that?"

"Because they're most likely to recognize his signature. Unless he's part of a real den of thieves, they're not all gonna lie for him. Sooner or later, one of them will acknowledge that it is his signature."

"And if they don't?"

He laughed. "Then we'll have a handwriting expert compare the signature to all of his signed checks and testify that they match. Won't cost us a thing, because the court will tax the expert's fees as court costs when we get a judgment against the guy."

Guidry had a way of explaining things that made them seem so obvious. It always left me wondering why I hadn't thought of it on my own. I had to remind myself that he had been practicing law 30 years longer than me.

After I returned to my office, I realized that I didn't even know how to set up a deposition, much less go about taking one. Gloria patiently explained the process to me. Once the other side agreed to a date, she would arrange for the court reporter.

"What if the other side won't agree to any date?"

She smiled at what she no doubt thought was a stupid question but answered patiently, "Then we pick a date, send out a notice, and serve them with a subpoena."

That made sense, of course. Like her boss had predicted, she had already begun to save my ass.

I called the other lawyer. He seemed a little surprised that I wanted to depose his client. However, he eventually agreed to a date. Gloria prepared the notice, arranged for the reporter, and put it on my calendar.

I sat down at the computer in my office to begin preparing my questions. While Emile Guidry could have taken this deposition off the top of his head, I needed to prepare for it. I opened the word processing program and began to type out my questions. After a couple of hours of drafting and redrafting, I had everything down exactly as I wanted it.

I was printing it out when the next letter from my mysterious pen pal arrived. There was still no return address on the envelope or signature on the note. The scribbling hand was the same. All the note said was, "Jones did what Greeley said. I've seen it in the moonlight."

This time, I became genuinely irritated. Enough of this game playing, I thought. If someone wanted something from me, why couldn't they just come out and say so?

Impulsively, I wadded up the envelope and paper and threw both in the trashcan. But one of the first things that Gloria had taught me was to file everything. She said that any paper you threw away could turn out to be the most important document in the case. She was certainly right about that; I had learned the truth about Beau Stedman from otherwise meaningless scraps of paper scattered in some of Bobby Jones's old files. For that reason, I knew that discarding the note was a mistake almost as quickly as I did it, so I retrieved the whole thing, smoothed it out, and placed it with the earlier ones. I had a feeling I would need all of the pieces if I was going to solve this puzzle.

Chapter 4

THE WORLD IS full of people who believe pro wrestling is real but the moon shot was fake. I tried to keep that in mind as I struggled to decipher the bizarre notes I was receiving. I had to be careful, I told myself, not to take this stuff too seriously. I could have been trying to make sense of something that had no sense to it to begin with.

By now, though, I was becoming more and more distracted by the whole thing. Every few days, I pulled out all of the notes and placed them in front of me. I guess I thought reading them together would reveal their meaning in a way that reading them one at a time had not. But nothing ever came to me.

I then changed their order, moving the notes around like a carnie in the midst of a shell game. That didn't help, either. Nothing.

For all I knew, they could have been written by Ernest T. Bass, the Mayberry village idiot from the "Andy Griffith" television show. Telling myself that the notes probably meant nothing at least allowed me to put them away.

Unfortunately, my curiosity wouldn't stay put. Sooner or

later, I'd have to dig them out and lay them in front of me all over again. I tried to remind myself that, just because my curiosity about Beau Stedman had been rewarded didn't mean there was a great mystery to be solved behind every odd circumstance.

I suppose that, to a normal person, my inability to let go of this might be difficult to understand. But the truth is that the need to make sense out of what appears to be senseless is part of being a lawyer. If you're not that way initially, law school will make you that way. For three years, every exam question consists of a confusing scenario of various facts that bring two or more parties into conflict. Each of these complicated problems has been created by a law professor who finds a good deal of amusement in testing your ability to distinguish between what's relevant and what's a so-called "red herring." Unless you can figure out the difference, you can't solve the problem.

This exercise is repeated on a daily basis after graduation, when lawyers are required to sift through confusing and conflicting stories from their clients. This time, however, the process was in reverse. Unlike law professors, clients aren't terribly interested in how the law applies to their situations. They just want to win, and their lawyers must find facts in the tangled webs they've been given that can somehow be used to reach that result. To quote an old saw, ask a lawyer what's 2 + 2, and he'll ask you: "What do you need it to be?"

For that reason, when a lawyer gets any kind of information, his or her first instinct is to analyze it from every angle. So when I received the next note, immediately I noticed that its tone was more direct than the others. In the same awkward hand, my anonymous tormentor had written: "What if the National had another course?" And there, for the first time, was a signature: "Moonlight."

Given the Augusta postmark, I quickly surmised that "the National" probably referred to the Augusta National Golf Club. During my search for Beau Stedman, I had learned that the locals there referred to Augusta National as "the National," partly to distinguish it from the Augusta Country Club, which was simply called "the country club."

It took me a while, but I eventually also recalled that the word "Moonlight" had appeared before. An earlier note had mentioned seeing something "in the moonlight." Was it coincidence? Or was there some hidden meaning in the repeated use of the word?

I didn't have any more time to think about it. Gloria burst into my office and breathlessly exclaimed, "Have you forgotten? You've got five minutes to make your ten o'clock pretrial with Judge Welsh!"

I bolted upright. I had forgotten all about the conference scheduled for that morning. Grabbing my coat and the file out of Gloria's hand, I sprinted down the hall to the elevators.

The state courthouse was three blocks away. If I ran, I could just about make it.

No lawyer wanted to be late for an appointment with a judge, least of all Judge Harold R. Welsh. The joke was that his breath smelled bad because he was always chewing on someone's ass. He was also a man unable to distinguish between mortal and venial sins. The slightest breach of his rules often provoked a blistering and humiliating dressing-down.

According to reputation, Judge Welsh's bad temperament was matched only by his mediocre intellect. It was a deadly combination. Although I hadn't personally experienced the sting of his whip, all the lawyers in the firm considered him to be ill-suited for the bench.

I briefly wondered how someone with such an unappealing disposition could ever get elected to the bench in the first place. Judges like him were Exhibit A in the argument for merit selection. It seemed to me that having the public elect judges made about as much sense as having *Playboy* pick All-American football players.

Judge Welsh's propensity for bad humor weighed heavily on me as I bounded out of our building onto the street and headed west toward the courthouse. I was sweating profusely by then, and it wasn't from the summer heat reflecting off the pavement beneath me. I couldn't help thinking that there I was, with the ink not yet dry on my law license, and I was already in trouble. And all because of those damned, distracting letters.

I ignored the light that flashed "Don't Walk" at the intersection and only broke stride in order to avoid a red convertible. Its driver yelled a curse at me which was probably a preview of what Judge Welsh had in store for me. I didn't even look back.

Halfway up the block, some lady pushed a flower cart unexpectedly in my path. I tried to dodge her, but Marshall

Faulk couldn't have made that sharp a cut in the Weejuns I was wearing. My trailing leg did me in, catching the back edge of the cart. It spun around and went crashing over on its side. I didn't know what they were, but some awfully pretty flowers ended up all over the street. I didn't have time to stop and apologize, but I did yell "Sorry!" over my shoulder as I continued my sprint up the street.

The courthouse soon came into view. It was a half block ahead of me on the right. I shot across the street, halfway hoping a passing truck would put me out of my misery. No such luck.

As I scampered up the front steps to the main entrance, I saw the large clock overhead. It read 10:08.

Judge Welsh's chambers were on the fourth floor. There was no time to wait for the elevator, so I headed up the stairs. By this time, I was wringing wet and breathing hard to boot.

I started taking two and three steps at a time and just as I reached the landing for the fourth floor, fatigue took its toll. I missed a step and fell heavily, tearing my pants and scraping my knee, which began to bleed. The contents of my file scattered across the floor. As I scrambled around retrieving them, I tried to ignore the throbbing pain in my leg. Unfortunately, most of my clothing was now stuck to my body either from perspiration or blood, and that would be more difficult to conceal from Judge Welsh.

I was now not only late but unsightly, and I knew that Judge Welsh was going to have a field day with me. I paused at the door with gold lettering that read "The Honorable Harold R.

Welsh" and for a moment considered not going in. Maybe I could check into a hospital and plead illness as an excuse. Or I could just leave town, never to return. I rejected both acts of cowardice and pushed the door open.

The first thing I saw was my opponent, Shaun Abercrombie, sitting on the couch in the judge's reception area. Abercrombie wasn't much older than me. He had only been practicing a couple of years and was an associate at another downtown law firm. His expression told me that I must have been quite a sight.

I was a little surprised to see him still sitting in the anteroom. Judge Welsh usually started on time whether all parties were present or not.

"Well, I'm relieved to see y'all didn't start without me," I managed to say.

Abercrombie's eyes were still wide in amazement at my appearance. "The judge is marrying someone right now. He should be done in a few minutes." He then paused for a moment before asking, "What on earth happened to you?"

I was about to make something up when the door to the judge's chambers opened. A smiling couple walked out, followed by the judge's secretary and law clerk (who presumably had been the witnesses). The secretary, whose disposition sharply contrasted with that of her boss, invited us inside. I followed my opponent in, hoping he would shield me from view in some way.

The judge was already seated at his desk looking at his file on our case. He looked up over his reading glasses at the two of us and was nodding an invitation for us to be seated when he stopped abruptly, gave me a second look, and said, "You look like crap."

The pretrial conference pretty much went downhill from there. I should have expected as much. It is too painful to repeat here all that Judge Welsh told me. Suffice it to say that his ranting included pointed advice about laundry and dry cleaning as well as personal hygiene.

Whenever I went through a particularly unpleasant experience as a child, my father often consoled me by saying that I would someday look back on the experience and see the humor in it. He was wrong. It's been quite some time since that pretrial, and I have yet to laugh about it, although I will admit that story has entertained a number of my friends.

The best I can say is that I managed to survive. As I stumbled out of the courthouse and back onto the street, I consoled myself with the thought that Judge Welsh had neither sanctioned me nor thrown my case out of court. We still had a trial date, and except for my personal humiliation, neither the case nor the client had suffered any real harm in the process.

As I continued my walk back to the office, however, I was surprised to find myself thinking about the notes again. If anything, my experience with Judge Welsh should have taught me that I could ill afford such distractions. If this was any indication, I had to decide whether I was going to be a lawyer or the golfing version of Don Quixote. It didn't look like I could do both.

At least that's what the sensible side of my brain was saying. On the other hand, I couldn't seem to push away these mysterious notes. As I limped back to the office, I began thinking again about the one I had just received and the clues it contained.

This had something to do with the Augusta National Golf Club—that much was clear. Several people—most of whom were apparently dead—knew something that my note writer seemed to want me to bring to light. I wondered whether that was the reason for his nom de plume, "Moonlight."

Was the secret that Augusta National had another course? I had never heard of Augusta having 36 holes. I was no expert about the place, but it seemed hard to believe that a course that was subjected to as much media scrutiny as Augusta National could operate another golf course in total secrecy. Then, again, if Congress could build a bomb shelter in the middle of the famed Greenbrier resort and keep it a secret, why couldn't Augusta National do the same thing with a golf course?

And who was "Moonlight," anyway? What did the name signify? Then it hit me. During my adventures with Beau Stedman, I discovered that virtually every caddie at Augusta National seemed to have some kind of a nickname. Carter and Eumont either were caddies or worked with caddies at Augusta National. If this Moonlight character knew them, chances were that he had been a caddie as well. "Moonlight" may have been the nickname he was given in the caddie yard.

At first, I decided just to sit back and wait for more mail that might answer these questions. After all, I had plenty of other things to do in the meantime. But I couldn't help but feel that whoever was behind this wanted me to make the next move. If this was some kind of a test, and I failed to respond, he might decide that I wasn't interested—or capable of helping him—and disappear altogether. Too, it occurred to me that, if this was an old caddie like Carter and Eumont, his time might be running short, and he might be too old to come to me. What if he were in a nursing home somewhere and unable to travel? (That might also explain the shaky handwriting.)

All that aside, I guess I was kind of like those Civil War buffs who spend their time and money visiting old battlefields just for the fun of it. As the saying goes, there's no accounting for taste, and after all the fun I had with Beau Stedman, the idea of once again traveling back in time was hard to resist.

At that point, I suppose my next step was obvious. There was only one thing to do. I had to go to Augusta and find a caddie named "Moonlight."

Not just yet, though. Gloria took one look at my bloody knee and insisted that I immediately go to the hospital for stitches.

Chapter 5

THE DRIVE FROM Atlanta to Augusta on I-20 is a pleasant one. The landscape has enough changes in elevation to maintain interest—certainly much more than the flat delta country in South Louisiana where I spent three years attending law school at Tulane.

Still, the scenery wasn't enough to distract me from thinking about the silliness of what I was doing. Like any new lawyer, I had precious little spare time. Instead of relaxing with a girlfriend or watching a ball game, I was chasing after someone—or something—for reasons that even I didn't understand. The absurdity of it all made me laugh out loud at one point. What would Emile Guidry have thought of his new protégé if he knew what I was up to? Perhaps he would have thought that I lacked the down-to-earth pragmatic sense of reality that a Butler & Yates lawyer should have—and shown me the door. Of course, I preferred to think that he would have congratulated me for my intellectual curiosity and said it showed that I had the instincts of a good trial lawyer. Frankly, I wasn't sure what his reaction would have been.

Even with a brief stop for gas and a sandwich, I made the hundred-mile trip in two hours. Although I had plenty of time to think during the drive, as I exited onto Washington Road in Augusta, I still wasn't sure just how I was going to find "Moonlight"—if, in fact, that was his name.

I knew better than to try to drive down Magnolia Lane at Augusta National. Security there was tighter than it was at the Pentagon. No matter what story I offered, I knew that I would be politely but firmly turned away. I had to find out where the caddies gathered when they were away from the course.

Augusta National is located on the west side of Washington Road. The east side (across from the club) consists of small shopping strips, restaurants, taverns, and souvenir shops. I didn't think I would find any caddies there, but I had to start somewhere.

While most of these places are jam-packed during the Masters, their business falls off considerably during the rest of the year. I pulled into a mostly empty parking lot at a place called the "Green Jacket Tavern." The building was probably a little too upscale to be a caddies' watering hole. When I walked inside and saw the vast array of imported beers behind the bar, I knew that I wouldn't find anyone I was looking for, and I was right.

I tried a couple more places down the street. Still no luck. No one seemed to know where the caddies could be found. I was coming out of a little old hamburger shack about a mile or so down the road from the club when a slightly built elderly black man came up behind me as I was unlocking my car.

I hadn't heard him approach, and I must have jumped three feet when he spoke.

"Say, Mister, did I hear right that you're lookin' for some caddies from the National?"

I turned around and looked at his broad smile, which revealed two gold teeth.

"Yes, I am. I need to find one of them badly. I'm a lawyer from Atlanta, and a relative of his died and left him some money." It was a lie that I hoped was not too obvious.

If the fella didn't believe me, he didn't let it show. "You might find some of 'em at Phil's Bottle Shop over on Wade Street. It ain't far from here." He pointed over my right shoulder. "Go back toward the National two blocks, turn right on Hamilton. It's about three blocks down on the left, on the corner. You can't miss it."

I thanked him and started to get in the car. He touched my sleeve and said, "Think you might help a fella buy a beer?"

I dug in my pocket and handed him a couple of dollars. He turned without thanking me and headed back down the street.

Phil's Bottle Shop clearly sounded like a neighborhood joint. If so, there wouldn't be any tourists there. I had no trouble finding it, and I was right. Phil's Bottle Shop was not a place for out-of-towners. There weren't many cars around, so I had no trouble parking right next to it.

When I walked into the bar out of the bright afternoon sunlight, I couldn't see a thing. In fact, I thought my eyes would never get adjusted. I managed to feel my way over to a stool at the bar.

That's when I noticed it had gotten quiet. I looked around and realized I was the only white man in the place.

An older man appeared from the back of the room, walked behind the bar, and came over to me. He eyed me more out of curiosity than suspicion and finally said, "Can I get you sump'n?"

I smiled nervously and asked for a Miller Lite.

He pushed a can in front of me. "Gotta buck?"

I pulled a dollar from my wallet and handed it to him.

Trying to sound as casual as I could, I said, "I was told I might find some guys here who caddie at the National."

He frowned. "You a bail bondsman?"

"No."

"Repo man?"

I shook my head.

He narrowed his eyes. "Maybe you a cop then."

I shook my head again. "No, I'm not a cop, either."

"Then what you want here? You a writer or somethin'?"

I guess he thought that I might be looking to do another story like the one that had appeared a year or so ago in one of the major golf magazines. It profiled a number of the caddies who used to work for the pros during the Masters back in the years before Augusta National allowed the players to bring their regular caddies. "No, I'm not a writer, either." I knew it was time to tell him just what I was doing here if I was going to leave in the same state of health as when I arrived.

"I'm a lawyer, and I'm trying to find someone who has been sending me letters."

The bartender's eyes narrowed again. "What kinda letters

would a caddie be sendin' to a lawyer?"

"Well, they're kind of hard to describe. In fact, one of the reasons I'm here is that I can't figure them out. I was kind of hoping I could find the guy who wrote them, so that he might tell me what he meant."

The guy stared at me for the longest time. He then slowly turned away and began to walk down to the other end of the bar. That's when I noticed the two men huddled together there. He talked with them for a few minutes, and then one of them came walking over. Like the bartender, he was in no hurry.

Because the light was so bad, I didn't realize how big he was until he got within a few feet of me. This guy was huge—at least six-foot-five and maybe 300 pounds. He had a toothpick in his mouth. As he looked me over, I struggled to maintain bladder control.

I thought he was never going to speak. Finally, he reached up, pulled the toothpick out of his mouth, and said, "I hear you askin' about some caddie from the National. Is that right?"

"Yes, I am." For some reason, at that moment I wondered if my car would be on blocks when I went back outside.

"I might know him. If I did who would I tell him is lookin' for him?"

"My name is Charley Hunter. I'm a lawyer in Atlanta. I've been getting some letters. They're kind of strange, but I think they may be from a caddie here at Augusta." I paused long enough to see if he appeared to believe me. Sensing no reaction, I asked him, "Have you ever heard of a caddie called 'Moonlight'?"

Although he tried to hide it, I could tell that he knew something about Moonlight. He put his toothpick back in his mouth, chewed on it for a moment, and then said, "I may have heard that name somewhere, but I'm not sure. Let me check with my buddy over there."

He turned and ambled back over to his drinking partner. After he spoke to him for a second, the other fellow jerked his head in my direction and laughed.

This time they both walked over to me. I began to think that I may have made a big mistake coming to Phil's Bottle Shop. Feeling a little panicky, I looked around the room for a telephone, in case I had to call 911 if mayhem broke out. All I saw were a couple of well-worn pool tables and a jukebox.

Although my new friend's companion wasn't quite as big, he was still a lot bigger than me. He gave me a hard look before asking, "You play?"

I figured he was trying to hustle me into a game of eight ball. I looked over at the pool tables and back at him. "No, not really."

He shook his head in irritation. "No, man, *golf*. You play golf?"

"Oh," I answered nervously, "yeah, sure."

"You got a handicap?" His tone suggested that this was a test of some kind.

"It's around six, but I haven't been playing much…"

"Yeah," he broke in sharply, "they all say that." He paused for what seemed like a long time, looking me over. Finally, he asked, "Who won the tournament last year?"

He caught me by surprise. "You mean the Masters, right?"

He gave out a sarcastic laugh. "Man, what other tournament do you think I'd be talkin' about 'round here?"

Christ, I thought, this is worse than being called on in law school. After a moment of panic, I remembered and told him.

"Okay," he said grudgingly. He was quiet for a moment and then asked, "Now…who came in *second*?"

To my everlasting relief, I knew the answer to that, too.

Just as I began to wonder how long this would go on, the big fella with the toothpick broke into a grin and said, "You okay…but that man you just asked about is the craziest white man I have *ever* known." With that, he threw back his head and laughed heartily. So did his companion. "The only 'Moonlight' we know is teched in the head. You can talk to him, but you ain't gonna make no sense outta anything he says."

"What do you mean?"

He shook his head slowly. "That old man's stuck in the past. Used to talk about carrying for Bob Jones and his friends at some place we never heard of. Then he said he made it all up. I don't think he knows where he is half the time."

"Really?"

There was a great deal of sympathy in his voice as he continued. "To hear him tell it, he's been on the bag for everybody from Jones on down to Arnold Palmer. But we know better. The man's got a bad case of the 'wanna-bes,' you know what I mean?"

Suddenly I knew that my earlier suspicions had been right on target after all. I *was* getting notes from Ernest T. Bass. And

I had wasted an entire Saturday to drive over to Augusta just to find that out.

I started to leave. I almost got to the door when something made me decide that, as long as I'd come this far, I might as well try to meet my tormentor face-to-face. Turning back, I said, "Do you know where I might find this Moonlight fella?"

The smaller companion nodded. "For all the good it'll do you, sure. He lives less than a mile from here."

They started laughing again at the thought of me trying to interview the "craziest white man" they knew.

The directions they gave me were easy to follow. I went back outside and was momentarily blinded by the bright midday sun. When I got my bearings, I was relieved to see my car sitting in the exact spot I left it with all its parts intact. It was a 10-year-old Chevy, and it wasn't much. But it was all I had, and I was at least a year away from affording a new car.

As I got in and drove toward Moonlight's house, I had no idea what lay in store for me.

Chapter 6

THE SMALL WHITE frame house needed paint, and a couple of its shutters were missing. The yard needed mowing, too. Its condition was no worse than its neighbors, however. This was obviously a part of Augusta that had seen better times.

I didn't see any house number, but this was where my friends at Phil's Bottle Shop had told me Moonlight's house would be. It matched the description as well. Still, I wanted to be sure before I approached anyone who had earned the vivid description they had given Moonlight.

The houses on each side had the numbers immediately before and after the address I had been given. This had to be the place. I pulled over to the curb, stopped my car, and got out. Before starting up the walk to the front porch, I righted a garbage can that had been turned over on its side. Climbing the three steps to the porch, I noticed several days' worth of newspapers lying near the front door. The mailbox next to the doorbell was overstuffed as well. No lights were on in the house, and there was no sign of activity. Even though there was an ancient-looking Ford Falcon in the driveway, it was apparent to me that whoever lived here had been gone for several days.

I was inclined to turn around and go back to my car. Still, I thought I should at least ring the bell, so I did. Even outside, I could hear its bright sound within the house. I waited a few moments, but heard nothing to indicate any activity in response. Then, out of the corner of my eye, I thought I detected the curtains moving in the window.

I began feeling a little uncomfortable, almost creepy. At that moment I realized that, even though this was a Saturday afternoon, I didn't see anyone else on the entire block. No one mowing their lawn, sitting on the front porch, visiting with neighbors, or engaging in any other typical weekend activity. There were no kids playing ball anywhere.

Maybe this was a crack house, I thought. Maybe the boys at Phil's were setting me up for something unpleasant. For the second time that day, I seriously questioned my own judgment at ignoring possible signs of danger while trying to find Moonlight.

That's when I heard a sound directly behind the door. Someone was removing the chain from the latch. Then I heard a bolt slide, and the door opened just wide enough for me to realize that the person on the other side was holding a double-barreled shotgun.

I jumped back quickly. A voice crackled from behind the door. "Who are ya' an' whaddya want?" Before I could answer, the voice added impatiently, "C'mon, speak into my microphone."

Although the shotgun wasn't pointed at me, it was close enough to start an adrenaline flow that doubled my heart rate in an instant. I immediately regretted that I had not rehearsed some kind of introduction that would have explained my presence. If this was Moonlight, and he was half as crazy as they said, I should have prepared something to announce my approach.

I would like to claim that I was too brave to consider backing away, but the truth is that I was frozen where I stood. I couldn't have moved my legs if I had wanted to. I decided to speak even though I wasn't sure any sound would come out. "Look, I'm not here to cause any trouble. My name is Charley Hunter. I'm a lawyer. I drove here from Atlanta, and I'm looking for someone they call Moonlight."

For a second, I thought it might have been a mistake to disclose my occupation. Lawyers aren't the most popular people on the planet, and whoever was holding this shotgun might have thought that I was in season.

When there was no immediate answer, I added nervously, "I don't mean to bother you, but I was told a fella named Moonlight might live around here. And that's all I'm here for."

After what seemed like an awfully long time, the door slowly began to open a bit more. I prepared to duck or jump if the gun barrel moved abruptly, but it slowly swung in the other direction. Then I saw a figure step from the shadows into the light.

The first thing I noticed was that he was very old. Short, too. Bald on top, with disorganized wisps of hair sticking out oddly from the sides of a Ben Hogan-style cap. He was dressed in an old, dirty, short-sleeved, plaid cotton shirt and beltless double-knit pants—the kind that golfers wore during the disco era. They were too short and revealed a pair of old running shoes with laces knotted in several places. I now know that you can take in a whole lot really quickly at a time like that.

The little man finally spoke again. "Who sent ya' here?" That's when I noticed a faint accent. I couldn't tell what it was.

"Some of your friends over at Phil's." I knew they weren't exactly his friends, but it was no time to split hairs.

He put the shotgun down. I felt my heart rate slow appreciably.

"Well, if they sent ya' here, they must've decided ya' were okay." His stern expression softened. "Hope I didn't scare ya' too much. Ya' can't be too sure in this neighborhood." Then a slight smile appeared. "It wasn't loaded, anyway."

Neither are my bowels anymore, I thought to myself. At the same time, something clicked inside my head, and I recognized the traces of a Scottish accent, its sharp edges dulled by years of life in the States. The little man gave out a funny kind of laugh that was part giggle and part cough. In an apparent reference to my chinos, polo shirt, and Weejuns, he said, "We don't get too many come through here lookin' like you. Thought ya' might be from the government or somethin'."

I forced a laugh in an attempt to get us on friendlier terms. "No, sir, I'm not from the Government. In fact, no one has *ever* mistaken me for that. I don't know if…"

"Well, step back a little bit so I can get a better look at ya'." His tone was less threatening. I stepped away from the door.

He had propped his gun against the wall by then and had walked out onto the porch.

"Now, ya' better tell me ag'in what you're doin' in this neighborhood."

I looked him straight in the eyes. "I've been getting some anonymous letters in the mail that I can't figure out. Someone has sent me a couple of obituaries of people who used to work here at Augusta National. They've put little notes in with the newspaper clippings saying things that I don't understand. But it looks like whoever wrote these things wants to talk to me about something. I'm just not sure what it is."

He seemed to be studying me intently as I spoke. "What makes ya' think I'd know anythin' 'bout that?"

"Well, one of the notes was signed 'Moonlight.' Since all the notes were postmarked from here in Augusta, I drove over and asked some caddies from the club whether they knew anyone named Moonlight."

I looked at his face closely, but his expression did not change. "They told me I could find someone named Moonlight here at this address, so here I am."

"Here ya' are," he repeated. "What'd they tell ya' 'bout this fella named Moonlight?"

I wasn't about to tell him that they said Moonlight was crazy. I shrugged nonchalantly. "They just said they knew someone by that name and thought he lived here."

I began to worry whether this little question-and-answer session was going anywhere. Suddenly, he turned sociable. "Look, I can't invite ya' in. But lemme fetch a coupla chairs, an' we can sit here on the porch an' talk if ya' want."

He disappeared inside and came out holding two rather dilapidated folding chairs. He handed one to me. I took it, opened it, and waited for him to set his down before I located mine. I had no choice but to let him lead me through this dance because he was the only one who could hear the music.

After we sat down, he asked to see the notes. Fortunately, I had thought to bring them along. I went to my car and got them. He glanced at them quickly.

"Can I see your driver's license?"

I pulled it from my wallet and obediently handed it to him. He looked at it for just a moment and read my name out loud before passing it back to me. He then stuck out his right hand and said, "My name is Seamus McIntyre. I'm pleased to make your acquaintance."

I shook his hand and said, "I'm glad to meet you, Mr. McIntyre."

"Just call me Moonlight. Everyone else does."

Chapter 7

WE TALKED FOR over an hour. It was a rather delicate—and sometimes taxing—negotiation. My new acquaintance seemed to be testing me over and over, trying to gauge my credibility. I took it as a challenge.

He also liked to talk in riddles. At times, his oblique way of communicating made me think that he was every bit as crazy as the guys at Phil's said he was. At other times, though, I thought I could see a method to what he was doing, as if our dialogue was an examination to see if he could trust me with something larger.

As we talked, I remembered something that one of my psychology professors in college had once told me. He said that genius was a form of madness. According to him, truly creative people who saw the world and the things in it differently were biological freaks whose brains functioned abnormally. It was just their good fortune that the abnormality made them creative rather than criminal.

Moonlight sometimes twitched as he talked, which made me wonder where he fit into that analysis. He liked to bounce around a lot, and his conversation had no straight lines. Getting from point A to point B wasn't a simple thing. There were a lot of hairpin turns to be negotiated along the way.

After I had asked him for perhaps the fifth time whether he was the one who sent me the mysterious notes and clippings, he finally admitted that he was. Of course, I asked him why, but it was obvious that he wasn't quite ready to tell me. He appeared to enjoy fending off my questions. For a brief moment, I wondered whether he was just an old man in need of attention, but that wouldn't have explained why he picked me to be his pen pal.

In what I took to be a breakthrough in our standoff, he abruptly stood up and asked me if I wanted a beer. I knew better than to reject the offer, as it was a gesture indicating we had made some kind of progress. He disappeared into the darkened house and returned a minute later with two bottles of Rolling Rock.

As he handed me a bottle, I commented that it was not a brand I had seen often.

He laughed. "Second most famous thing to come outta Latrobe, Pennsylvania."

He looked expectantly at me. I quickly responded, "The first being Arnold Palmer."

He cackled delightedly. "Very good, young man. So far you're all they said you'd be."

Of course, I had to ask who "they" were. Once again, he withdrew as if he was afraid to say too much. "Never ya' mind who 'they' might be. Just know that they're people who are good enough for me to trust."

I fell silent for a time, thinking that might draw him out. However, he seemed just as comfortable sipping his beer and quietly taking in the afternoon sun.

Eventually, I became a little exasperated by it all. "For goodness sake, Moonlight, if you didn't want me to know what this was all about, why did you send me all that stuff in the mail?"

He drained the last of his beer and put the bottle down beside his chair. Looking at me, he said in an even tone, "A fair question." He paused for a while, perhaps to let the drama build.

"Beau Stedman was a friend a' mine. Ya' did a good thing for him. He was very grateful to ya'." He paused briefly. "So am I."

I couldn't help but smile at the compliment. I was happy to be reminded of the great pleasure Beau took from finally being recognized for his accomplishments.

"I thought I might be able to trust ya'. Anyone who did for Beau Stedman what ya' did has to be a good man. But *my* secret is a sacred pledge. I didn't think I'd ever want to tell anybody, but I just can't let the secret die with me. There's no one else to carry it on."

I didn't want to say anything for fear of spooking him. I just sat there, almost afraid to breathe.

"Like many a' the great ones, Mr. Jones was a very private man. He saw an' understood things that other men knew little about. It set him apart, if ya' know what I mean."

I nodded, although I really didn't understand what he was

trying to say. After a moment, he continued. "Mr. Jones didn't much like bein' famous. It attracted a lotta people who tried to take things from him. His privacy, for one thing. His time with his family an' his friends, too. People just wouldn't leave him alone."

Moonlight was looking off in the distance now, almost as if he were in a trance. He was quiet again for a time, but finally spoke.

"Golf was always the main thing, ya' know? It wasn't the money or the trophies. He never talked 'bout any a' that much. For him it was the game an' the other players." He paused before adding, almost as an afterthought, "He really liked the players 'cause they seemed to understand him better than anyone else."

As hard as I tried, I couldn't quite figure out where Moonlight was headed with this soliloquy. He kept making sharp turns in the conversation that I neither predicted nor expected, much less fully understood.

"The tough part for him was gettin' sick. He didn't like hero worship, but he damned sure didn't want pity, either. Hell, he wouldn't even let his friends talk 'bout his problem."

Finally, he turned back to me as if coming out of the trance. Fixing me with a hard look, he said, "That's where the secret comes in. First, though, I've gotta know that I can trust ya' with it."

It was hard to imagine that this strange old coot was privy to a secret of any great importance. Still, it didn't hurt to humor him, so I just said, "I sure hope so, Moonlight."

He seemed disappointed by my lukewarm response. "I

won't tell ya' the story—an' I got proof of it all—unless I know you'll 'do right' by it."

I must have had a queer expression, because he laughed and said, "I know they think I'm crazy. They tol' ya' I was crazy, didn't they?"

I shook my head from side to side, but before I could say anything, he said, "Oh, don't deny it. I don't mind, really. It's my own damned fault. I once let the secret slip out an' then had to deny everythin'." Without telling me what the "secret" was, he explained that it gave him a reputation for spinning yarns and indulging in fantasies.

"That's alright," he said after awhile. "It's a small price to pay for what I did."

I thought about the notes and asked him quietly, "Does this have something to do with another course at Augusta National?"

"No," he said.

"Then why did you write something about another course in that note?"

I saw the beginning of a wry smile appear. "In this law business you've gone into, do they warn ya' 'bout jumpin' to conclusions?"

Another hairpin turn. Now we were talking about my new profession. "Well, they tell you to look at the evidence to learn the facts."

"You've gotta be careful doin' that, don't ya'?"

"Well, sure," I said defensively.

"Then go look at your note ag'in. I didn't say anythin' 'bout another course at Augusta National."

I pulled the note back out. He was being evasive—not to

mention sarcastic—but I had to admit he was right. The note simply asked, "What if the National had another course?"

Moonlight seemed just as pleased as my law professors had been to have caught me in a mistake. I had just failed one of his tests.

In another abrupt change of subject, he said, "You've never even asked me why they call me Moonlight. Don't ya' wanna know?"

Again, he had me on the defensive. "Sure, I want to know," I offered apologetically.

"Never lost a ball. They said I could find 'em even in the moonlight."

As I sat there watching Moonlight do his verbal bob and weave, I suspected that I would encounter few witnesses during my career who would be tougher to follow than Moonlight McIntyre. There was so much more I wanted to ask him, particularly about how he came to know Stedman and Jones. Based on what I knew, I assumed that he had caddied at Augusta National for many years and met them there, but Moonlight was cautioning me not to make assumptions like that. However, I didn't want to distract him from the topic at hand, so I continued to ask him about the notes.

"You said you'd seen something in the moonlight. What did that mean?"

He continued with his riddles. "What did the rest a' the note say?"

I pulled them out again and found the note. "It says that Jones did what Greeley said."

He fixed his eyes on me. "Okay, what did Greeley say?"

"Well, if you're referring to Horace Greeley, he is supposed to have said 'Go west, young man.'"

"An' what does that tell ya'?" he demanded.

At this point I almost wanted to hit him. "I suppose it means that Jones went west at some point. Is that what you're saying?"

He laughed that thin cackle that I was becoming familiar with. "An' where do ya' think that fits with the rest a' what I said in the notes?"

Maybe it was the beer, maybe it was the heat of the day, and maybe he had just confused me past the point of understanding. Whatever the reason, I couldn't keep track of the floating pieces of the puzzle. I looked back down at the notes, but my eyes wouldn't even focus on them.

Then it hit me. "Are you telling me that Augusta National had another course out west? Is that your secret?"

Moonlight smiled. He seemed to be thinking of what to say next. Finally, he said in a low but friendly voice, "Charley, I didn't think you'd ever get it. I was beginnin' to wonder if ya' were as smart as Beau said ya' were."

If Augusta National had a golf course somewhere out west, I'd never heard about it. Why would the club have another course? And why didn't anyone know about it? Where was it? Was it still in use?

Just as quickly, I caught myself. There was no reason to put any stock in such a far-fetched story. It was precisely this kind of nonsense that no doubt earned Moonlight the distinction of being the "craziest white man" the regulars at Phil's Bottle Shop ever knew.

But that didn't quell the curiosity rising within me. Just suppose, I thought, this punchinello was telling the truth. If I walked away, I would be turning my back on one of the most fantastic golf stories of the century. The odds, of course, were against that being the case. But I remembered what one of the trial lawyers at Butler & Yates once told me: You can't win the lottery without buying a ticket.

So, I decided to stay and play. If Moonlight was telling the truth, I had a hundred questions. I didn't know whether I would eventually discover the answers to them, but I wasn't in charge of this expedition. It was clear that we were going to do this at Moonlight's pace, and that I would have to get used to his hairpin turns.

Chapter 8

I SAW A lot of Moonlight over the next several weeks. Much of my available time during the weekends was spent sitting on his front porch, drinking Rolling Rock, and trying to hold up my end of our conversations. It wasn't easy; Moonlight *never* said anything directly. It was like he had an aversion to declarative sentences.

I have to admit that he kept me on my toes. My understanding of this odd little man was coming in bits and pieces, often without warning. I had to be careful not to miss something.

I did manage to unearth some of his background, though. He was born in central Scotland, not far from the Gleneagles resort where his father was the caddie master. He said he began toting bags for the resort's guests there when he was only ten years old and immediately knew that he wanted to spend his life walking golf courses. His father brought the family to the States in 1932 when he got a job at Pinehurst through Donald Ross, the great golf architect from Dornoch who designed and ran the courses at the North Carolina resort. When the call went out for caddies at the new course that Bob Jones was building at Augusta, a teenaged Seamus McIntyre packed his bags and never looked back.

As further evidence of his independent streak, Moonlight had always lived alone and appeared to like it that way. Besides, he once told me, at his age his friends were all gone anyway.

Needless to say, the old man's peculiar ways sometimes made me question the sanity of what I was doing. The skeptical side of my lawyer's brain said it was possible that Moonlight's nickname may have come from his habit of howling at the moon, rather than his ball-finding skills as he claimed. But the truth was that his story had an irresistible pull to it, and I was having a good time listening to his tales about Jones, Stedman, and an assortment of other characters from the early days of golf.

Moonlight never invited me inside his house. Although the worst part of summer was over, it was still uncomfortably warm on that porch. I could see window units protruding from the side of the house, so I knew he had air-conditioning. However, our relationship was still too fragile for me to invite myself inside.

Sometimes we would spend as much as three hours talking on the porch. Like most folks his age, he was fond of reminiscing about the past, but never in a way that consciously revealed anything intimate about himself. At the end of some of our chats, I would walk away thinking we had gone backward rather than forward and that I had learned nothing new about Moonlight's secret.

I did learn at one point that Moonlight, Chico Carter, and Eddie Eumont were the last three of the prewar caddies who worked at Augusta National. According to Moonlight, the rapid growth and success of the Masters tournament in the early years surprised even Jones and Cliff Roberts, Jones's confidante and autocratic ruler of Augusta National. Jones had originally conceived of the tournament as a reunion of sorts for his friends throughout the golf world. He scheduled it in the spring as a way of kicking off the golf season. No one associated with the inaugural Augusta National Invitational Tournament (as it was originally called) foresaw it as a major championship.

Apparently, Jones vastly underestimated his own influence. Virtually no one declined an invitation to compete at his tournament. The best professionals and amateurs of the day began making the trip to Augusta every spring.

The course had something to do with it, too, but the Augusta National Golf Club in the early years was very different from the way it is now. For one thing, it was not as well groomed then as now. Too, virtually every hole has been tweaked more than once, if not totally rebuilt, to improve its playability. For instance, the par-3 16th hole, which has been the scene of so many great moments in Masters lore, didn't even have the pond that has sunk Corey Pavin's Masters hopes more than once. In the beginning, the green was on the other side of a scraggly ditch and wasn't much to look at.

In addition, a large part of the tournament's success can be traced to the way it is structured. For one thing, the field is smaller than it is in other tournaments, which tends to focus more attention on individual players. Invitations are limited to players who have achieved real competitive success. Although space for amateurs in the field has shrunk over the years, a small number of amateur champions still tee it up every year with their professional counterparts.

In addition to preserving the amateur tradition in golf, Augusta awards its Masters champions a lifetime invitation to compete in the tournament. Thus, long before there was a Senior Tour, the Masters provided a showcase for golf's legends.

All of these factors converged in a magical way to lift the Masters to the status of a major championship in a few short years. This was remarkable, because the tournament has never been an official championship of anything. Unlike the other majors, which are either national championships (U.S. Open, British Open) or professional championships (PGA), the Masters has always been nothing more than an invitational tournament staged by a private club. Yet for many, it is without question *the* best golf tournament in the world.

According to Moonlight, that was the problem.

When Jones originally founded the Augusta National Golf Club, he did so with the idea that it would serve as a retreat for him and his friends. One of the reasons Jones retired at the age of 28 after winning the Grand Slam in 1930 was his desire to escape the intense pressures of competition, as well as the weight of the enormous expectations that dogged him every time he entered a tournament.

Even when Jones tried to play a casual round with friends, word would spread quickly and no matter where he was, a crowd would soon appear. Once, while playing the Old

Course at St. Andrews on holiday, he was confronted with as many as 5,000 spectators before completing the outward nine.

But if Jones expected privacy at Augusta National, his little reunion tournament did him in. The Masters captured the public's fancy in a big way, and Augusta National became perhaps the country's most prominent golf club. As a result, it became evident by the late 1930s that any appearance by Jones at the club attracted far more attention than he wanted.

Apparently, neither Jones nor Roberts anticipated that the Masters would have such a profound effect. While other major championships brought the bright glare of the media spotlight on the host club for the week of the event, the eyes of the world moved on after the tournament concluded. Thus, the uproar of a U.S. Open at Baltusrol or Winged Foot would quickly die after the champion was crowned, and the club would then resume its quiet ways until its next turn on the national championship rota—usually ten years or so down the road.

But the Masters became the only one of golf's four major championships with a permanent site. As a result, the tournament focused the attention of the golfing world on the same club year after year. This caused Augusta National and the Masters to become inseparable in the public's mind. Mention of one inevitably required mention of the other, giving the club a kind of cult status, and the scrutiny it received from the golf media became unrelenting.

Moonlight and I were discussing it one afternoon on his porch. I remember the day well because it was the first time

I had bought the beer. I had iced down a case of Rolling Rock in a good size cooler and hauled it onto the front porch from my car when I arrived. I told Moonlight that it was time that I bought a round, so I brought my own.

We were both on our fourth or fifth bottle, and the conversation had become much easier. I remember looking directly at Moonlight and saying, "So Jones had to find another course if he wanted some privacy, huh?"

"Lookin' back, it was Mr. Sarazen's 4-wood at 15 in 1935 that changed everything. When that ball rolled into the cup for a double eagle, the media fell in love with the tournament. It just took off from there."

I knew he was referring to the shot that earned Gene Sarazen a tie with Craig Wood in the final round of the second Masters tournament. Sarazen defeated Wood the next day in a 36-hole play-off. There is perhaps no more celebrated stroke in the history of golf than Sarazen's double eagle.

Moonlight took another swig of beer. "That's 'bout it, Charley. A few of us went an' caddied at the new place. Only the ones who could be trusted. We were all sworn to secrecy."

Even half-drunk, I found his story difficult to believe. "How do you keep something like that a secret?"

"Just like ya' keep most of the details 'bout Augusta National a secret," he shot back.

He had a point. Despite being the most intensely scrutinized golf club in the world, the inner workings of Augusta National have always remained largely hidden from view.

"Okay, you've got to tell me. Where is this course?"

He laughed. "Not so fast, Charley. I've got terms, lad." I noticed then that, the more Moonlight drank, the more evident his accent became.

"What terms?"

"My terms," he said in a suddenly fierce tone. "We gotta do this the right way…my way…or we don't do it at all."

"Okay, then, what are your terms?"

He had obviously given this some thought. Leaning forward, he said, "First, ya' only use this information the way I let ya'. Can ya' agree to that?"

I could tell from the tone of his voice that his terms were not negotiable. "Agreed."

He continued. "Second, neither of us makes any money doin' this." He paused and then added by way of explanation, "Makin' money off a' this would desecrate Mr. Jones's memory, an' I won't do that no matter how much beer ya' bring me."

I nodded again. "Fair enough." I raised my bottle as if making a toast. "We're doing this for golf and golf history."

He relaxed. "Ya' know, I saw what ya' did for Beau Stedman. That's kinda what I had in mind."

I finished off my beer and opened another. I offered one to Moonlight, but he shook me off. "You'd better be careful," he said. "You've got some drivin' to do."

I put the beer down.

"Okay, *now* will you tell me where this new course is located?"

"Was," he corrected me.

I was disappointed.

"It's not there anymore?" I asked the question even though I didn't know where "there" was.

"No, lad, that's the sad part. It was a holy piece a' ground. The site a' some a' the greatest golf ever played on the planet. But no one has struck a shot there in a long, long time."

"Do you think you can still find it?"

"Oh, I can find it, that's for sure. I could find it in my sleep. Ya' never forget a place like that."

I stood up. "Take me to see it."

He just laughed. "It's a long, long way from here. Don't ya' remember what I tol' ya' 'bout Horace Greeley?"

Too much beer had made me forget that Augusta National's secret course was supposedly somewhere out west. Of course, I wasn't really certain that any of these wonderful stories the old man was telling me had any truth to them at all. If—and it was a big "if"—Augusta had another course, it seemed most likely to me that it would have been on the same grounds as the other course. At the time when Jones and Roberts bought the property in Augusta, it was a nursery called the Fruitlands and consisted of nearly 400 acres—plenty of room for two courses. For all I knew, Moonlight's talk of a course somewhere else was his way of trying to throw me off the "secret" until he was sure he could trust me. In the meantime, I had no other choice but to play along.

"If we went there, do you think we could walk the course or has some shopping center or office building been built over it?"

He shook his head. "I dunno. It's been years since I was

there. But we do need to go. There's things there ya' need to see, Charley."

"What kinds of things?"

"The most beautiful land you've ever seen, for one thing. I pray to God it hasn't been spoiled."

He looked off in the distance as if imagining himself back there. When he spoke again, he said, "There's so much to tell ya', Charley. So many wonderful things happened there. It was as if the good Lord blessed that place for golf like no other."

I could tell he was dead serious. So I asked him, "In what way was it blessed?"

"The people who came there were some a' the most fabulous characters you'd ever meet. An' the golf—why, it was magnificent. An' then there was the course. If ya' think the course at the National is somethin', ya' should've seen this one."

A broad smile appeared across his face. He laughed. It was obvious he was remembering something very funny. "We had some great times there. There must've been somethin' in the air. A stranger bunch a' folks there never was, but I loved each one of 'em."

"Sounds to me like you have some stories to tell."

He laughed again. "Ah, yes, Charley, I *do* have lots a' stories to tell ya'. 'Bout some a' the greatest matches ever played, includin' one that nearly changed the course a' history."

I couldn't imagine a place more exciting than the one Moonlight was describing. But it was hard for me to believe that such a place could have existed in secret. "How come no one knows about this but you?"

"'Cause just 'bout everyone else is dead. Besides, anyone who ever went there wouldn't've given up the secret if ya' tortured him. It was that special."

"It sounds like a helluva story," I told him.

He smiled and winked at me. "It is that, Charley, as ya' say, a helluva story. An' it's a story I want ya' to tell the world before it dies with me."

I realized that this would be no simple project. "And how do you propose to do that?"

"There's only one way," he said evenly. "We've gotta go there. You've gotta walk the course." He paused and then added as a smile spread across his face, "More than that, you've gotta play the course."

Another hairpin turn. "But you said that the course no longer exists. And for all you know, the land may be paved over with a highway or parking lot."

The little man gave me the kind of look a bishop would give an unbeliever. "We'll find a way, lad, make no mistake 'bout it. You're gonna play that course. I've gotta do a loop there one last time. It's the only way to make ya' see an' feel what it was like."

From the way he talked, I suspected Moonlight had already booked our starting time.

Chapter 9

NOTHING WAS EASY with Moonlight. Even planning to travel together required negotiation.

In the first place, he wanted to keep the location of the course a secret until we got there. His idea was that we would drive across country by car. Still playing along with the notion that Moonlight's secret course was somewhere out west, I had to tell him that there was no way I could spend that much time away from work. As it was, I felt uneasy taking time off so soon after starting the job. One of the things I liked best about Butler & Yates was that it didn't pressure new associates with quotas for billable hours like some of the megafirms that had tried to recruit me out of law school. The emphasis there was on learning how to be a good lawyer, not on churning files.

Still, I knew that taking a vacation in my first few months on the job wasn't the best way to impress the partners at the firm. So I told Moonlight that we would have to fly to wherever his secret course happened to be and that, in order to purchase tickets at a fare that I could afford, I had to know in advance where we were going. Besides being the truth, it was a good way to call his bluff.

He wanted to argue about it. "I tol' ya' we were goin' to do this my way. We'll drive there, an' you'll know where the course is when we arrive."

"Moonlight, I just don't have the time. By all rights, I shouldn't have any vacation time coming yet. I just can't be gone that long."

He grunted. "Ya' can't get a feel for the country when ya' climb into one a' those steel birds an' get whooshed away."

I was getting a little outdone by all this when it dawned on me. I looked at him and asked, "Moonlight, are you afraid of flying?"

"You're damned right I am."

I laughed.

"It ain't funny," he said.

"I'm sorry. But that's the first thing I've seen you afraid of." I tried to reassure him. "Look, your chances of dying in an airplane are less than in a car. The statistics have shown that year after year. Flying is easy. We'll get you something to calm your nerves."

"I dunno," he said uneasily.

I half-plead with him and half-scolded him. "Look, we don't have any choice. It would take us three or four days each way to drive out west. That would leave us no time at all to look the place over."

His shoulders slumped. "Are ya' sure ya' can gimme somethin'?"

"I promise. The flight will be the easiest part of the entire trip. Just tell me, where do we fly to?"

He still didn't want to tell me exactly where the course was located. "If ya' get me to San Francisco, I can find it from there."

After scouring the Internet, I was able to locate two cheap fares for a round trip flight from Atlanta to San Francisco, and I reserved a rental car for our arrival. We were set to leave in two weeks.

Had I not been so busy at work keeping up with the mounting pile of collection files that threatened to take over my office, I might have had time to realize how crazy it was to chase the ghost of a golf course. But the days at work flew by, sometimes without my ever looking up from my desk. After a week without hearing from me, Moonlight must have feared that I was having second thoughts about our trip. One morning at work, I found another envelope addressed in his now-familiar handwriting in the mail. I opened it and found a scorecard with a note from Moonlight that said, "Don't let your faith slide, Thomas. I ain't making this up."

The scorecard was yellowed with age. Unlike modern scorecards, which are gaudy with all kinds of colors, this one had the style and elegance of the classic cards I had seen from grand old courses like Winged Foot. It was small enough for a player to fold and place in his pants pocket while he walked the course, unlike the larger cards nowadays that attach to a clipboard in the middle of the steering wheel of a golf cart.

The front of the card read "Bragg's Point Golf Links" and featured a modest but attractive crest showing a putter and driver crossed like an "X" over several golf balls. There was no address or other information that disclosed the club's location.

I opened the card. The course measured 6,767 yards—modest by today's standards but plenty long for championship courses back in the days when steel had only recently replaced hickory as the material of choice for golf club shafts.

The card was marked with the names and scores of a foursome. Only the players' first names appeared: Bob, Ben, Jimmy, and Gray. The scores were quite impressive; all four players broke 70. Bob had 67, Ben and Gray shot 68, and Jimmy was one stroke back at 69. In the bottom corner of the card read the date: "3/22/46."

I noticed that the card wasn't signed or attested. Still, it was tangible evidence of some kind. I picked up the telephone and called Moonlight.

He answered after the second ring. When he heard my voice, he immediately knew why I was calling.

"Ya' got the scorecard, didn't ya'?" His voice had an "I told you so" tone to it.

"Yes, I did. May I assume that it's from this magical place you've been telling me about?"

"That's the place, alright, lad. An' that card shows ya' what a special place it was, don't it?"

I looked again at the card. "Well, it shows that either the course played easy or some pretty good players were in this group."

He cackled over the line. "I'd say they were some pretty good players. Do ya' have any idea who they were?"

"Do you mean to tell me that the Bob on this card was Bob Jones?"

"One an' the same, lad. Who do ya' think was in the rest a' the group?"

"Don't tell me that Ben was Ben Hogan."

He laughed again. "You're startin' to catch on now. An' just so ya' know, Jimmy was Jimmy Demaret."

I whistled. "That was some group. Whoever this fella Gray was could play, too."

"He was just 'bout as good as the rest of 'em, lad. I saw the whole thing, 'cause I was on Mr. Hogan's bag that day. His name was Gray Little, an' he was from somewhere down in Louisiana. He was a friend a' Mr. Hogan's. I think they had come up together on the ol' Texas tour." There was a pause. "Mr. Jones didn't know him well, but he let him play there on Mr. Hogan's say-so. Mr. Jones thought a lotta Mr. Hogan."

I was staring at the card while we talked. I noticed some pluses and minuses across one column at the bottom of the card. "This must have been a four-ball match of some kind."

Moonlight let out a soft whistling sound. "Yeah, it was, an' one a' the best ever played. The sparks really flew that day. Mr. Hogan an' Mr. Little skinned Mr. Jones an' Mr. Demaret outta two hundred bucks. That was a lot a' money back then."

Moonlight talked as if it were yesterday. I had to admit that I was a little moved by his reminiscence. "You still remember it well, don't you?"

"That I do. It was the best golf Mr. Jones'd played in a long time. An' he never really played quite that well ag'in." He suddenly sounded sad.

"I take it you sent me this because you thought I didn't believe you."

"I don't mean to be sacrilegious, but ya' kinda needed to see the nail holes in the hands, didn't ya'?"

I didn't want to admit that he was right. At the same time, I wondered how he could otherwise expect me to believe the fantastic story he was telling me. There were so many gaps in it.

All I really knew was that Jones needed privacy and that he built another course that remained a secret to this day. There were still a lot of missing pieces to this puzzle. Golf courses cost money to build and maintain. Who paid for all of this? And who got to play there? Beyond all of that, how on earth could the world's most famous golfer keep an entire golf course a secret?

There was only one person who could answer those questions. The card I was looking at told me he had the answers, but he preferred not to solve the puzzle for me. Perhaps this was the only way that Moonlight could be sure that I would believe him.

I was determined to outfox Moonlight in some way. Maybe it was just ego, but I wanted to show him that I could figure some of this out on my own. At the very least, I wanted to discover where this course was located before he finally had to tell me.

Someone at the office told me we had a road atlas in our law library. Since Moonlight had us flying into San Francisco, I figured that the almost-forgotten course was within a day's drive of the airport there. I told myself that he wouldn't expect us to drive more than 300 miles to get there, although it did occur to me that it would be just like him to pick a distant city as a diversion. For all I knew, the course might be located in Arizona. I hoped, however, that Moonlight believed me when I told him I didn't have time to gallivant around the country by car.

Ignoring Rand McNally's copyright warning, I photocopied a map of the western states. I then drew a semicircle based on a 300-mile radius from San Francisco. To the north, it extended almost to the Oregon border, and it reached Santa Barbara to the south. Parts of Nevada, including Reno, Carson City, and Lake Tahoe, were also inside the radius. It was quite a bit of ground to cover.

As I studied the map, I realized that there were an almost unlimited number of spectacular sites for a golf course in that part of the country. It would be difficult to narrow things down. I assumed that, to fulfill Jones's desire for reclusive privacy, the course would be far off the beaten path.

I was no expert on geography of the western United States. I knew that California was one of our most heavily populated states, but I also knew that it was a big state and that far less of it was developed 50 years ago when all of this was going on.

There was no shortage of scenic terrain in that part of the country, either. Jones might have found any number of wonderful venues for his ultraprivate playground.

As I scanned the map, I listed some possibilities. The Yosemite National Park was within a couple hundred miles of San

Francisco, and the land surrounding it was supposed to be gorgeous. It would've made a great site for a golf course. So would the Lake Tahoe area (which in fact has now seen the construction of several great courses in recent years). Then, of course, there was the Napa Valley region, as well as perhaps dozens of other sites up and down the coast.

I knew that Jones loved the Monterey Peninsula. Pebble Beach was one of his all-time favorites, and Alister MacKenzie's beautiful design of Cypress Point compelled Jones to select him to design Augusta National.

It was hard to imagine, though, that Jones might have been able to build a course anywhere around Carmel without attracting enormous attention. As much as he liked the area, he never would have had the privacy he craved. Besides, even back then, the cost of land there had to be prohibitively expensive for something as indulgent as the golf course Jones desired.

I then began to scan the map in the opposite direction, moving up the coast to the north of San Francisco. It showed Fort Bragg to be almost 200 miles away. Could Fort Bragg be related at all to the Bragg's Point Golf Links? To the south of Fort Bragg was something called Point Arena. I wondered. Could Bragg's Point be a combination of Fort Bragg and Point Arena?

There was perhaps 50 miles of coastline between the two points on the map. I felt a sudden surge of hope that my search had narrowed. I just might have scooped Moonlight after all.

Chapter 10

AFTER I MANAGED to finish an appellate brief for one of Emile Guidry's toxic tort cases that was due three days before we left, I got enough of a breather to spend some time thinking about our trip. As a result, I began to bombard Moonlight with questions. It seemed that the more I learned about this remarkable oasis created for Jones, the more I wanted to know about it. While I still wasn't totally convinced of Moonlight's story, by now I wanted to believe him.

Moonlight never became irritated by these cross-examinations. In fact, he seemed to enjoy them.

I didn't ask Moonlight again about the exact location of the course. (He wouldn't have told me anyway.) Nor did I let him know that I had some ideas of my own about where we might find it. Instead, I asked him all manner of questions about how Jones chose the location, acquired the property, designed and built the course, and paid for it.

He spoke about those things late in the afternoon on the Sunday before we left. We were sitting on his front porch drinking beer and watching the sunlight fade into shades of orange and yellow.

"Ya' remember those movies Jones made?"

I figured that he was referring to a series of instructional short subjects Jones made in Hollywood in the early 1930s after retiring from competitive golf. It was, technically, Jones's formal forfeiture of amateur status, because he was paid a handsome sum to do the project. Although Jones was the leading character, each installment featured a cameo appearance by one of Hollywood's leading stars. The black-and-white movies were reissued in the mid-1980s on video and, to everyone's amazement (except, perhaps, the true Jones believers) the 50-something-year-old films became the biggest selling videos on golf instruction in the entire country. My friend Ken Cheatwood had the complete set, and I had watched them with him.

"Yes, I know what you're talking about," I told him.

"Ya' remember that big fat funny man that was in 'em?"

"You mean W.C. Fields?"

"Yeah, that was his name." He leaned back in his chair on the porch. "As I understand it, he loved to talk with Mr. Jones 'bout golf. He asked Mr. Jones 'bout his favorite places to play. Mr. Jones tol' him he loved Pebble Beach an' Cypress Point near Carmel."

Moonlight paused, as if trying to recall the precise details of the conversation. "The fat man supposedly tol' Mr. Jones that there were other places in California that were just as beautiful as the Monterey area. The way I heard it, he was braggin' 'bout how California had property like that all up an' down the coast. Mr. Jones must've challenged him to show him a place as beautiful as Pebble Beach an' Cypress Point. The fat man showed him a spot, an' that's where Mr. Jones eventually built the course."

I didn't know whether Moonlight had intended to do so, but he had provided me with one more clue. Jones's private sanctuary was on the coast. If true, it was certainly consistent with my hunch.

"What would a comedian know about golf course locations?"

Moonlight stroked the stubble on his chin. In the short time I had known him, he appeared to shave no more than once a week.

"What can I tell ya'? Like a lot of us, he loved the game, even though he couldn't play a lick. He also had a lotta money. Ya' gotta remember, he was a big, big star. All those Hollywood types were tryin' to outdo one another to see who could build the biggest mansion. I dunno whether he was lookin' for a place to build a house overlookin' the ocean or what, but he knew 'bout this place somehow."

"What made him think that Mr. Jones wanted to build another golf course? I'm surprised that Fields didn't want in on the deal."

He opened another beer and took a pull from the bottle. "Don't know that he didn't. Wouldn't've mattered anyway. Mr. Jones didn't trust anyone he didn't know real, real well. Besides, I don't think he thought a whole helluva lot 'bout that Hollywood crowd."

"So…what happened next?"

"Well, Mr. Jones went an' scouted the area. Took Mr. Roberts with him. They found a wonderful place. Problem was, it was owned by the government. They got a lotta land out there, ya' know."

He emptied his beer bottle and reached for another before he continued. "Mr. Roberts had some friends in New York who had plenty a' stroke in Washington. In less than six months, the property was deeded over to these high-powered guys in New York. They then turned it over to Mr. Roberts."

"How was Jones going to keep this a secret with that many people involved?"

"These people were already members at Augusta National. Ya' gotta remember, most a' the early membership came from New York. They loved Mr. Jones an' feared Mr. Roberts. They wouldn't do anythin' to risk gettin' tossed outta the club."

I wanted to keep him talking. "When did all of this take place?"

Moonlight thought for a minute. "By the time Mr. Jones decided he needed another place away from the National, it must've been 'round 1935 or so." He looked at the ceiling and then said, "Yeah, that would've been 'bout right. I know that he waited a year or two after that fat man tol' him 'bout the property before he really did anythin' with it."

"Did Alister MacKenzie design the new course, too?"

"Nah, Mr. MacKenzie died right 'round the time they opened the course at Augusta. Heart attack, I think it was. I believe that Mr. Jones had talked to him 'bout the new place, though, before he passed on. Mr. MacKenzie may've even seen it. But he died before he did any work on it."

"Then who *did* design the course?"

Moonlight seemed to enjoy my persistence.

"When Mr. Jones was workin' with Mr. MacKenzie on the National, there was a young Scotsman who was an associate a' Mr. MacKenzie's. He offered some thoughts a' his own 'bout the design that apparently impressed Mr. Jones. Turned out to be a pretty fair architect in his own right. Name was Maxwell."

"Are you talking about Perry Maxwell?"

"Yeah, that was him."

"So he designed the new course?"

"Yep."

I thought about how active Jones had been in the design of Augusta National. "Why didn't Jones design the new course himself?"

Moonlight shrugged. "Oh, he'd a lot to do with it, just like he did at the National. But he wouldn't go it alone. He wanted someone who did it for a livin'. Mr. Jones was great 'bout the golfin' part—ya' know, where he wanted shots to be played an' that sorta thing—but he knew there was more to buildin' a golf course than that. Besides," he added after taking a swig, "he had a law practice, ya' know."

Later on, I looked up details about MacKenzie and Maxwell. Moonlight's memory was pretty good.

Maxwell worked with MacKenzie during the early 1930s in the last years before MacKenzie died. During their brief time together, the two of them collaborated on the design of several outstanding courses, including the University of Michigan Golf Club.

After MacKenzie's death, Maxwell went on to design a number of impressive layouts on his own and then, in later years, with his son Press. His courses can be found in virtually every part of the country. Perhaps his best work was Prairie Dunes, a links course built in the plains of the Midwest that remains to this day one of the great courses in America. From what I read, Jones would have had good reason to be impressed enough with Maxwell to hire him for his special project.

But were it not for a great amateur golfer from Nebraska named Johnny Goodman, Jones would probably never have known about either MacKenzie or Maxwell. Goodman is perhaps best known as the last amateur to win the U.S. Open, which he did in 1933. But his decisive victory over Bobby Jones in the first round of match play at the 1929 U.S. Amateur at Pebble Beach actually had much greater impact on golf history.

Faced with time on his hands after his unexpectedly early exit from the championship (and with a hotel room already paid for), Jones accepted an invitation to play a new course just opening nearby known as the Cypress Point Golf Club. He was impressed by what he found. While there, Jones somehow also met the course's architect, who happened to be Alister MacKenzie.

MacKenzie was a physician-turned-golf architect. Although he advertised himself as Scottish, the truth was that he was raised in England. He did have a Scottish mother, however, so there was some truth to his boastful claim of a connection with golf's birthplace.

MacKenzie was an avid but not particularly talented golfer. Like most mediocre players, he had a rather healthy respect for those who possessed real talent at the game. No doubt, he revered a world-class player like Jones.

Jones probably found much to admire in MacKenzie as well. For one thing, MacKenzie proudly proclaimed that he did not design courses so much as "find" them in the land. MacKenzie's more subtle method of taking what nature gave him helped make certain that the new course at Cypress Point would accentuate the great natural beauty of the property.

Although MacKenzie was certainly not as prolific as Donald Ross, the other great golf architect of the day, he did as much as Ross to make golf architecture a respected profession. As early as 1920, MacKenzie had published a book titled *Golf Architecture*. In it, he articulated what he considered to be fundamental design principles and described his philosophy of preserving the best natural features of each site.

It probably didn't hurt MacKenzie's chances at being eventually selected by Jones for Augusta National that this approach was also the most economical way to build a golf course. By preserving the most attractive natural features of the land, MacKenzie moved less dirt, which meant less expense. When one considers that Augusta National was built in the throes of the Great Depression, the resulting economy could not be ignored.

So it made sense that, if Jones was going to build another course out west—particularly one overlooking the Pacific Ocean—he would have wanted MacKenzie to design it.

Unfortunately, that didn't happen because MacKenzie died unexpectedly at the age of 63 in 1934. From all accounts, he never even saw his completed handiwork at Augusta National before he fell ill. As a result he wouldn't have been available to help Jones with Bragg's Point, so Maxwell was apparently tapped for the job.

I was interested in knowing more about Maxwell's design work. Could he possibly have matched MacKenzie's brilliant work at Cypress Point? There wasn't enough time to run that to ground at the moment, however, because it was time to leave for San Francisco.

Chapter 11

MOONLIGHT AGREED TO meet me at the airport. I found him at the ticket counter just as I was checking my bags. He sported his familiar Hogan cap, polyester pants, and caddie's sneakers. And he looked nervous.

I smiled and tried to reassure him. "All set?"

He looked at me, licked his lips, and said, "I could use a drink."

I laughed. "Did you take the Dramamine I gave you?"

"Nah, I thought I'd wait an' wash it down with some Scotch."

I recalled his fondness for Rolling Rock. "I thought you liked beer."

"At a time like this, I need somethin' a little more potent."

I looked at my watch. "Well, we've got an hour before our flight leaves. Let's find a bar."

I knew that there was one down on our concourse. I headed him in that direction. As we approached the security station, he stopped short. After looking around nervously, he asked, "What's all this?"

His question reminded me that he had never flown before. So naturally he hadn't ever been through the security screenings or metal detectors that have become a necessary aspect of air travel. As skittish as he was, I didn't want to tell him that these security measures were a response to the threat of terrorist skyjackings.

"It's just a routine thing."

We got in line. As we approached the portal, we could hear the security guards directing everyone ahead of us to place all jewelry and other metal objects in a plastic tray to avoid setting off the sensors. At about the same time, I saw Moonlight carefully reading the warning signs announcing that it was a violation of federal law to carry weapons onto an airplane. The next thing I knew, he had pulled me out of line and said in an agitated voice that I needed to follow him. I did, to a nearby restroom.

To my astonishment, he then opened his jacket to reveal a small .22-caliber handgun. I grabbed his coat, closed it, and shoved him into a stall.

"What the hell are you doing with that?" My voice was louder than I would have liked, but it was difficult to whisper under the circumstances.

"I didn't know…" he said lamely before I cut him off.

I fought off visions of sitting before a hearing committee trying to avoid disbarment for a federal firearms violation. "For God's sake, why are you packin' a gun?" I didn't wait for his answer. Reeling off a long strip of toilet paper, I grabbed the gun from him, wrapped it up, and then opened the stall door. At that point, another man entered the room, but he walked straight over to a urinal, which put his back to us. I moved quickly to drop the wad of paper into the trash receptacle and then pulled Moonlight by the scruff of the neck out of there as fast as I could.

I was too nervous to return to the security station, so we headed back toward the lobby. As luck would have it, there was a lounge at the far end. I made a beeline for it, literally dragging Moonlight with me.

"Now wait just a damned minute," he said finally. "Ya' don't have to get crazy, ya' know."

I turned on my heels to face him. "You're calling *me* crazy?"

I saw from his reaction that I had hurt him. I patted his shoulder in a gesture of reconciliation. Pointing to the bar, I said, "Look, let's duck in there for a drink. I need one now even more than you do."

After Moonlight promised that he had no more unpleasant surprises for me, I bought a round of Scotch. One drink led to another, and we were both pretty lightheaded by the time we boarded our flight.

The combination of whiskey and Dramamine took its toll on Moonlight shortly after we were airborne, and he slept most of the way. I was grateful that we encountered no turbulence to disturb his restful sleep. He didn't wake up until we were beginning our descent into San Francisco.

Even after he was fully awake, Moonlight wouldn't look out of his window. He preferred to stare straight ahead as if he were counting the minutes until we would be back on the ground. I don't think he really began to relax until we had retrieved our luggage and located the rental car. By that time, the incident with the gun seemed to be behind us, although I never did get a straight story about why he had it to begin with. He did tell me later that it wasn't loaded and that he wasn't even carrying any ammunition for it. Like so many other things about Moonlight, that didn't make any sense either.

As we exited the San Francisco airport, I turned to Moonlight and said, "Do I take 101 North?" I was referring to Highway 101, which runs north and south along the West Coast from Tijuana to Canada.

He gave me a wry smile. "So ya' think ya' know where to go, do ya'?"

It was my turn to be coy. "I may have some idea," I said, leaving him to wonder how much I *did* know about his big "secret."

Moonlight was not to be outdone. He let me drive on for a bit before commenting, "Well, this is at least in the right direction." After a pause, he added, "But it ain't the only way to get there."

We soon came upon a sign indicating an exit one mile ahead to California Highway 1. Pointing to it, Moonlight instructed me to take the exit. "This way's better."

And it was. Where Highway 101 strayed inland as much as 40 miles or more, Highway 1 hugged the coastline for a hundred miles or so before it eventually looped back into 101. The view along the way was breathtaking. Lots of beaches, bluffs, cliffs, and ocean.

I saw any number of remarkable vistas for golf courses. Depending on how much of the area was still unclaimed by developers nearly 70 years ago, Jones could have found his golfing nirvana virtually anywhere along the Northern California coast. I could only hope that there was something left in the area to identify the location of Bragg's Point. Otherwise, I would soon have to rely on Moonlight for further directions.

I engaged him again in another history tutorial. "Tell me how they were able to finance the new course."

He grunted. "We've been over that, Charley. Mr. Roberts took care a' that. He did it the same way they built the National. Mr. Roberts could lay his hands on a lotta money up North. Ya' know, they built Augusta National in 'bout three months. The man could really mobilize the troops when need be."

"And even with all those people involved, they kept it a secret?"

Moonlight laughed. "You're havin' trouble with that part of it, ain't ya'? Ya' had to know Mr. Roberts. He didn't tell ya' anythin' he didn't want ya' to know. An' no one questioned his authority. Not if they wanted to stay in the club at Augusta. Besides, things were different then. People kept their word 'bout things, ya' know?"

He watched some seagulls hovering over the beach to our left. "Mr. Jones put a lotta his own money into this project, too. He got paid big money for makin' those movies. He had family money, too, an' owned a Coca-Cola bottlin' plant in Massachusetts."

I knew that Jones came from money. His grandfather owned virtually all of Canton, Georgia, including its main bank and cotton plantation. And his father, a lawyer nicknamed "The

Colonel," had done well, too. Jones was an only child, so everything had gone to him.

The Coca-Cola plant was news, however. I figured it must have come through Jones's connections with the founding family of the Atlanta-based company. I made a note to ask Moonlight about that part again later.

Moonlight was suddenly in the mood to talk. "Ya' know, another thing that Jones liked 'bout it out here was that he could play all summer. Hell, sometimes ya' had to wear a sweater'n July. Back'n Georgia, ya' wouldn't think 'bout stayin' out in the sun very long in the middle a' the summer. That's why they always closed the National from May to October."

"But what about Jones's law practice? Was it a problem for him to be gone for long periods of time?"

"Nah," Moonlight said lightly. "Just to have Mr. Jones's name in that firm you're workin' for was money in the bank for 'em. Ya' don't think they objected if he took off to play golf, do ya'?"

Not if they wanted to play Augusta National or enjoy the considerable financial benefits of being associated with the greatest golfer in the world, I thought.

"They began to call the course at the National 'the tournament course,'" Moonlight explained. "An' those who knew 'bout the new course referred to it as 'Bob's course.'"

Knowing Roberts's penchant for promotion, especially in the early years of the tournament, I asked Moonlight why they didn't refer to it as "the Masters course."

"Ya' know, Mr. Jones never really liked that name. He wanted to call it the Augusta National Invitational Tournament. Mr.

Roberts kept pesterin' him to call it the Masters. Mr. Jones eventually gave in, but he never used that name. He just called it 'the tournament,' an' that's what the members called it. At least, the older members did—an' still do."

I was becoming more and more fascinated by the idea of the world's most famous golfer hiding away and playing on his private playground. I had to admit that what Moonlight was telling me made sense. Everything I knew about Jones was consistent with Moonlight's story. Jones was, as Moonlight suggested, a very private person who was drained by public attention. How else could you explain his decision to step down from the top of the sporting world before his prime?

I remained skeptical, however, about keeping such a remarkable secret from the media. Moonlight didn't seem to think that was such a difficult thing. "If ya' think 'bout it, ya' could do it then. The news media wasn't so snoopy. They didn't have no television, ya' know. An' reportin' was different back then. I guess they felt they needed famous people more'n famous people needed them, so they looked the other way when asked. Besides, Mr. Jones an' Mr. Roberts had some powerful friends in the media."

I recalled that Grantland Rice, perhaps the preeminent sportswriter of the day, was one of the original members of Augusta National. Jones's influence ran deep into the American Establishment.

Moonlight gave me a mischievous look. "I guess I should tell ya'. There was one fella who came close to figurin' it out. Never knew what happened to him."

"What do you mean?" I sensed that there was a great deal more to be told from the tone in his voice.

"Not long after the course opened, we heard that some guy was snoopin' 'round town askin' questions. He was some kinda reporter or investigator. I really don't know if he was with a newspaper back East or from the government." He gave me a sideways look and cocked an eyebrow. "Ya' know, I don't think the land deal went through normal channels, if ya' know what I mean. Maybe some bureaucrat was gettin' nosy, for all I know."

"Okay, so what happened?"

"Mr. Jones was worried that the course'd become public knowledge. He thought it'd look bad, not to mention probably shut the place down. He tol' some a' the others who were out here playin' 'bout it. One a' the caddies in the group was a guy named Clarence Henderson. His nickname was 'The Cleaver.' I never knew why. Frankly, didn't wanna know."

What an ominous handle, I thought.

"Anyway, the man was fanatically devoted to Mr. Jones. Apparently, he loved bein' a caddie 'cause it was the first thing that ever kept him outta trouble. The guy had done three stretches in prison before he somehow caught on at the National."

I interrupted Moonlight to ask why anyone at Augusta National would hire a three-time felon nicknamed "The Cleaver."

"They don't check references in the caddie shack. If a guy is willin' to show up, keep up, an' shut up, he's got the makin's of a good caddie."

I laughed.

Moonlight apparently thought I was making light of the caddie's job. "It ain't as easy as it sounds, lad. You're either hurryin' ahead or behind the player, gettin' a pin or repairin' a divot or bunker. An' in between you're givin' out yardage an' tellin' him what club to hit or how much a putt breaks. Ya' never get credit when you're right—the good shots are always the player's doin'. But when you're wrong, ya' hear 'bout it, ya' know what I mean?"

I tried to make amends by saying sympathetically, "Sounds like being an umpire. When you do a good job, no one notices. Blow one call, though, and everybody's all over your case."

Moonlight just grunted, as if still a little upset at me for not appreciating the demands of his profession. I needed to get him back on track, so I asked about Clarence Henderson again.

"He had somethin' inside his head, kinda like a gyroscope. Never seen anythin' like it before or since. The man could measure yardage without ever pacin' anythin' off. We'd check him, an' he was right on the money every time."

He paused and stroked the permanent stubble on his chin. "That wasn't the best part, either. He did the same thing with the wind. At the National, the wind can kill ya' on the back nine, especially at number 12."

Moonlight was referring to the adventurous par 3 whose meager 153 yards had often proved to be too much for some of the world's best players. The hole challenges the player with a shallow green that is nestled against the back edge of the property, where the wind direction above the tall loblolly pines is often different from what the player feels against his cheek or sees at the flag. As a result, the slightest miscalculation can mean that a tee shot finds the pond guarding the front of the green or gets lost in the dense brush covering the hill immediately behind it. In virtually every Masters tournament, at least one contender has encountered disaster on Sunday because he was deceived by the air currents swirling above the 12th green.

There have been any number of novel theories advanced by Masters veterans about how to figure the wind at the 12th. Ben Hogan supposedly ignored the tips of the pines swaying above and instead looked at the flag on the nearby 11th green to determine which way the wind would blow his tee shot. Ken Venturi has claimed that a limp flag at 11 means the wind is moving above 12 and that a flag waving in the breeze there means there is no wind above the par 3 at the moment. Neither one of them ever adequately explained the basis for their theories.

At any rate, I understood the enormous value of having a caddie at Augusta National who could decipher which way the wind was blowing, particularly down at Amen Corner.

"So Henderson had the wind figured out, huh?"

"It was amazin', I tell ya'. Whenever we were on a bag in his group, we'd look to him at the 12th before we said anythin' to our man. Even when we had a bet, he never lied to us. Got it right every time."

"How'd he end up at the new course?"

"Mr. Jones an' Mr. Roberts didn't want to take a chance an' hire people out here they didn't know. They took several of us from the National. They didn't need many; wasn't gonna be that many playin' the course anyway. Anyhow, Clarence wanted to get away. He was tryin' to live down a bad reputation, an' people in Augusta knew all 'bout his past. Guess he felt he'd be gettin' a fresh start out here."

He pointed toward the ocean. "Can ya' imagine havin' a caddie who can figure out what that wind's gonna do comin' in off the ocean an' bouncin' 'round in these trees?"

I took it to be a rhetorical question and continued with the interview. "So what did Henderson have to do with the guy who was snoopin' around?"

He took a long time answering. "I got no evidence a' what I'm 'bout to tell ya'." He hesitated again, carefully choosing his words. "The man had an almost religious attitude 'bout Mr. Jones, like he was his savior or somethin'. He must've felt like workin' for Mr. Jones at the National turned his life 'round, if ya' know what I mean."

I nodded. A lot of people back then had made a religion out of following Jones.

"Like I said, Clarence was in the group when Mr. Jones shared his fears 'bout what this fella might find. The next thing we knew, the fella disappeared. Never heard from ag'in."

"What makes you think Henderson had anything to do with it? Maybe the guy just went back to wherever he came from."

Moonlight shook his head. "I don't think so. Clarence tol' another one a' the caddies, Gra'm McNulty, 'My man won't have to worry 'bout that snitch no more.' It don't take a genius to figure the rest out."

"Did they ever find a body or any evidence of foul play?"

Moonlight laughed softly. "Ya' lawyers all sound like you're a book. Ya' got that lawyer-talk down, Charley, I'll say that for ya.'"

I took no offense. "Well, they pound it into you for three years, night and day. Either you learn it their way or you don't become a lawyer."

He nodded agreeably. "To answer your question, they never found nothin'." He paused a moment before adding, "An' that was the end a' that."

"You don't think Jones had anything to do with it, do you?"

He shook his head vigorously. "Oh, no, nothin' at all. Clarence would never've said anythin' to him 'bout it. He protected Mr. Jones. Besides, he knew Mr. Jones would never had stood for anythin' like that. It was just his way a' takin' care a' his man."

"Did any of you ask Clarence about it?"

He looked at me wide-eyed. "I don't believe so, lad. Some things ya' don't want to know 'bout. What was I gonna do 'bout it, anyway?"

There was clearly no point in answering that question.

It was getting late in the afternoon. I figured we only had maybe an hour or so of daylight left. I had no idea of how much farther we had to go to reach our destination, and we had made no arrangements for the night's lodging.

As if he had read my mind, Moonlight directed me to drive all the way to Fort Bragg. "We'll stay the night there an' get a fresh start in the mornin'." Seeing my inquisitive expression, he added, "It ain't far from there."

I smiled as if I had been vindicated. Before I could say anything, he mumbled almost to himself, "I get the feelin' ya' maybe knew that already."

It was almost 8:00 P.M. when we pulled into a Holiday Inn just east of Fort Bragg on Kaspar Boulevard off Highway 20. By venturing inland a few miles, we avoided the higher room rates of places selling ocean views or beach access. After checking in, the two of us were directed to a small diner across the street, where we ate our evening meal.

At dinner, I tried to get Moonlight to tell me more about the course, but he was clearly determined to keep me in the dark. "Ya' gotta see it first," he said. "Ya' can't begin to understand the magic a' the place until then."

He then distracted me by asking about what it was like to grow up in Birmingham, why I went to law school, and how long I had been playing golf. We had talked about some of the same things on his porch. Since I wasn't sure if he just didn't remember or was deliberately changing the subject, I played along. In typical fashion, Moonlight wasn't going to show his cards until he was ready to do so.

Chapter 12

I HAD RENTED one room with two beds to save money. By sharing a room with Moonlight, I quickly learned two things about him that I hadn't known before. He snored, and he was an early riser.

I don't know whether it was Moonlight's snoring or the excitement of knowing I was about to see Moonlight's secret course, but I wasn't able to fall asleep until the early hours of the morning, when exhaustion finally overtook me. As a result, I overslept. By the time I woke up, it was close to 7:30 A.M. Moonlight wasn't in the room.

It turned out that he had been up since 5:00 A.M. In that time, he had showered, read the paper, eaten breakfast in the coffee shop, and had gone for a walk. I figured that he was scouting the area to regain his bearings from years past.

He returned to the room just as I was getting dressed. I couldn't resist a dig.

"I'm sure so much has changed," I said indulgently. "Are you sure you'll be able to find this place?"

He gave me a stern look. "I know exactly where it is, believe you me."

I asked him how long it had been since he had been on the course.

"The last round was played on October 17, 1970. I was there 'til the end."

I was surprised by the date. "Was Jones still playing golf then?"

He shook his head. "Nah, he hadn't played in years. But he still loved bein' out there. Rode 'round the course in a golf cart. It was the only one allowed on the grounds."

If Jones was no longer playing the course, I wondered who was. His face took on a mischievous smile when I asked him.

"That's the interestin' part. Best I could tell, it came down to whether Mr. Jones an' Mr. Roberts trusted ya' with the secret. An' there weren't many they did. So we'd go days at a time without anyone playin'. Toward the end, those were the days Mr. Jones liked. He'd ride out on the course by himself an' be gone for hours. We used to worry that somethin' might've happened to him."

"Why would he do that?"

He seemed almost annoyed by my question. "I've tol' ya' before, Mr. Jones didn't like a lotta attention. An' he didn't like people seein' him all crippled up like he was. But to his dyin' day, he loved bein' on that golf course."

Moonlight's voice had faltered, and he paused for a moment to collect himself before continuing. "Ya' see, he couldn't do that at the National. Whenever he was on the grounds, it attracted a lotta attention. All the members an' the people who worked there wanted to touch him, talk to him, whatever. He just didn't want to be asked how he felt."

I felt his slight rebuke. "I still want to know who all played this private reserve."

He ignored me. Instead, he asked if I was hungry for breakfast. I was, so we headed down to the coffee shop.

After we settled into a booth, I confronted him.

"You know, Moonlight, you've asked me to help you tell this story, but I feel like I'm having trouble following you. It's almost like we're playing some kind of a game. That's okay, but I can't tell the story you want me to tell if I don't understand it. You've got to help me a little more."

He seemed to appreciate my predicament. Putting down his coffee cup, he said, "I'm sorry, lad. Believe me, I'm not tryin' to confuse ya.'"

Sensing that I had an opportunity, I tried to take advantage. "What I really want to know is, who got to play there? Did they ever hold any tournaments of any kind there? Was there a clubhouse of any kind? Where did you and the other caddies live? And what did..."

He held up his hand. "Whoa, son, I can't keep up with ya.' Believe me, you're gonna understand it all in the next few days."

I had finished my breakfast by that time. He drank the last of his coffee and said, "It's time to complete your education."

I noticed that his eyes were suddenly brighter. As he stood up, Moonlight's thin gray lips spread into a wide grin, and he said with unmistakable pride, "C'mon, ya' need to see it."

I followed him out of the coffee shop and into the parking

lot. We climbed into our rented Taurus. As I pulled out of the parking lot, he directed me back to Highway 1. When we reached the highway, he told me to follow the signs to Fort Bragg.

For the first time, I felt a surge of childlike excitement, like the kind a seven-year-old feels on Christmas morning. I was about to become privy to a remarkable piece of golf history. I felt fortunate that Moonlight had decided to share his secret with me while he was still on this side of the grass.

There were pictures in my head that had been developing slowly as Moonlight revealed more and more about the place. Thus, even though I really didn't know what to expect, my imagination had conjured up some fairly graphic images of the secluded course. Now that I was about to confront the reality of it, I wondered how it would compare with the photo album in my brain.

I was so deep in thought that the sign for Fort Bragg almost startled me. Moonlight pointed left and said, "Turn here." We left the highway and headed down a large boulevard. A sign appeared every few hundred yards to warn that we were approaching a security checkpoint for Fort Bragg.

Soon a huge gate and guardhouse appeared a quarter of a mile ahead of us. Another sign instructed us, "Please Have Appropriate Identification Ready."

I turned to Moonlight. "What do we do now?"

He looked straight ahead. "Just keep drivin'."

I slowed as we approached the main gate. An MP waved us forward. As we stopped by his side, he leaned down at my open window and asked for our credentials. Before I could tell him that we didn't have any, Moonlight reached across me and handed him a tattered old card of some kind.

I'll never forget the look on the MP's face when he saw that card. He turned toward the guardhouse and yelled, "Hey, Joe, come take a look at this."

An older MP with a look of foreboding appeared almost immediately. As soon as he saw Moonlight's card, he blanched. Then he looked at me and said, "Sir, would you mind pulling your vehicle over to the side there for a minute?"

I did as I was told, although I really didn't know what to think of it all. I had never been put in a military stockade, but I wondered for a minute whether that was where we were headed.

As I turned off the engine, I heard the older MP say, "Man, it's been years since I've seen one of these." He then disappeared inside the guardhouse. I imagined that he was calling for reinforcements in the event we resisted our imminent arrest.

In what seemed like a long time but was probably only a couple of minutes, he reappeared. As he was walking toward us, I heard him say to the other MP, "It's still good." He then reached across me to hand the card back to Moonlight.

In an apologetic tone, he said to Moonlight, "Sorry to detain you, sir. But that's an unusual card you're carrying. It has one of our highest clearances, but it's so old I had to check and see if it was still current." Looking at me, he said, "That card is good for anyone in this gentleman's company, but I must ask you to remain with him at all times while you're inside the gate." Turning back to Moonlight, he said, "Sir, if you will check with us here when you leave, we'll have a new card for you with a bar code on it. It'll make things easier for you in the future."

Moonlight had remained respectfully quiet the entire time. He simply nodded toward the MP and said "Thank you."

Needless to say, I was completely dumbstruck by this. After we cleared the gate, I turned to Moonlight. "Did you get that from a general or something? And why didn't you tell me about it?"

Moonlight just cackled. He had thoroughly enjoyed the scene at the gate, especially my befuddlement. After he let me dangle a bit, he said, "Probably for the same reason ya' didn't tell me 'bout the stuff at the airport."

Okay, we were even, I said.

He couldn't leave it at that. "I told ya' that Mr. Jones an' Mr. Roberts had friends in high places. I tol' ya' they got this property from the government. Ya' gotta listen, Charley."

Turning back to the road, he pointed ahead and said, "There should be a road up here a coupla hundred yards ahead. It won't be marked, so ya' better slow down or we'll miss it."

Sure enough, a road appeared right where he said it would. It wasn't very wide, but it was paved. It obviously hadn't been used very much, because weeds now grew tall through the cracks and expansion joints in the pavement, some as much as three feet high. Trees and other assorted vegetation encroached on both sides, effectively narrowing the road to the width of our car. As the brush scratched its sides, I caught myself wondering if I would get any of my security deposit back when we returned it to the airport.

The road began a gentle and prolonged turn to our right. Combined with the heavy overgrowth, the result was that I couldn't see more than 20 or 30 yards in front of us.

Without taking my eyes off the road, I sought some reassurance from Moonlight. "Are you sure this is the way to go?"

"I told ya', I remember it like it was yesterday."

Just then we encountered a tall, fenced gate across the road. It was padlocked, and there was no way around it. It appeared to extend indefinitely into the woods on both sides of the road. It looked like we had reached the end of the road, literally and figuratively.

I stopped the car and turned to Moonlight. "Well, what do we do now?"

He was opening his door and pushing it into the brush that was against our car. As he struggled to get out, he said, "Just wait here a minute." It then occurred to me that Moonlight hadn't been surprised by the gate.

I watched as he fought his way through the brush around to the front of the car. He walked confidently toward the gate, reached into his pocket and pulled out a key. Inserting the key into the padlock, he flipped it open and pushed the gate back. Standing aside, he then waved me through. Once I was past, he closed and relocked the gate.

Moonlight then got back in the car as if nothing unusual had occurred. I just sat there staring at him. He finally turned to me impatiently and said, "Well, let's get goin'. We don't have much more to go."

"How long have you had that key?"

"A long time," he said. He then looked back toward the road. I took this to mean it was time to continue.

After a couple of hundred yards, the trees and bushes became so thick that I had slowed the car to no more than 10 miles per hour. I was becoming pretty apprehensive about continuing. We were in the middle of a rather dense stand of trees, and I had lost all sense of direction. Even though there was no place to turn around, I asked Moonlight if we should turn back.

He never took his eyes off the road and said, "Nah, it's just up ahead." It seemed like we had been driving a long time, but we probably hadn't covered much distance given our slow rate of progress. We suddenly entered a clearing, and I saw it.

Chapter 13

I WAS TOTALLY unprepared for the magnificent scene that appeared before me. From where I stood, the land fell away for several hundred yards to the Pacific Ocean. Some of the ground swept down close to the water's edge, while other portions abruptly terminated at rocky cliffs. I could see and hear the surf crashing on the rocks below. An occasional California fir, redwood, or cypress tree stood out above the native brush as the land cascaded down to the sea. The trees appeared to be separated by fire lanes of some kind. Then I realized that they weren't fire lanes at all. They were fairways.

Our visual feast was accompanied by an array of fragrances more potent than any scent from Paris. I tried to sort them out, but there were simply too many. It was as if someone has opened the door to a massive nursery that had been kept under seal. The aroma was deep, rich, and various shades of green.

The next thing I saw was the clubhouse off to our left about a hundred yards away. It was small but elegant—and remarkably well preserved under the circumstances. I noticed that all of the windows were intact and that, aside from the aging white paint that was peeling in spots, it was in surprisingly good condition for property that had been abandoned over 30 years ago.

There weren't any signs of vandalism, which I would have expected to see. But then I remembered that this place was protected by two of the greatest forces known to man: Uncle Sam and Mother Nature. The chances of anyone making it back here with mischief in mind were minuscule.

I stood there for quite some time. When I finally turned and looked over at Moonlight, he was watching me intently, grinning from ear to ear.

At that moment, all of the questions and lingering doubts I may have had about our crazy mission—and about Moonlight—were suddenly gone. And I was very, very glad for whatever instinct had persuaded me to trust him when logic and common sense told me otherwise. I wanted to say that much and more to him, but the words wouldn't come.

"This is the damnedest thing I've ever seen," was all I could manage to say.

He laughed. "It's more than that, Charley. There's magic in this place. You're gonna see it, believe me. An' you're gonna feel it, too." He paused a minute before asking, "Are ya' ready to do some explorin'?"

"Lead the way."

Moonlight started walking toward the clubhouse. Without looking back, he began giving me a tour of the place. "The clubhouse here was different from anythin' I've ever seen before or since. The caddies were allowed inside with the players. Everyone who shared the secret was equal."

The small white building had a large front porch typical of the Southern style of architecture with which Jones was so familiar. It faced the ocean, offering an inspiring vista to the players and caddies who must have gathered there after the day's play.

I entertained myself with wonderful thoughts of Jones and his friends drinking whiskey and conducting postmortems on the round they had just concluded. This porch, I speculated, was probably the place where money changed hands as bets were paid in full.

As we stood there, Moonlight showed me where the first tee was located to our right and the eighth tee to our left. In front of us, he said, was the large green for the 18th hole. Anyone sitting on the front porch could see a lot of golf—a lot of damned good golf.

I started to ask a number of questions about the course, but he dismissed them. "Later," he said and, pulling another key from his pocket, unlocked the front door of the clubhouse. I was trying not to be surprised by anything he did at this point.

The door creaked as he pushed it open. As we stepped in, I was struck by the fact that the interior was as well preserved as the outside of the clubhouse. I turned to Moonlight. "Somebody's been taking care of this place."

Moonlight shook his head. "No way, lad. I tol' ya', there ain't no one else left."

"But this place is in really good shape for a building that's been deserted all this time."

Moonlight just shook his head. "That's part a' the magic a' Bragg's Point, lad."

To our right was a door that led into a small but comfortable locker room. The lockers reminded me of Shinnecock Hills, which I had played the previous year with a friend. There were no more than a dozen of them, as well as three card tables, and what must have been a small bar. On the other side of the room were the showers and toilets. The place looked like it could be reopened with just a good spring-cleaning.

Pointing to the tables, Moonlight said, "There used to be some hellacious gin games there. Mr. Hagen loved to take 'em all on. What he didn't win on the course, he won at cards."

"Walter Hagen played here?"

Moonlight smiled. "They *all* played here."

As we left the locker room, I saw a staircase to our right. "What's up there?"

"The bedrooms. An' Mr. Jones's room."

"I've got to see that," I said and started walking to the stairs.

Moonlight grabbed my arm. "Careful, lad. I don't know if those stairs are safe."

I ignored his warning. "They look pretty good to me," I said over my shoulder. Dust rose from the carpeted stairs with each step I took.

Moonlight hesitated at first, but quickly followed me. At the top of the landing, he pointed down a hallway. "It's down there."

I took "it" to mean Jones's quarters. "Show me."

Moonlight seemed nervous for some reason. His eyes darted around. He looked back at me and said, "Ya' really wanna see it?"

I was taken aback by his skittish manner. "Are you afraid of ghosts or something?"

He didn't take it as a joke. "Remember, Charley, I've tol' ya' several times. This place isn't like any other."

Reluctantly, he started down the hallway. For the first time, I noticed that the floor creaked as we walked. It reminded me that the building was made almost entirely of wood. As far as I was concerned, a good clubhouse had to be made of wood to have the proper feel to it. If it was made of concrete and steel, it was too new to be of any use to me.

As we made our way down the hallway, clouds of dust accented the shafts of sunlight streaming in through the windows on a diagonal in front of us. At the end of the hall was a door. Moonlight started to turn the knob. It wouldn't move. He uttered a single word, "Locked," and reached inside his pocket. Producing still another key—again I suppressed my surprise—he inserted it into the lock and turned it. I heard the bolt slide, and Moonlight swung the door open.

We stepped into the sitting room of a small apartment. Through a door on the left was a bedroom with a single bed, small dresser, and night table. To the right of the sitting room was a small bath.

It all seemed neatly preserved. Too neat, I thought. Although there was no bedding or other linen, much less toiletries and such, the place seemed perfectly habitable.

"Moonlight, someone could be living here."

He gave out a funny laugh. "Now, lad, ya' gotta cut that out. You're startin' to spook me, ya' know?"

What I was really thinking was that, if someone was living in Jones's old apartment, they would have good reason to regard us as intruders. If anything happened to us out here, it might be months before we (or our bodies) were discovered.

I thought I heard something move down the hall. I spun around, but saw nothing.

Moonlight seemed irritated. "Would ya' stop that, for Chrissake?"

I didn't tell him that I was becoming afraid too. Still, as much as I wanted to leave, I couldn't forget that I was standing where the great Bobby Jones had been. "How often did Jones stay here?"

Moonlight shrugged. "He'd come for a week or two at a time. Every once in a while Mrs. Jones came with him, but that was rare." He paused before adding, "I guess there wasn't much for her to do here. It was really a man's place, ya' know what I mean?"

He pointed to the bedroom. "Didya' notice the view through the window in there? Mr. Jones liked to say it was the best seat in the house."

I walked back into the bedroom and looked out the window. It did, indeed, offer a splendid view of the entire property and the ocean. I stood for a minute and took it all in. Just as I was about to turn away, I thought I saw something move in the shadows of a tree outside the window. I didn't say anything to Moonlight.

I suggested to Moonlight that it was time to take a look at the course. He seemed a little surprised that I didn't have more questions about Jones's quarters, but led me back outside.

As we stood in front of the clubhouse, I peppered Moonlight with questions about the golf course.

"How much land did they have?"

Moonlight thought for a minute. "I dunno. Not a lot. They had to squeeze it in. There's no range. 'Course, they didn't need one; if anyone wanted to practice, they hit balls to a caddie in one a' the fairways."

I looked around. "Looks like a pretty tight fit for 18 holes."

Moonlight nodded. "It's plenty enough, though, you'll see. Remember, they didn't need any space for anythin' else. There wasn't any pool, no tennis courts, or parkin' lot. Only a few people ever came here, an' when they did it was for one reason: to play golf."

Looking out over the property again, I said, "God, this is a gorgeous place."

"That's why Mr. Jones was determined to fit a course in here. That fat man was right when he told him he knew of a place that was as pretty as Cypress Point."

He gestured out toward the ocean. "Come with me, lad, you've gotta see the view out there." We walked down toward the rocky cliffs that lined the edge of the property overlooking the ocean. Although I had expected the brush to be heavy, even in what I had first mistook for "fire lanes," the walk was surprisingly easy. Part of that was due to the fact that the property dropped a good 50 feet or so in elevation from the clubhouse to the cliffs several hundred yards away. As we walked, Moonlight commented, "This was the eighth fairway. Ya' just walked past the green for the finishin' hole."

I stopped and looked back. If I had been paying attention, I would have made out the contours of the green without Moonlight pointing it out to me. I also now saw quite clearly the remains of a large bunker that stretched almost all the way across in front. I imagined how often it must have collected wayward approaches.

I also noticed that the green was barely overgrown—as if it had been unattended for only a few days, as opposed to three decades. I also thought it was curious that the fairway on which we were walking seemed much the same way. In fact, as I looked about, I realized that all of the fairways within sight remained fairly distinct and easily recognizable.

I would have expected nature to reclaim the fairways and greens quickly after the course had been abandoned. Yet there weren't any trees, much less heavy underbrush, to speak of where Jones and his friends pitched and putted years before. Apparently, even the forces of nature hesitated at the thought of taking back a golf course that had once belonged to Bobby Jones. Maybe that was part of the "magic" that Moonlight said inhabited the place.

Before I could give it more thought, I heard Moonlight's voice calling out to me. "C'mon, now." I hurried after him.

The trees ended abruptly 50 yards or so from the edge of the cliffs, where the soil began to turn to rock. At that point, you could see up and down the shoreline. It was breathtaking.

As we broke away from the trees, the cool ocean breeze stiffened noticeably. Every once in awhile, a gust of wind sprayed us with the surf crashing into the rocks nearby. It felt cold.

I looked out at the ocean and marveled again at its vastness and its deep blue color. There was nothing back home in Birmingham, Alabama that compared to this.

The shoreline was jagged along the edge of the property. There were crevices running deep into the land and points jutting out as much as a hundred yards. In some places, the land descended more gently down toward brown, sandy beaches. In others, it had been sheared off by some ancient geological event, leaving a rocky cliff. As I looked north and south, I could see that the entire property extended out into the Pacific almost like a peninsula, exposing itself to the ocean's winds on three sides.

It occurred to me that the property could be seen from the air. "How did they keep this place a secret when a plane or balloon could fly by and get a bird's eye view of the whole thing?"

Moonlight shook his head. "Normal folks weren't allowed to fly over the property because a' the base. Ya' know, military security. They had a name for it…"

I suddenly remembered. "Protected airspace?"

He smiled. "Yeah, right."

As we looked around, I also wondered what challenges Perry Maxwell designed along here as he "found" the course that the property presented to him. I could see several areas that looked like more green locations. Again, they appeared as if they had only recently been returned to nature. In fact, from where I stood, the greens seemed remarkably healthy and free of weeds. It was almost as if one pass with a greens mower would have them ready for play.

I started to ask Moonlight about it, but he was standing a few yards away, looking out at the ocean as if transfixed. I couldn't tell what he was looking at.

After several minutes, he turned slowly away from the sea and walked back toward me. As he reached me, he said, "There's so much to tell ya', lad."

With that, he turned and walked back toward the clubhouse. He still had the fast-paced walk of a caddie, and I was forced to hustle to keep up. As I scurried along behind him, I thanked God for allowing me to be in such a wondrous place.

Chapter 14

I CAUGHT UP with Moonlight at the top of the hill just before he reached the clubhouse. I figured he was headed over to the first tee so that we could finally begin my round on the course.

"You want me to get my clubs out of the trunk?"

He shook his head slowly. "Nah, you're not ready yet. Ya' can't play the course without preparation, lad."

He lost me there. While I wasn't a great player, I didn't need a lesson just to tee it up, not with my own caddie with me.

"What kind of preparation do I need?"

"Prob'ly more'n I can give ya', but I'll do the best I can." He looked around as if searching for something. "We need to leave here now."

With that, he turned and began walking toward the car.

"But the day's still young," I protested.

He didn't even turn back to answer me. He just kept walking, shaking his head and saying something to himself that I couldn't understand.

He remained quiet during the ride back to the hotel. As we passed through the gate and stopped to relock it, I thought I heard the sound of an engine of some kind behind us in the distance. Although it was hard to tell, it seemed to be coming from the course, or at least from that general direction.

I turned to Moonlight as he was getting back in the car. "Do you hear that?"

He gave me a puzzled look. "Hear what?"

"That sound," I said. "Doesn't it sound like some kind of motor?"

He shrugged it off. "We're next to a military base. They got all kinds a' machinery here. That could be anythin'." He paused before adding, "But I don't hear nothin'."

I didn't say anything more for fear that he would accuse me again of an overactive imagination. We rode in silence for a while. It seemed as if the place had a spell on Moonlight that wouldn't loosen its grip until we were almost back to the hotel. We were several miles down Highway 1 before he spoke.

"The magic's still there. I could feel it."

"Tell me about the magic, Moonlight."

"It's a hard thing to describe. The place's been touched with greatness. Ya' can feel it in the ground as ya' walk the course. Ya' can taste it in the sea air as ya' breathe. And I could smell 'em in that clubhouse—Mr. Jones, Mr. Roberts, Mr. Hogan, Mr. Nelson, Mr. Hagen, Mr. Sarazen. President Eisenhower, too, only he wasn't the president when he first started comin' there. Mr. Snead, Mr. Armour...they came, too..." His voice trailed away as he retreated into his memories.

I didn't want him to stop.

"But those guys played at a lot of places. What made this place so different?"

He was quick to respond. "The golf was pure, lad. No gallery, no television like they have now, just the players. An' no one was bein' paid to play there. Everyone who came had only one purpose: To play the game for the sheer love of it. Some of 'em even skipped tournaments to come play while Mr. Jones was in residence."

I couldn't resist playing the devil's advocate. "But you sent me that scorecard from a four-ball match Jones played for money. Remember that? Something about Hogan and his friend Little beating Jones and Demaret out of two hundred bucks?"

He shook his head and smiled. "I didn't say they never played for money. These boys couldn't play golf unless some-thin' was on the line. That ain't the point. They weren't paid to be here. They were here first an' foremost for the love a' the game an' Mr. Jones."

We turned into the hotel parking lot. It was still early after-noon, and I realized that we had missed lunch. I was hungry.

I pointed to the diner across the street. "Want to get a bite?"

"Sure," he said, and took off at the brisk pace that appeared to be his only walking gear.

The place was nearly deserted. The greeter told us to pick any table we liked, so we found a booth near the back of the dining room.

I was starving by the time the waitress arrived to take our order. "Must be something in that salty air," I said to Moonlight as if to explain my choice of a steak and baked potato instead of a sandwich for lunch. He was too busy studying the menu to reply.

He finally looked up at the waitress and said, "I'll have the same thing."

While we waited for our food, Moonlight began my "preparation" for playing the course.

"The trick to golf, lad, is to keep it simple. People poison their minds—an' their games—with these crazy notions 'bout how they should swing the club instead a' where they should hit the ball. There's no one swing; we're all different. Mr. Nelson didn't hit it like Mr. Hogan. Mr. Snead didn't hit it like either one of 'em. Yet they were all born the same year an' came up at the same time. An' they all won their share a' championships."

He was looking directly at me.

"It's all 'bout gettin' the ball in the hole. Ya' don't get points for form. Look at Mr. Jones's swing. My God, he let loose a' the club with his left hand at the top a' his backswing. Claimed it gave him more power. If anyone else ever tried to let go an' re-grip like that, they'd miss the damned ball altogether. But it worked for him, didn't it?"

I tried to imagine Jack Nicklaus letting go of the club with his left hand right before starting his downswing. It was too ridiculous for words.

He continued his dissertation. "It's a game a' feel, not form. It's 'bout sendin' the ball where you want it to go, not posin' for pictures on your follow-through."

What he said made sense.

"You came up at a time when there were no videos to analyze a player's swing. There weren't any golf schools, either. Golf wasn't so much theory as it must've been trial and error."

He laughed. "Ya' think Mr. Hogan an' Mr. Snead could afford 'swing doctors' when they were comin' up? They were caddies, lad. They learned the game by watchin' others an' then sneakin' on the course when they were done carryin' bags. Get a few holes in here an' there. Practice? Hell, they were thrilled just to play a little whenever they could. Same for Mr. Nelson. He was in the same caddie yard as Mr. Hogan."

"That must have been one helluva caddie shack."

"Those Texas boys came up in the wind. They learned to keep it low, like we did back in Scotland. It was a matter a' survival. They tried hittin' the ball every way imaginable 'til they found a way that worked for 'em. No fancy theories. They learned what worked through sweat an' blisters. Mr. Hogan said it best: Ya' gotta dig it outta the dirt."

I thought about Hogan winning the British Open in 1953 in his first and only try, at fabled Carnoustie, no less. There wasn't a harder course on the entire British Open rota. And I remembered that Snead had won at St. Andrews at 1946, also on his first trip "over the pond," as they used to say.

"I guess when you're standing over the ball in a major championship, you'd better be thinking about where it needs to go instead of some swing theory."

"Exactly, lad." Moonlight seemed pleased at my comprehension.

I was quick to disappoint him, though.

"But what's all this got to do with playing the course?"

He frowned. "Everythin', lad, everythin'. Ya' can't take it all in if you're worryin' 'bout pronatin' your wrists, now, can ya'? You'll miss the magic if your mind is busy frettin' 'bout the mechanics a' the golf swing. Ya' can't waste an opportunity like this. Ya' won't catch the magic if ya' don't open your mind to it."

"You've never seen me play. What makes you think I don't play by feel?"

"'Cause you're not ol' enough to be past all those 'quick fixes' an' 'snake oil' cures they throw at ya'. They tell ya' how to be a pro overnight. It's a bunch a' hogwash, I tell ya', an' they oughta put those people in jail. You Americans...you'll say anythin' to make a buck, won't ya'?"

Moonlight had again put me on the defensive. "We've done alright with our system."

"That ya' have, lad. You've shown the world. But it don't make ya' perfect, now does it?"

It seemed pointless to argue. "No, no one's perfect." Our food had arrived. The conversation ceased as we both tore into our rib eyes, which were surprisingly good.

I waited until we were both halfway through our steaks before saying anything more.

"So, have I learned enough to rate a round on the course tomorrow?"

"Tomorrow afternoon, lad, 'bout 2:00. The course should be ready for ya' by then." He cut another bite of steak before adding, "And let's hope you're ready for it."

I laughed and said, "I'll have the best caddie in the yard. How can I miss?"

Back at the hotel, as the emotions of the day died down, I thought again about what I had seen. Moonlight had been fully vindicated, that much was certain. He might be a lot of things, I thought, but crazy ain't one of them. Bragg's Point was right where he said it would be.

Now that I knew that the place truly existed, I wanted to know everything about its connection to Bobby Jones and the golden age of golf. And I knew that I wasn't going to be satisfied until I did. At that point, I could only imagine what had taken place on that marvelous piece of ground. It was up to Moonlight to pass the folklore of Bragg's Point on to me before it was lost forever.

Of course, he had promised to tell me as much while we played. As he put it, "Each hole has its share a' stories, lad, but ya' can't really understand what I'm tellin' ya' unless we're there at the time."

By the time we were done, it was late afternoon. We went back to the hotel. As we were headed to our room, Moonlight abruptly took his leave. He didn't say where he was going, and I didn't ask.

When he returned a few hours later, we ate a snack for supper and watched a little television in the room. He didn't speak much and seemed preoccupied. I guess I was, too, because I didn't push for conversation.

As I turned out the lights that night, I knew I would have trouble sleeping again. Only this time, it wouldn't be

Moonlight's snoring that would keep me awake. My mind was crowded with questions about the splendid place called Bragg's Point.

Chapter 15

I AWOKE THE next morning to find Moonlight sitting in the only chair in the room. He was cleaning my golf clubs.

"What are you doing?"

"My job," was his terse reply.

"Since when is that your job?"

"Since today it's my job."

I was now fully awake and able to understand what he meant. He was going to caddie for me today, and cleaning his player's clubs was part of a caddie's job.

I glanced over at the clock on the table next to my bed. It was only 6:15 in the morning.

"It's kind of early to be doing that, isn't it?"

"Beats layin' 'round in bed all day."

"Touché."

Moonlight softened his attitude. "Nah, it's alright, lad. When ya' get as ol' as me, ya' can't sleep much anyway. Dream those sweet dreams while you're young."

I got up, showered, and dressed. By the time I was done, he had finished with the clubs. "Ready for some breakfast?"

I told him that I was, and we left for the coffee shop.

Moonlight ordered eggs over easy, with bacon, toast, orange juice, and coffee. He also wanted grits, but they didn't have any. I was surprised he didn't ask for haggis, too, and I asked him if he always ate like that.

"Nah. Too much trouble to cook like this at home. Besides, this stuff'll kill ya' if ya' eat it all the time."

It didn't take long for our conversation to turn to Bragg's Point. I had laid awake thinking about the course until the wee hours of the morning, and I had questions.

"Moonlight, who owns the property now?"

"Good question. It was supposed to belong to Mr. Jones, but Mr. Roberts always handled all the paperwork. I once heard Mr. Jones refer to a foundation, an' I gathered that the land was under the control a'…whaddya call it?"

I tried to think of whatever word he might be searching for. "Are you talking about a trustee?"

"Yeah," he said brightly. "That's the word he used."

"I wonder why they would do that?"

"Beats me." He bit into a slice of bacon. "I guess they figured that puttin' Mr. Jones's name on it would attract attention, an' that'd defeat the whole purpose a' what they were doin'."

I considered how ironic it was that Jones took such great pains to remove himself from the public eye. Celebrities almost always crave attention, no matter what they may say otherwise. And public adulation is apparently as addictive as any drug. The most difficult adjustment most famous athletes are forced to make upon retirement is not so much the loss of competition but the loss of the constant ego-stroking from adoring fans.

But Jones not only embraced a world away from the limelight, he went to extremes to wall himself away from public view. He found the perfect architect for a new private life in Cliff Roberts, a man who had many acquaintances but few friends. Nor did Roberts have family obligations to distract him from serving Jones; a series of unhappy marriages produced no children.

During my tossing and turning the night before, I had also wondered why we were waiting until two o'clock in the afternoon to play. As I quipped to Moonlight at breakfast, it wasn't as if all the morning starting times were booked.

"When ya' see what the afternoon sun does to the place, you'll see why we're playin' then. The spirit a' the course becomes most evident in the settin' sun."

So we were back to the magic. I wondered if I would ever understand it. It was becoming clear that the most important part of the story of Bragg's Point, that Moonlight wanted me to relate to others, was not so much its geography but its spirituality. Jones had found a piece of ground that was holy to him. To be sure, the gorgeous setting was important, but Moonlight clearly believed that it was only a small part of what made Bragg's Point so special.

That Sunday, he wanted me to envision that other layer, the one beneath the marvelous physical beauty of the place. I guess he felt like I could only take in so much at a time. So the day before had been my first view, and I had needed 24 hours to get over the splendor of it all.

I recalled that Jones had hated the Old Course at St. Andrews at first. He had to play it several times before he began to understand and appreciate its subtleties and charm. By the time he finished his career, he would rate it as the best course he had ever played.

Moonlight obviously believed that, just as with Jones at St. Andrews, a true appreciation of Bragg's Point would take time. The first sight, though spectacular, didn't reveal all that was there. I only hoped that I would eventually see everything I was supposed to see.

I shared my misgivings with him as he was finished the last of his toast.

"You'll see it, lad. Ya' won't be able to miss it."

"I hope you're right."

"Once ya' play the course, you'll be under its spell."

I hadn't considered our round to be part of a ritual, but Moonlight apparently did. Play the course, say abracadabra, and the spell is complete. It was kind of a scary thought.

Back in the room, I began to consider what I was supposed to do with this discovery that Moonlight was sharing with me. He had always said that he wanted me to tell the story. Now he had shown me the secret place. That proved the place existed, but not the truth of all the stories associated with it. If we could prove them to be true, Moonlight's tales would reveal the "magic" that was the *real* story of Bragg's Point.

The only tangible evidence I had of any activity at the place was the old scorecard Moonlight had given me. The lawyer part of my brain began to compile a list of exhibits to prove

Moonlight's case for Bragg's Point. I needed to research the public records here to document the conveyance of the property and to show its present ownership. Beyond that, I had to find some paper trail to connect the deeds to Jones and Roberts.

We would also need mementos from the secret club, physical evidence that would prove what took place there. Were there other scorecards? Maybe a guest register of some kind existed. Old photographs would be the strongest evidence.

Moonlight had promised from the beginning that he could prove what he was telling me. I hoped he understood that the world was not going to believe his fantastic story just on his say-so. Like the crowd at Phil's Bottle Shop, they might well dismiss him (and me) as crazy if we couldn't back up our claims.

We left for the course right after eating a light lunch. As we drove along, I shared with Moonlight my concerns about having adequate evidence to give "our story" credibility.

"Didn't I tell ya' I'd lots a' proof?"

"Yeah, you did, Moonlight. But I think we need more than your testimony. The world is a cynical place, you know? People will think we've got an angle when we tell them about Bragg's Point. They'll say we're just trying to make money somehow, and they'll use that as an excuse not to believe us."

He nodded. "That's the beauty of our story. It's *not* 'bout money. It's 'bout much, much more. An' I've got all the proof you'll ever need, so put your mind at ease."

We passed through the security checkpoint (Moonlight's new card worked just fine) and onto the winding road that had been so difficult to negotiate the day before. For some reason, the brush didn't seem quite so dense this time. I assumed it was due to the fact that I now knew my way and wasn't quite so uneasy about what lay ahead.

When we arrived at the gate, Moonlight got out to unlock it. As he pulled out his key, he suddenly stopped. I saw him reach up to the padlock and take it into his hand. He turned it over, as if he were looking for its serial number or checking for damage. He then flipped it open, pushed the gate back, and waited for me to drive through.

He was quiet when he got back in the car.

"What were you looking at?"

He shook his head side to side slowly. "I dunno. I could've sworn I locked that gate when we left here yesterday."

I felt a little unsettled. "What do you mean?"

"The lock was open."

"Maybe you didn't push it all the way closed yesterday. Maybe it didn't catch."

He nodded. "Or maybe someone's expectin' us."

I stopped the car. Suddenly, I recalled again how I had heard strange sounds while we were in Jones's quarters the day before and had seen something move below when I looked out of his window. I didn't like what I was feeling at that moment.

"You want me to turn around?"

He was quiet. After staring ahead for a minute, he said, "Nah. Maybe you're right. Maybe I didn't close the lock." He shook his head as if to clear it of bad thoughts. "I don't mean to go buggy on ya', lad. I'm okay now. Let's get goin'. We're due on the first tee shortly."

I wasn't quite so keen on playing anymore, but I put the car in gear and continued down our narrow path toward the clubhouse. In a few moments, we were clear of the brush again.

But there was one difference: There was a flag on the 18th green in front of the clubhouse. Looking closer, I saw, too, that the green had been mowed. So had the first and eighth tees that flanked each side of the clubhouse.

Without thinking, I jumped out of the car and ran to the front of the clubhouse for a better look. I could see several more greens from where I stood. Each one had a flagstick and appeared to be ready for play. The same for every teeing ground in view.

I felt Moonlight standing next to me.

"I told you I heard something when we were leaving yesterday." I looked at him closely. For the first time, it dawned on me that my newly found trust in him may have been misplaced. Maybe I was being manipulated in some way. Lawyers are trained to be a little paranoid; it helps to avoid being surprised at trial. But as I looked at Moonlight, he appeared to be as bewildered as I was.

"Glory be. The magic's stronger than I thought."

"Magic, hell. Moonlight, I hate to tell you, but you're not the only one who knows about this place."

He shook his head, still looking around in wonderment at what was before us. "I'm tellin' ya', lad, the spirit here is strong. Stronger than anythin' you've ever seen. Don't let go a' your faith. Not now, when we've come this far."

He turned to me and said simply, "I'll get your clubs." He left me standing there and headed back toward the car.

In a few minutes, he returned with my golf bag slung over his shoulder.

"Follow me."

We walked to the first tee. Unless we turned back, I was about to put myself under the spell of the Bragg's Point Golf Links.

Chapter 16

AS WE STOOD on the first tee, Moonlight must have sensed my lack of faith, and I could tell he was disappointed.

"Do ya' wanna call the thing off?"

I knew he was testing me.

"No," I assured him. "But it's kind of hard to concentrate with something as weird as this going on."

"Show your faith, lad. The course has been made ready for ya'. It don't matter who or why. When it comes right down to it, all ya' can do is play. Whoever—or whatever—did this wants ya' to play. Can't ya' see that?"

I treated his question as rhetorical, mainly because I didn't have an answer. Moonlight took my silence as an agreement to continue.

Although the tees and greens were prepared for play, the fairways looked exactly as they had the day before. The grass was tall and thick—perfect for rough at a U.S. Open, perhaps, but unsuitable for much of anything else.

I pointed down the first fairway and asked Moonlight, "How are we going to find a ball in that stuff?"

He smiled in a condescending way, as if disappointed in my continued unbelief. "Remember what I told ya' 'bout my nickname? Leave that worry to me, lad. Ya' just hit the ball where I tell ya'. I'll take care a' the rest."

He started walking toward the clubhouse, telling me over his shoulder to loosen up. I started stretching. In a few minutes, he reappeared, wearing the white overalls worn by the caddies at the National.

"Where'd you get that?"

"Ya' don't think Mr. Roberts would have us dress any differently here than at the National, now do ya'?"

When he bent down to pick up my bag, I saw that my name was on his back. Before I could comment, he began emptying the pockets of my bag on the ground.

"What are you doing?"

"Ya' got all kinds a' stuff in here ya' don't need. I'm gonna lighten my load a little."

He started dropping balls, head covers, an umbrella, and other unnecessary baggage right there in a pile on the tee. He was down to the essentials, nothing more than my clubs, a couple of tees, a glove, and a ball. Pointing to the pile, he said, "We'll get this when we're done."

"But you only left me with one ball."

He clucked disapprovingly at me. "One ball's all you'll need. Stop that whinin', will ya'? Ya' need to embrace the spirit, lad. It'll tell us what to do. Don't worry. I'll hear it even if ya' don't."

As we stood there on the first tee, I began to swing my

driver back and forth to loosen up. Moonlight was watching me intently.

"Ya' got a good-lookin' swing there, Charley. What are ya'—'bout a five or there'bouts?"

I was impressed. Actually, I told him, I was a six, although I had been a semipermanent twelve until I got serious about the game a couple of years before.

"Well," he said, "You'll be just fine today, so long as ya' do what I say. Ya' got plenty a' game, if you'll just take what the course here gives ya'. It rewards virtue, especially patience. Get greedy, an' she'll slap ya' down hard."

"I'm in your hands," I assured him.

"Fine. Now listen to me. The key here is to stay outta the brush. You'll find that it runs up an' down the sides a' every hole. Sometimes it takes your ball an' won't give it back."

I looked out at the wiry grass and thickets of brush that appeared to form a gauntlet at each hole. It was clear what he meant.

"An' another thing. Mr. Jones tol' that Maxwell fella he wanted a thorough test a' golfin' skills. Some holes turn left; others turn right. Some short, an' some are long. Some a' the greens break toward the water, but not all of 'em. The trick is knowin' which ones. That's my job."

I nodded to indicate that I was paying attention. He took it as a sign to continue.

"But the real killer out here is the wind. It's like the devil; it'll lie to ya'. Ya' think it's comin' in from the ocean, but it'll swirl over the brush, bounce off these trees, an' do tricks with your ball."

Again, I let him know I would heed his warning.

He continued with his briefing of the course. "Mr. Jones knew that the course had to be maintained by a small staff. That's why he told Maxwell to keep bunkers to a minimum. So ya' won't see quite so many out here as ya' might expect."

He snorted. "Not that it matters; 'tween the trees an' the wind, you'll've all the challenges ya' can handle."

He watched as I continued to make dry swings, trying to knock the rust off. It seemed to inspire one more bit of advice.

"Can ya' knock the ball down?"

I suppose I was feeling a little intimidated. After all, Moonlight was a veteran who had caddied for the likes of Bobby Jones. I hesitated, not sure of what to say.

Sensing my unease, Moonlight pulled my 7-iron out of my bag, took a stance with it, and said, "It's easy, lad. Ya' just play the ball back in your stance a coupla' inches. Pick the club up quickly on your backswing"—here, he demonstrated—"an' hit down steeply. Then cut off your follow-through, keep'n it low. The ball'll come out on a clothesline. It'll bore right through the wind an' stop the minute it lands." He gave me a wink. "An' that's how ya' cheat the devil."

I couldn't resist a quip. "I never thought golf was so theological."

He laughed. "You're closer to the truth than ya' think, Charley. Anyway, Mr. Hogan knew how to play that shot better'n any man alive. Mr. Palmer was almost as good. He could hit a 9-iron a 140 yards, an' it never got higher'n your chest."

I gave a slight whistle in appreciation.

"Is there anything else I need to know about the course?"

He thought for a second. "Just one more thing."

"What's that?"

"Remember you're walkin' with the great ones." With that, he handed me a scorecard. It was identical to the one he had sent me earlier, only this one had no scores. He had written my name on it. It was an eerie feeling seeing that same shaky handwriting I had first seen on his mysterious notes. It was as if I was now becoming a part of the story.

Somehow, he could tell what I was thinking. "When we're done, lad, we'll put your card in the box with all the rest. You'll leave your mark on this place, too."

He then handed me my ball and a tee. "Ya' can play away now." Pointing down the first fairway, he said, "Favor the right side if ya' can. It'll make it easier to get 'round the corner."

Moonlight was referring to a dogleg that swung gently right about 275 yards down the fairway. As I considered my tee shot, I began to look critically at the hole for the first time. It was a generous and forgiving starting hole that measured 471 yards, according to the card. From the tee, the hole ran downhill to a wide fairway, encouraging—and rewarding—big hitters.

Before I addressed the ball, Moonlight favored me with one last bit of advice. "See that creek that runs 'cross the fairway? It's 'bout 230 yards to carry it."

The magic of Bragg's Point made its first appearance when my tee shot rocketed off my driver straight down the right side of the fairway, exactly as Moonlight instructed. It cleared the shallow creek and bounced just once before disappearing in the tall grass of the fairway.

As he took the club from me and we began to walk off the first tee, Moonlight gave me a wink and said, "Mr. Jones himself couldn't have done it any better. Well done."

I couldn't help but notice that the air seemed to have a special fragrance, perhaps from a combination of the lush green grass and the spray from the ocean. Not only did it smell sweet and fresh, but the atmosphere seemed ionized with positive energy. Every breath taken at this place was invigorating.

As we walked along, I asked Moonlight about the first round ever played on the course.

"Ah," he said. "That would've been sometime in '38. 'Course Mr. Jones struck the first shot. Hit it 'bout where yours went, only longer. He played the round with Mr. Roberts. It was just the two of 'em that very first time. An' I was on Mr. Roberts's bag."

"No kidding? Who carried for Jones?"

"Slats Reinauer."

"Interesting name," I commented.

Moonlight sniffed. "One a' the best I ever saw."

"How'd he get the honor of carrying Jones's bag?"

I noticed that Moonlight was staring straight ahead, like a bird dog pointing at quail. He wouldn't take his eyes off where he apparently had spotted my ball, but he continued to talk.

"Oh, Mr. Jones loved Slats. Brought him out from the National. Slats knew Mr. Jones's game, an' Mr. Jones trusted his club selections entirely. But the main thing was, Slats could read greens like nobody I ever knew."

"He was good, huh?"

Moonlight chuckled. "He had his own way a' doin' it, too. Everybody else always measured the break by usin' the cup or a ball. Ya' know, they'd say 'Play it half a cup to the right' or 'It's two balls on the high side.'"

He paused, as if to catch his breath. I reminded myself that Moonlight was 80 some-odd years old.

"Slats wouldn't talk like that. He used money to measure how high he wanted ya' to putt it. He'd say, 'Gimme a dime out,' or he'd hol' his hands this far 'part an' say, 'I need a dollar bill above the hole.' If Slats tol' ya' a putt was expensive, he wasn't talkin' 'bout the bets that were on the line; he meant it had a lotta break. Mr. Jones loved that. If he thought Slats was readin' too much break, he'd ask him, 'Ya' sure it costs that much?'"

Moonlight laughed as he recalled those happy times. "Slats also loved to read the financial papers. Even carried 'round a copy a' the *Wall Street Journal.* Word was that he'd invested his savin's an' gotten rich. Some a' the members even got to askin' him 'bout different stocks."

I found it hard to believe that a caddie moonlighted as a financial guru. If Slats had done so well, I wondered, why was he still caddying? I didn't say anything, however, for fear of offending Moonlight.

My friend must have read my mind. Grinning at me, he said, "Turns out Slats didn't have a dime in the stock market; he was just havin' fun all those years makin' those guys think he did."

"What was Mr. Roberts like?"

Moonlight's face suddenly took on a sad expression. "That was an unhappy man. He wasn't much of a golfer, either. But he loved the game, I'll give him that."

He walked a few more steps and then stopped and put my bag down. I couldn't tell why.

"Are you alright?"

He pointed to the ground. I saw my ball right in front of where Moonlight was standing.

I don't know how, but the ball was sitting up nicely. From where we stood, the fairway climbed back uphill to a flag waving in the distance. The green appeared to be within reach.

"How far to the green?"

Moonlight looked around to get his bearings and said, "It's 'bout 185 or so to the front. Looks like the flag's back right. With the wind an' all, it'll play closer to 200, maybe 210."

Handing me my 5-wood, he said, "Land it in front a' the green an' let it feed down to the pin."

I did as I was told and hit it flush. We watched as the ball bounced twice and began to roll toward the rear of the green.

Moonlight grinned at me. "You're coachable, I see."

"Do you think it's close?"

"Yeah. I think we've gotta chance to start this one off with a bang."

When we arrived at the green, I saw even more clearly why Moonlight had me hit the 5-wood. Although it was wide, the green was shallow in depth, leaving little room for error on club selection. Any approach had to land short and run to the hole. The 3-iron I probably would have selected would have come in too low and run through this green into a deep grass bunker behind the green.

My ball was no more than 20 feet from the hole. As Moonlight removed the flagstick, I marked the ball. He held up his hand, and I tossed it to him. He cleaned it and flipped it back. As I replaced the ball, he said, "It'll move to your left, toward the ocean. Play it a cup out."

I jerked the putt a good three feet or so past the hole, but managed to slide the comebacker just inside the right edge of the cup.

It wasn't pretty, but I had made a four on the first hole at Bragg's Point. I was enormously pleased with myself. As we headed to the second tee, it occurred to me that I didn't know what par was on the first hole.

Moonlight just shrugged when I asked him. "Depends on the wind direction. I suppose you'd consider it a par-5. The only thing that really matters, though, is the number a' strokes it takes to play 18 holes, not one."

The second hole turned back to the left. According to the card, it was 381 yards in length, and I could see that it ran straight down toward the cliffs. Beyond that, the ocean was visible in the distance.

Although it was into the wind, Moonlight explained that the hole would play short because it was downhill. Pointing to the remains of a large fairway bunker, he directed me to avoid the trouble by hitting an iron off the tee. It was another play I would never have chosen on my own.

"Mr. Hogan always hit 3-iron here. Most a' the others did,

too, but he was the first. He said anyone who hit driver here was an idiot, what with the fairway so narrow down there an' that big trap waitin' to catch your ball."

Although I pushed my tee shot, it stayed inside the tree line and fell short of the bunker. I immediately saw the wisdom of Hogan's plan.

As we started toward my ball, I joked, "John Daly would hit driver here."

He belched out a disapproving sound. "Not if I were on his bag, he wouldn't. What would it give ya' even if ya' hit it straight? He'd still have a half-wedge to the green. No player a' mine is gonna be hittin' half-wedges for money, I'll tell ya' that. Toughest shot in golf. Ya' gotta lay up for a full swing an' leave those dicey little touch shots alone. Hell, even Mr. Snead hit an iron here, an' he was the straightest driver I ever saw."

I wanted to know more about the man most authorities consider to have had the greatest golf swing of all. "Did Snead play here much?"

Moonlight nodded. "Oh, yeah. He was here as much as anyone." He chuckled at a sudden memory. "He was easy to caddie for, too, when he was workin' his favorite bet."

"Which was?" I asked.

The old man cackled again. "He loved to play what he called 'one-club.' He'd let ya' pick any club ya' wanted, an' he'd play ya' with his 5-iron." He pulled the strap of my bag over his shoulder. "Made for a pretty light load, not to mention easy club selection."

"I bet he was good at it, huh?"

Moonlight nodded. "Shot 71 once when I was with him. He could do everythin' with that club, includin' remove your billfold."

The grass was thick where we were walking, and I began to fear that we wouldn't be able to find my ball. But Moonlight's stride was confident, and he took me right to it.

He looked at the tops of the trees, threw up some grass, and said, "Ya' can get there with a five—even if ya' don't hit it quite as good as Mr. Snead."

I took the club from him. The green below us was deeper than the one on the first hole, and the flagstick was in the middle. It was an easy location to reach. Whoever set the pins wanted us to get a good start.

I had another good lie. I made decent contact—a little thin—and the ball landed in the very front of the green. I had maybe 30 feet to the hole.

When we got to the green, I could tell that it brought us within teasing distance of the water's edge. The view was staggering. I now understood even better Moonlight's admonition to lay up and avoid any touch shots into the green. This was a heavily guarded green, with bunkers on three sides waiting to capture a poorly executed wedge. Maxwell may have kept the bunkers to a minimum elsewhere on the course, but he made up for it here.

As we lined up the putt, Moonlight said from behind me, "Remember now, it'll roll toward the water."

I took him to mean that the putt would be faster than it appeared, since an extension of my line through the hole ran directly toward the sea. However, I still ran it well past the hole.

He reminded me that the putt coming back to the hole would be much slower. "Hit it to the back a' the cup."

I did exactly as he said, rapping the ball so hard that it nearly popped out when it struck the back edge. Without saying a word, Moonlight picked up my bag and began walking away. I hustled along behind him.

The third hole was a one-shot hole. Moonlight estimated the yardage at 175 from where we stood, but the wind made that measurement almost meaningless. In fact, Moonlight told me the hole called for everything from a 2-iron to an 8-iron depending on the air currents.

Once again, Bragg's Point allowed little room for error in club selection. The tee wasn't far from the second green, no more than 30 yards from the cliff's edge. Whatever shot you hit from the tee had to traverse a cove to a green that was tucked onto a small point jutting out from the property. Any play that was short or left fell into the surf. It was a beautiful but terrifying hole.

Moonlight pointed to the right front of the green. "There's a bail-out area over there. Mr. Hogan always said that was the way to play it when the wind was up. He'd hit it over in that direction, short a' the green, an' chip on. Usually made three, never risked worse'n four."

"You want me to hit it there?"

He looked up in the sky, as if surveying the heavens for a sign. "Nah. The gulls look comfortable up there. Can't be much of a wind." Handing me the 5-iron again, he said, "Remember what I tol' ya' 'bout knockin' the ball down? This is where ya' wanna hit that shot."

I had my doubts about whether this was the time to try a new shot and said so. "Ya' gotta believe in your game, lad. Ya' got what it takes. It's the shot for this hole. It's the shot Mr. Nelson played. Ya' might get lucky an' do what he did here."

"What do you mean?"

"He made a one here."

"No kidding?"

"Knocked it in on the fly. Mr. Jones was with him at the time. He laughed an' said, 'Well, Byron, that eliminates the bad bounce, don't it?'"

"Were you there?"

"Nah. I was in the group behind. We were on the second green. Didn't know a thing 'bout it 'til Clarence Henderson yelled at us."

I set up for the shot just as Moonlight had shown me. I knew he was right; knocking the ball down would keep it below any wind that tried to trick us, and the ball would tear into the green and stop dead in its tracks when it landed.

But I was much too intimidated by the roar of the surf crashing below to release the club down the line that Moonlight had given me. Almost involuntarily, I steered the ball away from the water, pushing it right into Hogan's bail-out zone.

"Sorry," I apologized as I handed my club back to him.

"No need for regrets, lad. You're safe. We can get up an' down from there."

When we got to my ball, I was surprised that it had come to rest in short grass. Was this more of the magic that Moonlight had promised? If my ball had been buried in the tall grass surrounding the fourth tee just beyond, I couldn't have made clean contact and put enough spin on the ball to keep it from running too far. That was critical because, as Moonlight pointed out, the green ran away from us down to the sea. We had to stop the ball quickly after it landed on the green.

Fortunately, the excellent lie gave me the confidence I needed to play the shot. Using my sand wedge, I pinched the ball off the turf. It popped up, landed softly just inside the collar of the green, and rolled quietly toward the hole before stopping just a few inches from the cup.

Moonlight smiled appreciatively. He handed me my putter and went to pull the flag. I looked at him in mock offense and said, "What—that's not good?"

He shook his head. "We're playin' golf today, lad. We're gonna putt 'em all out."

I tapped it in for my three.

Chapter 17

MOONLIGHT HAD LEFT my bag on the fourth tee after I had played my chip to the third green. As we turned to walk back to play the fourth hole, I glanced uphill over brush and heather. At that moment, I thought I saw something white flash out of the corner of my eye near the top of the hill just beyond the double green. Although I turned quickly to look, I couldn't see anything.

I tried to get Moonlight's attention. "Did you see that?"

He was bending over my bag, pulling out my driver. "See what?"

Pointing up the hill, I said, "Over there. There was something over there. Something white. I couldn't tell what it was."

He waved me off with the back of his hand. "Don't be gettin' distracted now. The game is on. Keep your mind on why we're here."

He put the driver in my hands. It felt good just to hold it, and I knew I should heed Moonlight's advice. "Tell me about this hole."

Moonlight pointed down the fairway. "This is a two-shot hole that'll challenge your game. It's 'bout 400 yards or so, but it don't play quite that long. As ya' can see, it runs 'long the shoreline here off the tee an' turns back slightly toward the water for the second shot. We'll have to carry that cove ya' see there to reach the fairway, but there's a little more room for error than the last hole."

He didn't have to tell me about the large fairway bunker just to the right of the fairway because it was plainly visible from the tee. Maxwell wanted to make sure that players thought twice about cutting across the slight dogleg to cheat the hole out of its full length.

Backing away to give me room to hit my tee shot, his parting advice—unnecessary in view of the open sea on the left—was to favor the right side of the fairway. I did a little better this time, pulling the ball slightly but making solid contact.

Moonlight seemed satisfied. "We can git home from there, alright."

We had an unobstructed—and astonishingly beautiful —view of the surf on our left as we walked down the fairway. I couldn't help but think of how Jones's two courses—Augusta National and Bragg's Point—were every bit as extraordinary as the man himself.

As we made our way to my ball, it also occurred to me that this wasn't Jones's last creation. In the late 1940s, he organized and built Peachtree Golf Club in Atlanta. Supposedly, Jones's public association with a club other than Augusta National infuriated Cliff Roberts, but Jones wanted a place to play in town, and his boyhood course, East Lake, had fallen into disrepair as the neighborhood around it deteriorated.

Peachtree turned out to be a pretty fair track, too; it hosted the 1989 Walker Cup, a biennial competition between the leading amateurs of the United States and Great Britain/Ireland.

Roberts may have been miffed about Peachtree, but I couldn't imagine him objecting to Bragg's Point. For one thing, it was a secret. It didn't compete with Augusta National in any way. And, most importantly, Roberts was an integral part of the enterprise.

The fairway grass here was native bent and fescue, the same as the links in Scotland. It was not as thick on these seaside holes above the cliffs because the soil was too rocky to support much in the way of vegetation, and we could see my ball before we got to it. Once again, I had a good lie, thanks to Moonlight's magic.

I didn't like what I saw in front of me, however. The route to the green was fraught with problems in the form of two large bunkers that had to be negotiated. At least this green was bigger than the last one, and there appeared to be more land surrounding it. As I studied what I saw, I concluded that the challenge was more visual than anything else.

I made my best swing of the day with the 6-iron that Moonlight assured me was the right club. The ball finished safely on the green.

"This was Mr. Jones's favorite hole," Moonlight told me as we walked toward the green. "He liked it 'cause it required two good shots an' had great scenery. He said it reminded him a' the eighth hole at Pebble Beach, only it played north 'stead a' south."

I thought about Jones playing the hole.

"Was he as good a putter as people say?"

Moonlight nodded in agreement. "He could work wonders with Calamity Jane. He had a wristy stroke, like a lotta the players did back then. He liked to hook his putts, kinda the way Bobby Locke did. It made 'em roll better on those grainy greens."

I understood what he was saying. "I remember seeing old newsreels of Arnold Palmer winning the Masters in 1960. He would bend way over the ball, knock-kneed, and putt with his wrists. You don't see that any more."

Moonlight handed me my putter. "Yeah. Almost all of 'em putted that way back then. Billy Casper won a whole bunch a' tournaments, includin' two U.S. Opens, puttin' like that."

Moonlight shifted my bag to his other shoulder. "But we had a caddie who could outputt anyone on tour. Name was Jedediah Nash. He was one a' the original ones at the National. Mr. Jones had known him for years. In fact, Mr. Jones tol' people at the club that Jedediah was the one who taught him how to put that hook overspin on his putts to make 'em roll better."

This was something new. I had never heard of Jedediah Nash, much less that he helped Jones with his putting.

"So how come this fellow Nash never played the tour?"

Moonlight laughed. "'Cause he couldn't hit the ball a lick. But he won all the games of 'up and down' in the caddie yard. He had the damnedest short game of any man alive."

He paused as he recollected the caddie who was a short game wizard.

"Mr. Snead loved to bet with the caddies. After Nash beat him three days in a row on the puttin' green, Mr. Snead said he'd pay double if Jedediah would show him some a' his tricks."

"Did he?"

"Oh, yeah, Jedediah showed him, alright. Showed him how to cut his downhill putts to slow 'em down an' how to hook 'em to get 'em to run through the grain. Did the same thing with chips. An' he taught him how to dead wrist the ball on short pitches to take the air out of it. Jedediah could pitch the ball onto a downhill slope an' make it pop back into his pocket."

We arrived at the green as I pondered Moonlight's hyperbole. I had about 25 feet to the hole. It looked pretty straight. Moonlight barely looked at the line and said, "It'll break left when it loses speed. Play it a ball out."

I did as I was told and hit the putt. The result reminded me of the old joke: Other than distance and direction, there wasn't a thing wrong with the putt. It took me two more tries to get the ball in the hole. I would've been upset on any other day, but not today.

At that point, the course turned inland, as the fifth hole ran parallel and counter to its predecessor. It was ten yards or so longer and played slightly downhill off the tee before turning right and leveling out. As a result, it didn't play quite as long as it's listed 417 yards. Still, it was a healthy two-shotter, as Moonlight called it.

Pockets of scrub brush and fir and cypress trees touched both sides of the fairway, but they were considerably thicker on the left side, which was farther inland. As Moonlight pulled my driver from my bag, he said, "Take it down the middle, but favor the left if ya' have to."

I managed a good swing—thanks to his steady reassurance —and so we were off down the fairway again. Despite my earlier concerns, I noticed that Moonlight seemed to have even more energy than when we started. It was as if he was drawing something from the place.

Once again, he walked straight to my ball. I was no longer surprised to find that I had another perfect lie. Moonlight looked at the nearby bunker to confirm his bearings, and said quite simply, "It's right at a 160 yards to the middle. Pin looks left, behind the edge a' that greenside bunker. It's a sucker location. Ignore it an' play to the center a' the green."

I tried to follow his instructions, but I came over the top, sending the ball left of my intended line. It dove into the very bunker that Moonlight had warned me to avoid.

As I handed my 6-iron back to Moonlight, he said brightly, "Well, you're into a bit a' history there."

Seeing my puzzled look, he explained, "When we get there, you'll see what I mean."

I followed him quickly to the green. When we got to the hazard, he pointed to its contours and said, "Can ya' make out the shape a' the thing? Mr. Jones said it was what he liked best 'bout MacKenzie's work. At one time, ya' could see it all over the National, before they let every architect an' his brother tinker with the course. Mr. Jones told Maxwell that he wanted the bunkers at Bragg's Point to look that way."

I saw what he meant. The trap wasn't just a round hole dug

in the middle of the course. Instead, it had several fingers radiating from its center. I was immediately reminded of the large bunker on the tenth hole at Augusta National that sits about 75 yards or so in front of the green. Although it rarely comes into play, it offers a stunning visual effect as players round the dogleg and begin the long walk down the slope to the landing area.

"The players liked 'em, too. That meant a lot to Mr. Jones. Mr. Sarazen used to spend hours practicin' outta this very bunker. Ya' know, he had invented the sand wedge. Had a big contract with Wilson because of it. But he was forever tinkerin' with the design, tryin' to make it better. The Wilson people were always pressurin' him to come up with somethin' new they could sell. So he kept solderin' on the sole, addin' bounce, takin' off bounce."

I had heard that the famous Wilson R-90 wedge was one of Sarazen's designs. "They say that Wilson made Sarazen a rich man on account of that wedge."

Moonlight shrugged his shoulders. "I dunno what the numbers were, but I know one man who would."

"Oh, yeah?"

"Yeah. His name was Ivory Chavis. He was in charge a' the locker room here. Mr. Jones brought him out from Augusta with the rest of us. Mr. Sarazen talked him into lettin' him use his buffin' wheel to grind on his wedges. He'd wrap sandpaper 'round the wheel."

Moonlight put my bag down next to the bunker. "Chavis had to replace his wheel twice 'cause the motors would burn out. They just weren't made for the heavy pressure Mr. Sarazen was puttin' on 'em. Chavis used to say, 'Mr. Gene, ya' better 'splain to Mr. Jones why his shoes ain't as shiny as they used to be. Tell him why my wheel don't work.'"

He laughed at the thought of the bright little man they called the Squire using a shoe buffer to grind wedges. "Sarazen ended up givin' him a piece a' his royalty on one a' his new wedges. Made him the wealthiest locker-room man in America."

I saw that my ball was sitting on the upslope of the bunker. Moonlight had pulled my sand wedge from my bag.

I opened the face of the club until the grooves pointed past the front of my left foot, opened my stance, and swung. The ball rode atop the layer of old, compacted sand removed by my club as it sliced underneath it and dropped right next to the hole. Once it landed, it released into a lazy roll and stopped no more than six feet from the pin.

I was so pleased with myself. "How about that?"

Moonlight had already removed my putter from the bag and was exchanging it for the sand wedge. "Don't act surprised, lad. When ya' swing like you're supposed to, the ball knows it."

I got a little too casual on my putt and missed on the right.

Moonlight reproached me. "Let's keep our mind on what we're doin', now, okay?"

I had to laugh. Moonlight had spent a lifetime carrying clubs for serious players, and he wasn't about to take off his game face now. I hated to tell him, but I was a whole lot more interested in learning all about this wondrous place than I was in keeping score.

Chapter 18

THE SIXTH HOLE was a par 5. The card said it was 519 yards in length. (I found the odd yardages to be a curious thing. Why 519 instead of 515 or 520? After all, it wasn't as if the tee markers were never moved.) It doglegged to the left and required the player to choose between a high-risk second shot that had to carry a cove and at the same time avoid a deep bunker or a simple layup for a fairly routine wedge on the third shot. It was the kind of decision that Jones himself relished on three-shot holes.

The brush and thicket that lined the left side of the fairway were thick and heavy. As we stood on the tee, I reached for my driver. Moonlight placed his hand on it. "Not here, lad. This is what Mr. Jones called a 'USGA par 5.' He said it was like the ones he played in the U.S. Open. Ya' couldn't reach 'em in two, an' with the rough so high, there was no point in hittin' the driver."

He sorted through my irons, found the 3, and handed it to me. "Use this. All we want to do is keep it in play."

That's about all I managed, hitting it fat and sending the ball no more than 175 yards from the tee.

Moonlight was quick to comfort me. "That's alright. It's in the fairway. We're where we need to be."

As he picked up my bag, he asked me if I ever heard of "Bootsie" Beacham. I said no.

He laughed. "I didn't think ya' had. Bootsie was the first caddie they hired who was from out here. One a' the Augusta guys got homesick an' left. They needed someone quick. Mr. Jones asked 'round, an' somehow Bootsie got sent here."

He shook his head, still laughing. "One thing ya' knew the minute ya' met him; he was gay, although they called it somethin' else back then. Bootsie didn't really care what anyone thought; he literally skipped 'round the golf course. Ya' should've seen the reactions a' the players who'd never been 'round him. They'd drop their jaws in amazement. Mr. Jones would just grin. He liked Bootsie a lot an' tolerated his flitty ways—probably 'cause Bootsie read these greens better'n anyone but Slats Reinauer."

I wondered if it might have been Bootsie that I had seen in the shadows. "Do you think he's still around?"

"Nah. After a coupla' years, he went out on tour as a caddie for a pro a' similar persuasion, who for obvious reasons, I won't name. The guy won a few events, an' Bootsie ended up makin' some money, which he promptly spent on a sex-change operation."

"I didn't think they did those back then."

"Not in this country. Hell, he went all the way to Denmark or Russia or someplace. Anyway, that pretty much ended his career. Not that it mattered. I heard later he—or she—married some rich guy up East. They spent their time playin' golf all over the world." He chuckled. "I don't guess the guy ever did figure out why his 'wife' was such a strong player."

"What made you think of Bootsie?"

He kept looking straight ahead at the spot where he had located my ball. "Aw, I dunno. I just remember bein' on this hole when Bootsie was caddyin' in the same group. Bein' out here brings back a lotta memories, ya' know?"

When we got to my ball, Moonlight pointed to the fairway and said, "Ya' got 180 to the corner there. It's another 40 yards or so to the trees beyond that on the other side a' the fairway. We need to keep it between there."

I saw what he meant. The fairway made another turn right before presenting the green to the player. I needed to keep my ball within the bracketed yardage to have an open shot.

"Another 3-iron?" I asked hesitantly.

He nodded confidently. "That's the one. Keep it smooth an' let the club do the work."

I hit it better than my last effort.

As Moonlight wiped the club clean with his towel, he said, "Not much more'n an 8-iron in from there."

As we made our way along, Moonlight asked me about my clubs, which were the perimeter-weighted type that were marketed under the euphemism of "game improvement" clubs.

"Ya' like these?" I sensed from his question that he didn't think much of anything that wasn't a traditional blade.

"Yeah, I do," I said, trying not to sound defensive. "They feel good."

"Well," he sniffed, "they're popular 'nough these days. I just can't seem to get used to how they look." He walked a few more steps before offering, "'Course, ya' seem to hit 'em well enough."

As we stood at my ball, Moonlight pointed to a nearby cypress. "It's right at 130 yards from that tree there to the middle a' the green. We're a coupla' yards behind that. I think ya' can get there with an eight."

Which, of course, was the club he had called from 200 yards back.

The green at the sixth was guarded by two bunkers. The first was in front of the green. The other wrapped around the green's left side, extending from front to back. Since it was the side opposite the water, I imagined that the left-hand bunker had been a frequent destination for nervous approaches.

Before pulling my bag away, Moonlight offered his parting advice. "Ignore that front bunker. Ya' can't tell from here, but it's a good 70 yards in front a' the green. Maxwell learned that trick from MacKenzie. Changes the dimensions a' the green to the eye an' makes it harder to figure the right club. It ain't as tough as it looks. Just shoot for the flag; it looks like it's dead center. If the ball rolls right after it lands, that's okay. It'll leave us an uphill putt."

Beyond the green, I could see the clubhouse in the distance, sitting on the bluff above us. As I stood over the ball, I turned to take one last look at my target. When I looked at the flag, I saw something move off in the distance. I backed away and looked at Moonlight. I waited for him to say something, but he remained quiet. Finally, I said, "Did you see that?"

He looked puzzled. "Whaddya mean?"

Once again, I thought, I'm seeing things that Moonlight doesn't see, or at least won't admit to seeing. There didn't seem to be any point in saying anything more.

"Nothing. I guess the wind made something move."

But it distracted me. I had lost my concentration. What should have been an easy 8-iron turned into a spastic effort that pulled the ball so far left it even missed the bunker.

Moonlight seemed miffed. "Well, that wasn't your best effort, now was it?"

"No, it wasn't," I admitted.

To make things worse, I had missed on the high side of the green. I would have to pitch the ball over the bunker down onto a green that fell away from me. I knew it would be hard to get the ball close to the hole.

When we got to the ball, I saw that I had a fluffy lie. I tried a flop shot, but came too far underneath the ball and left it short, about five feet from the hole. I then pushed the putt just enough to miss it on the right side.

The seventh hole was a one-shot hole that played back toward the clubhouse. At only 131 yards, it was easily the shortest hole on the course. Because it ran slightly uphill, Moonlight warned me that it played a half a club or so more than its measured distance. According to him, most players either punched a 7-iron or hit a full 8.

As might be expected, Maxwell's design compensated for lack of distance by requiring great precision in the tee shot at the seventh. The green was small and elevated. On every side were deep swales that served as grass bunkers. Missing the green meant the player faced a very difficult up-and-down for par.

The view of the ocean behind the tee made it hard to turn away and focus on the target. From where we stood, the third and sixth greens and the rocks jutting up from the ocean floor just off the shore formed a spectacular backdrop. Throw in the crashing surf and daunting ocean breeze, and the player on the tee had more than enough distractions to make him forget whatever swing he thought he had when he teed his ball.

As I took it all in, I spoke what I was thinking. "This is a helluva place."

Moonlight nodded in agreement. "It's awe-inspirin', isn't it?" As he handed me the 8-iron, he cautioned me, "Keep your mind on your business now, lad."

He pointed out a line to the middle of the putting surface and told me to ignore the pin, which was tucked in the front right quarter of the green. "Aim for the dead center. Anywhere on the green will do just fine."

I made a good pass at the ball that sent it toward the middle of the green. However, the trade winds from the sea pushed it left, and I ended up in a grass bunker.

As we walked down toward the green, I asked Moonlight how Jones thought this course compared to the National.

He gave me a curious look. "Now, ya' don't think Mr. Jones would be so rude as to suggest that any course was better than the National, do ya'?" He chuckled and added, "Not if he ever wanted to face Mr. Roberts ag'in."

"Maybe not, but I was wondering if he ever made any comparisons at all."

"Well," Moonlight said carefully, "I heard him say more'n once that he thought both courses tested every club in the bag." After a moment, he added, "I can tell ya' that he changed some things at the National because a' the way some a' these holes played."

"Oh, yeah? Like what?"

"Well, he liked the forced carries on several a' the holes here. Ya' seen it on the fourth an' sixth holes. There's more on the back. So he turned what was nothin' more than a ditch into a pond at the 16th at Augusta. Plus, he thought havin' problems beyond the green, like the 13th an' 16th holes on the back side here, tested a player's ability to control distance."

He laid my bag next to the green. "That's why he had 'em slope the back a' the 15th at the National to run down to the new pond at the 16th. Overshootin' the green with a long second shot now will land ya' in the water. It wasn't always that way, but now there's greater risk in goin' for the green in two. Mr. Jones also had 'em cover the upslope behind number 12 with all kinds a' brush to penalize any shot over the green. Remember how it caught up with Greg Norman at the Masters in '99 when he was fightin' for the lead?"

I remembered how Norman had lost his ball in the dense vegetation behind the 12th green. Under penalty of stroke and distance, he had to return to the tee. Despite what must have been bitter disappointment, he hit his next shot on the green and made a lengthy putt for a heroic four.

Something else clicked inside my head. "I did read somewhere that Perry Maxwell was hired by Augusta National sometime after it opened to make some modifications to the course."

Moonlight laughed. "Now you're gettin' it."

I managed to escape the bunker, but just barely. I then lagged a 20-footer and tapped in for four.

The eighth hole ran slightly inland across the beach on a diagonal. As we stood on the tee, Moonlight explained that this 486-yard hole could be reached in two with a good tee shot, allowing the player a good chance at four when five was a good score. Because of higher ground on the left side of the fairway, the ball tended to run toward the right when it landed. For that reason, Moonlight directed me to aim down the left side of the fairway from the tee, keeping the ball inside a small group of trees on the left.

"See if ya' can hit it like Big Jim Barnes used to," he said as he handed me the driver.

"He played here, too?"

Moonlight just laughed. "You're standin' where he and Mr. Snead bashed drivers for three days once, tryin' to prove who was the longest. Mr. Barnes kept swingin' harder an' harder, while Mr. Snead just kept that smooth tempo a' his." He seemed a little sad all of a sudden. "Mr. Barnes ended up winnin' the money, but he lost his swing an' never got it back."

On that unhappy note, I pushed my drive to the right. The ball landed in the sandy dunes there. Because the brush began to thin out toward the bottom of the slope, I halfway hoped that I would still have a clear shot at the green.

Moonlight seemed to know exactly where my ball was. As usual, he kept his eyes trained on the spot as we walked from the tee, never turning his head even as we talked.

"We'll have to pitch out. Can't take a chance missin' the green with a long second shot from there. Bad angle—bunker an' trees come into play from here." I didn't need to be told twice to lay up. After all, I only had one ball, and I couldn't afford to lose it.

The decision became even easier once we got to my ball. A solitary tree on that side of the hole blocked our path to the green.

Moonlight handed me a 7-iron. "Just punch it out into the fairway an' let it run back to the right, 'bout a hundred yards down. That'll leave us an easy wedge in."

It was a low-risk shot, therefore easy to execute. The ball flew low for about 60 yards or so, and then ran along the center of the fairway before sliding back down the slope toward the right side. The shot wouldn't have been possible in the denser grass that matted the fairways higher up on the slope toward the clubhouse, but it worked to perfection down where we were. It looked like the ball came to rest right at a hundred yards from the green.

"Well done," said Moonlight.

When I got to the ball and was able to get a closer look at the eighth green, I saw the wisdom of Moonlight's advice. Any attempt to reach the green with a long second shot from where we were was foolhardy. If we didn't catch the large bunker defending the front left of the green, we might wind up in the sandy dunes to the right, which was an equally undesirable fate.

Moonlight spoke softly now, as if we were in church. "Time for another knockdown. Let's keep it safe ag'in." Handing me a pitching wedge, he reassured me. "This is just the club for the shot."

I made solid contact, and the ball took off on a low trajectory. It landed in the front of the green, skipped once, and then spun toward the right, stopping quickly. It appeared to be no more than eight feet from the hole.

Moonlight was beaming. "Startin' to like that little shot, ain't ya'?"

I returned his delighted expression. "I wish I had learned it years ago. It's like throwing darts."

As we walked to the green and away from the shore, the roar of the surf began to recede in the distance. At the same time, I noticed that the wind had picked up. Then I looked up at the sky and saw charcoal clouds rolling toward us.

I turned to Moonlight, raising my voice to be heard above the rumbling that was growing closer, "Looks like bad weather coming our way."

He didn't say anything, but pulled his Hogan cap down around his ears. I became a little alarmed. While I hadn't seen any lightning, I could hear thunder in the distance. I loved the game and what we were doing, but I wasn't ready to die for it.

In an urgent voice, I asked Moonlight, "Don't you think we should head in?"

Again, he didn't speak; he just shook his head in disagreement and stooped to read the line for my putt. When he stood up, he held his thumb and forefinger about an inch and then pointed out toward the surf.

As I bent over the putt, a gust of wind threw me slightly off balance. I rushed the stroke and missed on the low side.

I was a little disappointed until Moonlight slapped me on the back as we walked from the green. "Ya' just made par on what Mr. Jones called 'the best short par 5 in the world.'"

For a moment I forgot about the threatening weather. "You mean he thought this was a better par 5 than either 13 or 15 at Augusta?"

Moonlight arched his eyebrows. "All I can tell ya' is what he said. As best as I can recall, his near-exact words were that he knew a' no par 5 presentin' such a terrifyin' challenge to a player who wanted an easy birdie."

I was inclined to agree based upon what I had seen. "Even with a good drive, you gotta have pretty fair-sized coconuts to go for that green in two."

Moonlight laughed at my use of slang. "Well, Mr. Hogan was the best at workin' the course to his advantage, an' he said the play on the second shot was to the area in front a' the green. From there ya' had an easy pitch, an' ya' made either four or five. Anyone hittin' directly at the green risked six or worse." He winked at me. "He'd have liked the way we played the hole. Kinda reminded me a' the way he parred the hole the first time he played here."

"Really?" I had never heard my game and Hogan's mentioned in the same breath.

"Yeah. Hit his second shot to the bail-out area, chipped

'bout four feet past, an' lipped out." He paused. "I know, 'cause I was there."

"You caddied for Hogan?"

"Nah," he said. "I was on another bag. Mr. Jones was there, too, ridin' in a cart an' watchin' the play."

"I don't suppose Hogan let you in on the 'secret' that he supposedly had about the golf swing."

I had meant to be facetious, but Moonlight shook his head. "He didn't tell me anythin' except 'bout rakin' a bunker, but I heard him say somethin' to Mr. Jones that was interestin'."

"What's that?"

"He said that the one thing he worked on the most was keepin' his right knee from movin' durin' the swing."

As we came to the ninth tee, the weather calmed down almost as rapidly as it had flared up. I said something to Moonlight about how quickly it was clearing.

He laughed. "That's the way it is here, lad. You'll see a week's worth of weather changes in one afternoon. That's why I didn't say nothin' before."

Moonlight then explained how the ninth hole continued to move away from the clubhouse and that it would seem every bit as long as the 447 yards listed on the scorecard. Looking out from the tee, I saw that the fairway started left and then turned slightly right toward the green. Perry Maxwell had again strategically placed a bunker at the inside edge of the dogleg to challenge those players who tried to cheat the hole of its full distance.

I hit a terrible drive that went low and left into the trees.

When we got to the ball, I saw that I had advanced it a mere 200 yards or so, leaving me a virtual cannon shot away from the green. Moonlight didn't say much, apparently subscribing to my mother's favorite rule that, if you can't say something nice, don't say anything at all.

At first I was concerned about finding the ball, because I hadn't seen it land after it disappeared into the trees. Once again, Moonlight's certain stride indicated that he had a bead on its location. Sure enough, he walked right to the ball.

I also couldn't resist a dig about his ball-finding skills. "You got a beagle in your family tree?"

He just grunted. "If I ain't surprised that ya' can draft them contracts ya' lawyers are so famous for, why should ya' be surprised that I can find a golf ball? Caddies find balls. It's what we do, ya' know."

Even as he spoke, he started looking around for some fixture from which to reckon our yardage to the green. It took him longer than usual to come up with a number for this shot. Finally, he pulled out my 3-wood, and said, "It's all of 235, uphill all the way. Give it a crack. Anywhere in front a' the green'll work."

I was surprised that he hadn't recommended a more conservative play. There was a large bunker protecting the right front of the green and a smaller pot bunker about ten yards in front of the left edge. All I could figure was that Maxwell was having a bad day when he designed this hole and wanted to take it out on somebody.

I wondered if there was something to this shot Moonlight wasn't telling me. "You don't think I should lay up?"

He made a face. "Nah. Ya' can get close enough with this club to have an easy pitch. There's nothin' to fear up there with those bunkers. It's worth a chance to save your four."

I looked at the faraway green and saw that the flag appeared to be toward the left rear. I doubted that I could reach the green, but I figured that Moonlight wouldn't have given me the 3-wood if it could cost me strokes, so I decided to let her rip.

I didn't hit it as well as I wanted. The ball popped up on me, probably because I was swinging into an uphill lie. It took distance off the shot that I couldn't afford to lose. The ball dropped a good 50 yards in front of the green, the distance of the dreaded half-wedge.

Moonlight didn't seem that disappointed. Without saying anything, he put my 3-wood back in my bag and started walking. I guess I felt some comment was necessary, so I said something about putting myself in the position that he had been telling me to avoid—that of making a touch shot with a half-swing.

He dismissed my concerns with a wave of his hand. "There's no water up there, lad. An' you're pitchin' uphill. We'll be alright. Besides, ya' won't be hittin' the sand wedge. We're gonna bump an' run the ball with a 9-iron."

As we stood at my ball, he explained that a pitch with the sand wedge would have to be struck almost perfectly in order to finish near the hole. We could get just as close, he said, by taking a 9-iron and running it up to the hole.

I pitched the ball to within ten yards or so of the front of the green. It bounced up the generous alley between the bunkers and rolled toward the back where the hole was situated. The ball missed the flagstick by a matter of inches, but continued to roll a good ten feet past.

Moonlight seemed satisfied with my effort. "We got a shot at it. That's all we can ask for."

Although I took my time studying the putt, I knew I would follow whatever line he read. He read it right edge and cautioned me that the putt was slightly downhill and would be a little fast.

So of course I left the putt a foot short.

Chapter 19

MOONLIGHT SUGGESTED A short break before starting the back nine. We had taken barely 90 minutes to play the first nine holes, so the afternoon sun was still bright. As he sat down on a nearby bench, Moonlight seemed almost apologetic about taking a break.

"Hilly course. Just gimme a minute an' I'll be good as new."

I took advantage of the recess to use a rustic water closet just beyond the ninth green. It didn't strike me as odd until we were headed back outside that the urinal had flushed. How many of these places still had running water, I wondered, after being closed for 30-plus years?

As we made our way to the tenth tee, I asked Moonlight about some of the more interesting matches he had witnessed at Bragg's Point.

"There're so many to talk 'bout, lad. So many great players loved to come here. They'd play four-ball matches, an' the standard bet was a hundred bucks for the front, another hundred for the back, an' two hundred for the 18. Automatic presses at two down, with each hole countin' as a new bet."

I wasn't familiar with that kind of bet. "How did that work?"

"Let's say you're two down for the back at the 16th hole. That makes a press automatic, an' that hole is worth $100, which is the amount a' the back nine bet. If the team that presses wins the hole, there is no press on the next hole 'cause they're only one down. But they've won $100 in the meantime."

"What if they don't win the hole?"

"If they lose the hole, they're out $100, an' the press continues on the next hole 'cause they're three down. If they halve the hole, no money changes hands, but the press applies at the next hole 'cause they're still two down. Either way, the next hole is a $100 hole."

"That could get expensive."

Moonlight nodded. "Sure. Presses for the 18-hole bet kick in when you're two down for the round, too. That's $200 a hole. I saw over $1,000 change hands more'n once, an' that was back in the days when winning a four-day tournament on tour didn't pay much more'n that."

I wanted to know more.

"Who played here the most often?"

"Mr. Hogan, Mr. Demaret, Mr. Nelson, Mr. Snead, Jackie Burke, guys who had won the Masters. Mr. Palmer, too, a' course. An' Mr. Jones's close friends, like General, then President, Eisenhower. Not many foreigners. Mr. Jones an' Mr. Roberts worried 'bout keepin' this a secret, an' Mr. Roberts didn't trust many foreigners."

I knew that Cliff Roberts had been a man who was said to harbor many prejudices, so what Moonlight said didn't surprise me. What he said next did take me aback, however.

"He made an exception once, an' it was quite a deal. Back in the early part a' 1941, someone from Washington approached Mr. Jones 'bout havin' a team competition with the Japanese as a gesture a' goodwill. The Japs had been makin' noises throughout Asia, an' Washington had finally realized they were a real threat to peace. The president had just imposed a trade embargo, which apparently made 'em madder'n hell."

I knew a little bit about World War II history, particularly the controversy about our readiness for the attack on Pearl Harbor. I was also aware that, as recently as 1995, relatives of the two top-ranked military officers at Pearl Harbor had petitioned the government to clear them of responsibility for our apparent unpreparedness for the Japanese sneak attack.

Moonlight continued. "According to American intelligence, one a' the big Jap ministers, some guy named Nakimura, was a golf nut. The idea was to invite him over an' have him bring a team a' golfers with him. We'd send agents to try to talk with Nakimura while he was here."

I was intrigued at the thought of Jones trying to head off World War II. "So, did the match ever occur?"

"Yeah. It only served to prove that the government shouldn't mess with golf. Damned near started a war instead of avoidin' one."

"What do you mean?"

"Well, Nakimura went for it. Then, the bureaucrats started worryin' 'bout how it would look for Americans an' Japs to be playin' golf at a time like this. What if we beat the pants off 'em? That could only make things worse. An' what if we lost? That might hurt morale. What started out as a great idea suddenly became a big problem. So they asked Mr. Jones if they could keep the matches a secret. Mr. Jones an' Mr. Roberts eventually decided to play the matches here, 'cause it was the only way to keep the whole thing quiet."

"But wouldn't that destroy Jones's secret?"

"I reckon Mr. Jones thought it was worth it to avoid a war. Besides, it wasn't like the Japs were gonna tell a whole bunch of Americans 'bout the place, especially if they lost."

"Tell me about the matches."

Moonlight set my bag down. "They ran it like the Ryder Cup. Each team had 'round ten players or so. Our team was a bunch a' real all-stars: Mr. Hogan, Mr. Snead, Mr. Nelson, Ralph Guldahl, Horton Smith, Sarazen, Demaret." He paused a minute. "Hell, I can't remember everyone."

"When did they play?"

"I guess it was 'round the early summer of 1941. It was gonna be a two-day competition, four-balls an' alternatin' shots the first day an' singles the second. They had a banquet for everyone the night before at the officers' club at the base. I guess they wanted to impress the Japs with our military facilities."

So far, everything I heard sounded like typical government psychology.

"Anyway, they almost didn't get to play 'cause a' what happened at the banquet. The players sat across from one another at a long table. Before they were seated, the Japanese players bowed to the American players. Our guys had been briefed on how to return the bow."

Moonlight laughed as he recalled the story. "Only Mr. Hogan refused to bow. Said he wasn't there to dance with 'em, just to beat the crap out of 'em on the golf course. He stood there, ramrod straight. Everyone noticed that he wouldn't move an inch. This is apparently a great insult in Japan. The way I heard it, Mr. Nelson leaned over an' said in Mr. Hogan's ear, 'Ben, you're the only one who hasn't bowed.' Mr. Hogan supposedly looked at Mr. Nelson an' said in a fairly loud voice, 'These bastards are damned lucky I'm willing to eat with 'em.'"

"So what happened?"

"Mr. Hogan never bowed. The Japs got upset. Mr. Jones was called in to mediate the dispute. He assured the Japanese delegation that Mr. Hogan, like most Americans, was unfamiliar with Japanese ways an' didn't understand the significance of the bow. So the matches went on the next day."

"How did the Americans do?"

Moonlight grinned. "If the American navy had been that good, the war wouldn't've lasted a month. Mr. Hogan won every match he played, without breakin' a sweat. So did Mr. Nelson, Mr. Demaret, an' Mr. Snead. I think the Japs only won one match an' tied three others. A lotta them were makin' long walks in."

I understood that to mean the matches ended early, forcing the players to walk in from holes that were a good distance from the clubhouse. "Doesn't sound like we were very gracious hosts."

"Nah. But American bigwigs met with Nakimura durin' the tournament. He was supposed to be sympathetic. But he didn't have enough say back in Japan. Yamamoto an' others had the Emperor convinced it was his destiny to rule most of Asia an' Australia, not to mention every island in the Pacific clear to Hawaii. Ya' know the rest a' the story."

"Wouldn't it have been something if golf could have enabled us to avoid the war?"

"Yeah, but they didn't understand the game."

"What makes you say that?"

"More than anythin', golf's a game of integrity, lad. Players call penalties on themselves even when no one's lookin'. It's at the heart a' the game." He paused, and I saw a look of contempt on his face. "Ya' think people who start a war with a sneak attack on a Sunday mornin' can really understand a game where playin' by the rules is the most important thing?"

He wasn't done. "The way I see it, lyin' is a form a' weakness. A liar ain't strong 'nough to own up to the truth. An' I got no patience with liars. So ya' won't see me ridin' in a Toyota or playin' one a' them Sony radios, no, sir. If ya' ask me, Truman gave 'em what they deserved."

I was a little surprised at the harshness of his attitude. But then I remembered how one of my grandfather's friends had survived the Bataan Death March. The stories he brought back were horrifying, and he never forgave his Japanese captors for their brutality. Moonlight was old enough to have served in that war—and to have lost loved ones in it. My generation hadn't been through anything like that, and I decided that I

shouldn't be so quick to judge Moonlight for things I really
didn't understand.

Chapter 20

AS WE PREPARED to play the tenth hole, I asked Moonlight what to expect on the back nine.

He thought for a moment and then said, "Six a' the nine holes are by the sea, terrific holes, every one a' them. Maxwell must've been inspired by God when he did these. The greens're a challenge. Hard to read, an' they require the touch of a mother bathin' her baby."

Shouldering my bag at the tenth tee, he handed me my 3-iron. "This is where you're gonna shine, Charley." He then explained that the tenth hole was a two-shot hole that started slightly up the slope toward the right and then turned back left where it ran down to a deep but narrow green. The idea from the tee was to make certain that the first shot landed far enough right to have a good angle for the approach.

"Why not driver?"

"Ya' don't need a big stick here, lad. The ball will run enough when it lands, an' the second shot is downhill all the way. The hole's 379 on the card, but plays no more'n 350 or so. With a driver, you're takin' a chance on goin' through the fairway or into the bushes."

I hit the 3-iron clean. I saw what Moonlight meant when the ball bounced high on landing and finished in the middle of the fairway. A driver would have landed near the trees across the fairway where it turned back to the left.

When we reached the bend in the dogleg, I saw more clearly how Moonlight wanted me to use my drive to set up my second shot into the green. The hole had turned partially toward the ocean in a pronounced curve that would continue through the next two holes. We were still cutting across the slope at an angle, which meant that the shot would run right to left when it landed.

Moonlight's instructions were simple. "Aim on a line with the inside edge a' the bunker frontin' the right side a' the green." Pacing to a nearby tree, he said, "You've got 'bout 180 to the front a' the green. It'll play a bit shorter 'cause the green's below us. Let's hit a five."

I certainly wasn't going to quibble; Moonlight hadn't mis-clubbed me yet. The ball started right down the line, hung in the air at its apex for what seemed like an extra few seconds, and then fell onto the front edge of the green.

The tilt of the slope caused the ball to bounce forward and to the left. Moonlight quickly determined its eventual destination. "That's gonna be close," he said in a reverent but excited stage whisper.

The ball continued to curve slightly to the left, and I realized it was headed straight for the flag. We both stood there transfixed as it seemed to disappear into the hole, only to spin back out and stop no more than a foot away.

Moonlight gave me a broad grin. "I don't suppose you'll be needin' me to read that one, now will ya'?"

It was the kind of shot I used to dream about. But somehow, at that moment, I felt as if the spirit of the course had more to do with it than my muscles, talent, or dreams.

As we walked off the green, I asked Moonlight if he had always been that good at clubbing players. He just grunted and said, "It's just somethin' ya' learn. But I was never as good as Henry Bradford."

"Who was he?"

"Another one a' the guys who came out from Augusta." He finished cleaning my ball with his towel and handed it back to me. "Most of us could size up a player after they hit a shot or two. Henry had 'em pegged just by lookin' in their bag."

"How?"

"He'd look at their irons first—mostly the wedges. He always said that the wedges told him what kinda player he had. If the wedges were worn in the right spot from practice, he knew he was on a good player's bag."

The 11th tee was off to the left of the 10th green. As we walked over to it, Moonlight said, "You're gonna like this hole."

He was right. The 11th tee was set back about a hundred yards away, right on the cliffs. Although it was the second shortest hole on the course at 147 yards, the teeing grounds on this one-shot hole (there were two to choose from) directed the player across an abrupt break in the shoreline to a green perched on an opposite cliff. The hole fell away perhaps 20 feet or so below from tee to green and offered a small target that made club selection critical.

Any shot played right or too long became fish food, and anything struck offline to the left was collected by a greenside bunker that was deeper than any I had seen on the course. From where we stood, it was a scary, but magnificent, view.

I felt Moonlight at my shoulder. He had remained quiet as I took it all in. After looking around at the white caps and gulls, it seemed as though he wasn't sufficiently confident of the wind's direction, so he threw up some grass.

"I haven't seen you do that very often."

"Usually don't need to," he grunted. He appeared thoughtful for a moment, then said, "Let's hit the eight."

As I wrapped my fingers around the grip, Moonlight offered a final thought. "Ya' know, this is the only hole that Mr. Jones made a one on—an' the only one that Mr. Nelson didn't."

I pulled up short. "Did they hit the eight here?"

He avoided the question and said simply, "You've got the right club in your hands. Just hit it."

Although the swing felt good, I caught a bit of turf behind the ball. I knew immediately that I wouldn't be adding my name to the list of those who had aced the hole. At the moment, I would've been quite satisfied if my ball just stayed dry.

Moonlight could tell from the sound at contact that I had caught it fat. "C'mon," he murmured at the ball in a kind of prayerful tone. "Get legs."

Moonlight and I both exhaled audibly when the ball landed

in the fringe fronting the green. It had taken a gust of wind to clear the cove, but we were safely across.

Moonlight seemed unconcerned by my poor effort. Wiping off the club, he started walking toward the green. After reinserting my 8-iron in my bag, he commented dryly, "I didn't expect ya' to lay up."

When we reached the green, I realized how lucky I had been. There wasn't more than seven or eight feet from the scrubby brush that marked the beginning of the cliff and the front of the green. If the shot hadn't been wind-aided, I would've had to re-tee and play three—that is, if I had another ball.

But that was in the past, I told myself. It was time to think about the next shot. Moonlight handed me my putter. I had about 25 feet to the hole. I figured the putt broke toward the ocean. I hit it solid, and for a short time I thought it might go in. Unfortunately, I hadn't given it quite enough steam, and it fell hard to the right as it approached the hole.

I had about two-and-a-half feet for my three, just enough distance to make me cautious. Moonlight still had the flagstick in his hands. As he walked by, he said simply, "Dead center to the back a' the cup."

Like most golfers, I have trouble keeping my head down on short putts. I was too anxious about making my par on this one-shot hole not to sneak a look. When I did, I pushed the ball slightly offline. Instead of heading for the center of the cup, it was drifting toward the right edge.

Impulsively, I stepped toward the hole as if to rake the ball in as it missed on the right side. It caught the edge, but not enough to bring it into the hole. The ball spun around the lip and finished just on the other side of the hole, mocking me.

Chapter 21

THE 12TH HOLE was kind of quirky. It was listed as a 421-yard par 4, but didn't appear to be anywhere near that long. It headed straightaway down for about 260 yards or so and then turned right at almost a 90-degree angle. At that point, the fairway was interrupted by a cove that separated the player from the green on the other side. It reminded me somewhat of the sixth hole.

Moonlight pulled the 5-wood from my bag. I wondered briefly if I should offer to carry my bag, but he showed no signs of fatigue. The last thing I wanted was to insult him by suggesting that he wasn't up to finishing.

When I took the club from him, he could tell from my expression that I didn't fully understand the club selection. This was a long hole, and it seemed to call for all the firepower I could get off the tee.

Looking down the fairway, he said, "I dunno who measured this hole, but he must've been a drinkin' man. Ya' gotta ignore what the card says; if ya' hit much more'n this, we'll have to climb down on the rocks to play our second." He then pointed to the right side of the fairway. "If ya' play short to that side, ya' cut off most a' the cove, an' you'll be no more'n a 150 from the green."

I had done quite well by trusting Moonlight. Even though it didn't seem like much club to hit on a par 4, I took the 5-wood, lined up for the right side of the fairway, and let it fly.

I didn't catch it as well as I would have liked. Still, when the shot landed, I saw what Moonlight was saying. The ball continued to roll after I expected it to stop. It finally came to rest no more than 25 yards from the edge of the cove.

"That'll play just fine," Moonlight said encouragingly.

As we walked down the fairway, what Moonlight had told me on the tee about the deceptive distance on the hole became even more apparent. The ground dropped much more sharply here than elsewhere on the course as it ran to the sea, and the thin turf offered little resistance to the rolling ball. The combined effect shortened the hole considerably.

Approaching my ball, I couldn't help but wonder how far it was from tee to green as the crow flies. It seemed possible for a long driver to reach the green by cutting across the dog-leg. For a brief moment, I tried to recall the formula to determine the length of the hypotenuse of a triangle, but I had long forgotten most everything I had learned in Coach Postell's tenth-grade geometry class (probably because he spent most of our classtime drawing football plays). I asked Moonlight whether anyone had ever driven the green.

He looked at me with disdain. "Ya' got any idea how much carry that requires?"

His tone made me feel slightly stupid. "Not really," I said rather lamely. "That's part a' the mystery here. The place is full of optical illusions. Distances ain't necessarily what they appear to be."

He cocked his head back toward the tee. "First time Olin Dutra played here, he asked his caddie if he could clear the cove at the narrow side to the right a' the green. If I remember, Gra'm McNulty was on Dutra's bag at the time." He pointed toward the green to indicate the line. "Anyway, Dutra'd won the Open in '34, an' poor ol' Gra'm wasn't 'bout to tell a U.S. Open champ he couldn't clear the cove, so he let him try."

Moonlight paused to let me ask the obvious question. "So what happened?"

He grinned. "After the fourth try, he hit a 3-iron not far from where we are an' ended up makin' 12 on the hole."

"I guess no one was tempted to go for it after that."

"Not hardly," he said, chuckling at the memory.

As had been the case all day, my ball had found an excellent lie. Moonlight paced off the distance to the water's edge. Walking back toward me, he said, "Gotta be right on this one, Charley. We don't want to be 'bove the hole on this green. Mr. Jones made this one like he did the ninth at Augusta. It's a bugger to putt from past the hole."

He looked up, as if gauging the wind. "Not much air movin'. It's just shy of a 150 yards to the middle."

Moonlight pulled my 8-iron from my bag. "Let's try the eight. Favor the left. It's a good spot there."

I made solid contact, and the ball jumped off the club. It

seemed to fly higher than usual, and I worried for a moment that it would barely clear the cove. But it maintained its elevation, landed in front of the green, and stopped a few feet short of the edge.

I was disappointed at missing the green, but Moonlight seemed pleased as he took my club from me. "Easy chip from there. We may even be able to putt it."

We had a long walk to the green, because we had to veer left to get around the cove. It was getting to be around four o'clock by then, and for the first time I noticed that it had gotten cooler.

"Did you pull the sweater out of my bag when you emptied all that stuff?"

He shook his head. "Nah, lad, I left it in, knowin' ya' might need it." He reached around and unzipped the back zipper without removing my bag from his shoulder. He then pulled out the sweater and handed it to me.

When I got a closer look at my ball, I could tell that, once again, Moonlight had put me in a good position. The area in front of the green was relatively flat. Moonlight gave me a pitching wedge and told me to land the ball just inside the front edge of the green. It would trickle toward the hole from there, he said.

His strategy worked like a charm. The ball popped up and fell softly onto the front of the green before rolling to within two feet of the hole. An easy putt.

After replacing the flagstick, Moonlight simply picked up my bag and said, "You're gonna like the 13th."

He was right.

The 13th tee was just south of the 12th green and momentarily put us with our backs to the water. Like 12, it turned right for the second shot and again forced the golfer to carry another cove in the shoreline in order to reach the putting surface.

Moonlight began to explain what lay ahead. "This is the shortest two-shot hole on the course, only 'bout 350 yards or so. I watched Mr. Snead drive the green here, but it was dry, an' he had a tailwind. We'll hit 3-iron." As I stood on the tee, I saw another reason Moonlight took the driver out of my hands. Because the fairway took a sharp bend to the right, any tee shot hit more than 200 yards straightaway would probably cross through the fairway to the rough on the other side. Snead must have cut the corner and flown his ball across the cove that the fairway wrapped around. Even with a tailwind, that took a bigger blow than I was capable of delivering.

I lined up for a distant tree, just as Moonlight told me, and hit it solidly, albeit a little left of my line. The ball bounded down the fairway, running along the left edge. It stayed out of trouble, and it appeared to me that I would have no more than 150 yards to the green.

As he tucked my 3-iron back into my bag, Moonlight said with a trace of concern, "We've brought the bunker in front a bit more into play from there, but we're not shootin' for the pin anyway. It'll do fine."

As we walked along, Moonlight seemed inspired by another memory of things past. "One glorious afternoon here in the early spring, we had Mr. Sarazen an' Mr. Jones playin' with a fellow named Walter Ogilvie. They called him 'Chug.' He'd been an All-American at Stanford, an' the talk was that he was gonna be the next great amateur in the country. Mr. Jones knew his father somehow an' had taken a shine to the boy. Anyway, he invited him out to play, supposedly to help him prepare for the U.S. Amateur."

After adjusting my bag on his shoulder, Moonlight continued with his story. "He really put on a display for us. I never saw anyone hit it so close to the hole time after time, although they tell me that Johnny Miller in his heyday was like that, too. He didn't miss a green the entire time, an' I don't remember him ever being more'n twelve to 15 feet away from the hole. Shot 63. Course record. No one else ever came close."

"Good Lord," I said appreciatively. "How come I've never heard of him?"

Moonlight shook his head as if discussing someone who had died. "Ya' know, lad, the gods a' golf can bless ya' with it all, but they rarely let ya' keep it. Mr. Jones had enough, an' he was only 28 years old when he quit. He tried to come back to play in the Masters, but the magic was gone for him. Look at that fella Bill Rogers. Won the Open at St. Georges, named Player a' the Year, had it all. Someone decided that his time was over. Maybe the fire went out. Who knows? Johnny Miller. Same thing. Shot 63 to win the U.S. Open at Oakmont. Won the Open at Birkdale, too. For several years in the '70s, no one could touch him. Then his putter went bad."

He pointed up to the sky. "Someone up there decided to take it away from Ogilvie. Practicin' for the Amateur, he developed a twitch with the putter. The harder he worked to overcome it, the worse it got. He tried everythin', but nothin' worked. People would look away when he was puttin', an' he often took four to get the ball in the hole."

It was every golfer's nightmare. Most called it "the yips." For years, there was a raging debate on whether it was a physical or mental condition. Neurologists offered a variety of medical explanations for its cause. Players appeared unwilling to acknowledge that it could be physical in nature, because that might mean it was out of their control. Instead, they preferred to insist that the yips were all in the head, as if a strong mind could make them go away.

"So what happened to him?"

"Gave it up. Walked away from the game for almost 40 years. When the long putter came out, he tried it. Found he could putt reasonably well with it, so he started playin' ag'in." Moonlight allowed himself a smile. "Ended up winnin' the California State Seniors at Lake Merced."

We were now at my ball. Moonlight had already calculated the yardage by the time he put my bag down.

"I got it at 135. Ya' can see it's downhill. I expect it'll play a club less. I like the 9. Okay with you?"

It was the first time he had asked me to approve his club selection. "I'm not about to argue with you now."

As I stood behind the ball, he counseled me to ignore the pin tucked behind the yawning bunker in front. "Another sucker pin. An' it's not just the bunker. Ya' can't see it, but the green falls away behind the hole there. It's jail over there. Stay to the left."

I picked a spot toward the left half of the green and tried to imprint it in my mind. As soon as I felt the frame freeze on it, I pulled the trigger.

The ball flew straight at the spot I had selected, landed there, and stopped. "Well done," Moonlight said quietly as I handed the club back to him.

As we approached the green, I noticed that the large bunker in front had the classic MacKenzie crab-shaped design. My concentration had been such that I didn't recall seeing it as I played my second shot.

I had about 30 feet to the hole. For the first time, I saw what Moonlight meant when he told me how special the greens were on the back side. There was a sizeable ridge cutting across my line, rising up about ten feet in front of me and then falling away toward the hole. Beyond the hole, the green continued to fall away from us for ten feet or so. At that point, it ended abruptly. Beneath it was a large collecting area, or grass bunker, that appeared to be deep.

The bottom line was that this was one of the most difficult putts I could ever have imagined. Moonlight apparently could sense my apprehension; he was standing behind me and put his hand on my shoulder, as if to reassure me. He said softly in my ear, "Ignore the hump. The downhill side'll give back what the uphill side takes. Just look at the hole for your distance. I've got it two balls 'bove the hole for the line." He paused before adding, "Ya' can make this one, Charley."

Feeling Moonlight close by upped my confidence. I made two good practice strokes, addressed the ball, and hit the putt.

The ball slowed a bit as it climbed the ridge and then regained its speed as it fell across the other side. It seemed to accelerate a little as it approached the hole, and for a second I was afraid it would run way past. Then it started to drift left ever so slightly, just as Moonlight had read. I still thought it would miss the hole, though, but it turned left again just as it reached the hole and fell in at the right edge of the cup.

Chapter 22

ONE THING HAD become obvious to me about the links at Bragg's Point: Jones and Maxwell wanted to keep players off balance. On the back nine, the course seemed to change direction every other hole. A player was required to adjust to changes in elevation and wind direction at almost every turn.

There didn't seem to be any pattern in the layout of the holes, either. Some bent to the left, and others turned back to the right. As a result, the course forced the player to adjust his ball flight continually to the layout. I was beginning to understand why Jones, Hogan, and anyone else lucky enough to experience the magic of Bragg's Point believed it to be such a great test of golf.

The 14th hole was the longest hole on the course and ran to the far south end of the property. The card in my pocket said it was 571 yards long. Most of it ran slightly uphill. It was a subtle double dogleg, bending once each way. The first bend in the fairway appeared to be about 200 yards or so from the tee.

I saw Moonlight pull my 3-iron from my bag. Although I had resolved not to question him again, I couldn't help myself.

"Are you sure that's enough?" Then, before he could answer, I attempted to justify my question. "It's uphill, you know. Won't it play longer?"

He chuckled. "Lad, Helen Keller could tell that's uphill. Ya' don't think I can see it, too?"

I felt my face turn a little red, and it wasn't from the afternoon sun. He let me dangle a bit before adding, "A three's enough to get ya' to the corner. Anythin' more risks the sand dunes beyond. It's the right club; just trust it, now."

I teed the ball just above the grass to make certain I would make clean contact. I then lined up for the right side of the fairway, as Moonlight suggested, to make the most of the angle of the dogleg. "Always aim where ya' can most afford to miss," he told me.

The shot felt as solid as anything I had hit all day. Moonlight grunted his approval as he picked up my bag and began walking off the tee before the ball even landed. He didn't look back or otherwise wait for me. For whatever reason, he was still giving me lots of space.

We walked toward my ball without talking. Without the distraction of conversation, I was able to observe him more closely. He still seemed to move without any sign of fatigue, which I found remarkable for someone his age. I knew that the Scots were a tough lot, particularly those who were hardened by a lifetime of walking the links. But Moonlight was exceeding my expectations. Ever so briefly, I wondered if that was another sign of the magic of the place. It certainly appeared that coming here had rejuvenated him.

The silence between us had allowed Moonlight to do some thinking as well. Even though we were standing at my ball, he appeared to be in no hurry to play the next shot.

"I'm no Biblical scholar, lad, an' the Lord knows I'm not as devout a man as I should be. But ya' know there are a few places on this earth especially blessed by God Himself. It's always been that way with this place. The Good Lord brought Mr. Jones here if for no other reason than to give him the peace he deserved when he began to get sick."

He tossed some grass in the air but paid no attention to where it drifted. "Ya' know, I believe God blesses those who play this game. There ain't another game as spiritual as this one. No other game makes a man look inside himself like golf. You're forced to confront a lot of things 'bout yourself ya' may not like, ya' know?"

"Wasn't it Mr. Jones who said that golf didn't build character so much as reveal it?"

Moonlight smiled, this time genuinely. "That he did." He stepped back from my ball. I waited for him to hand me a club before realizing that I still held the 3-iron I had used on the tee.

Moonlight nodded his head at the club and said, "Ya' need it again, Charley. Just bump it down the left side, same swing ya' put on it back there. It'll leave us a wedge to get home."

Without thinking, I walked up to the ball and hit it. The shot flew exactly where I had aimed.

My friend Cheatwood was fond of saying that there was no other game in the world that could be so easy and so hard at the same time as golf. I had certainly experienced my share of the hard part, but never before had I been in that place where the game became so easy.

As we advanced toward my ball, Moonlight began to reminisce again. "Mr. Jones loved this hole 'cause it made ya' play right to left for the first time on the back nine. He said it exercised different golf muscles, an' that made it hard to adjust to. He really liked the green on this hole, too. He told us that Mr. Maxwell was tryin' to imitate some big architect up East on this hole, some guy named Tuckerhose, or somethin'."

"Tillinghast?"

"Yeah, that's the one."

I knew about A.W. Tillinghast. He designed a number of classic courses in the Northeast, including Winged Foot in Mamaroneck outside of New York City. I had played there once; it was a memorable experience. Winged Foot has hosted a number of U.S. Opens, as well as a recent PGA Championship, and with good reason. I made four birdies the day I played it and still shot 86.

When we turned the corner, the green came into view, and I immediately understood why Jones felt the way he did about the hole. If imitation is truly the sincerest form of flattery, then Maxwell flattered the hell out of Tillinghast's memory.

The green itself was a virtual copy of the tenth hole at Winged Foot, which is unusual for a starting hole on a back nine in that it's a par 3. Like its Tillinghast original, the 14th green at Bragg's Point was raised well above grade, sloped steeply from back to front, and was protected by deep bunkers that wrapped around its front and sides. This was apparently the one time Maxwell disregarded Jones's instruction to keep bunkers on the course to a minimum.

If so, it was an act of disobedience that was justified. The 14th green was small, but otherwise defenseless. Without the Tillinghast-like design of the green, the hole would not have posed nearly as much of a challenge for Jones and his friends.

As we arrived at my ball, Moonlight walked a few steps forward, looked left at a nearby tree, and pronounced that we had a 150 yards left to the green. That was almost perfect distance for my 7-iron.

The swing just felt right from start to finish. I barely felt the ball come off the club, and it headed for the middle of the green, right where I had aimed, like it was on sonar. For a moment I thought it might hit the flagstick, but it didn't. Instead, it landed just beyond the hole and spun back, stopping four feet below the cup.

"Well, now, I think that one'll do." Moonlight was grinning as I handed him the 7, which he began to wipe clean with his towel as we strolled to the green.

As we walked up the narrow path in the front of the green between two large bunkers, I saw how fortunate I was to have spun the ball back below the hole. Although the green wasn't very deep, it was considerably higher in back than in front. If I had been above the hole, I would have had one of those Michael DeBakey putts, the kind that required the touch of a surgeon. I was no surgeon.

Although my putt was long enough to be in my "throw-up zone," it was uphill, which forced me to stroke it firmly. Moonlight assured me there was no break in it and reminded me to hit the back of the cup.

I hit the putt solidly, and it went right in the middle of the hole.

Chapter 23

MOONLIGHT GAVE ME a look of feigned nonchalance as he replaced the flagstick. He kept to himself and didn't say anything as we departed the green.

The 15th tee was back down the hill about 20 yards from the 14th green. We had reached the south end of the course and now turned back toward the clubhouse and across the side of the sloping ground along that part of the property.

Moonlight handed me the driver. "I'm turnin' ya' loose on this one. It's all a' 400 yards an' change, an' you'll feel it before we're done. As ya' can tell, it turns to the right, but not 'til you're a good 250 out. For once, let's play the middle."

I picked a line based on an outcropping of rock in the distance that Moonlight pointed out. I teed my ball near the right marker to give myself the best angle toward the fairway. By playing from that side, I was trying to eliminate the extreme right side of the hole where I might be blocked from the green on my approach. The idea, as always, was to play away from trouble.

Unfortunately, that was right where my drive appeared to be headed. I held my breath as I watched the ball start dangerously close to the trees in the right rough. However, it began to draw slowly back toward the fairway, and I released my sphincter muscle when it finally landed just inside the right edge of the short grass.

Moonlight smiled at me. "Never a doubt," he said as he pulled the strap of my bag over his right shoulder.

As we headed down the fairway, Moonlight appeared to be in the midst of yet another memory. "Ya' see where the fairway crests over on the right side there?" I nodded as he pointed to the spot. "Mr. Jones brought these two brothers from Louisiana out here to play. Hebert was their name. They spelled it one way an' pronounced it another. Said they were Cajuns. Anyway, they both had won the PGA."

I knew who he meant. Their names were Lionel and Jay Hebert. The younger brother, Lionel, won the PGA in 1957, and his older brother Jay won the same championship three years later.

"Yeah, I've heard of them."

"One of 'em had just won the PGA. They'd both played the Masters an' had cooked up some Cajun food for Mr. Jones while they were at Augusta. The pepper almost burned a hole in his stomach, but he really liked those two boys. They were kinda 'down home,' as Mr. Jones said."

He reflected a minute. "Ya' know, Mr. Jones always seemed more comfortable with people from the South than he did with a lotta Mr. Roberts's New York buddies." He shrugged as if the reason were obvious. "Anyway, he wasn't playin' much at all by then, but he rode the course while the two brothers played. I carried for one of 'em, an' Slats carried the other bag."

We had arrived at the spot he had pointed out. "They were bettin' pretty heavy against each other, an' Mr. Jones was gettin' a kick outa watchin' the whole thing. They sure had a funny way a' talkin'. My man knocks it in the hole from right here, for a two, with four carryovers ridin' on the bet. His brother just looks at him an' says, 'Ya' really give me the *chou rouge.*'"

I squinched my face. "What does that mean?"

"That's what I asked. Mr. Lionel laughed an' said it was French for red ass."

I immediately thought of Emile Guidry. He would be pleased to learn that I had expanded my Cajun vocabulary.

We were now at my ball. I looked at Moonlight. "It looks like I hit it farther off the tee than the PGA champion did that day."

Moonlight laughed. "That ya' did, lad." He waited a moment before adding, "'Course, the equipment's a bit different nowadays."

To my surprise, my tee shot had finished in the "A" position, and I was pleased to see the green present itself squarely to me for my approach. I looked over at Moonlight for a sign of approval, but he was busy calculating the yardage. He walked ahead to a line even with a nearby tree and began pacing back to my ball.

When he was done, he looked at me. "It's a good 6-iron. Play it down the right side ag'in; the slope'll run it back to the left. That bunker on the left'll catch anythin' in the area, so keep it away from there."

Unfortunately, I came over the top and pulled the shot

left—straight toward the deep bunker that Moonlight had just told me to avoid at all costs. Like most golfers, I always found watching my ball headed for trouble to be a special kind of agony. Unfortunately, as everyone who's ever played the game knows, golf balls have an inexplicable attraction for hazards. Mine fell directly into the bunker.

Moonlight didn't appear to be particularly upset. He wiped off my 6-iron, stuck it in the bag as we walked along, and pulled out the sand wedge. As I entered the bunker, I noticed that, like the one I had played from earlier, the sand was packed. No surprise there, of course. There was a lot of grass growing in the bunker as well, but my ball was sitting in a clear spot, and there was nothing to interfere with my swing.

The hole was barely more than a flagstick from the edge of the green nearest the bunker. All I wanted to do was to clear the bunker's edge; with any amount of roll, the ball would get to the hole.

The ball came up quickly and softly, carried on top of a thin slice of sand that my open wedge had carved from the bunker. It dropped about six feet short of the hole and began a lazy, almost uninterested roll before finally coming to a stop three feet or so from the cup.

It was better than I expected, but I was left with another putt in the throw-up zone, the kind that caught up to you sooner or later. And from the way Moonlight was circling it, I judged that it had a nasty little break to it.

As I exchanged my wedge for my putter, I asked him what he thought the putt would do.

"I got it a ball out to the right. It wants to run toward the front a' the green."

I made my two practice strokes down the line, took a quick final look at the hole, and made a firm stroke. The ball took the break just as Moonlight had read it and snuck in the left side of the cup.

There wasn't much time to enjoy the sand save. The 16th tee was right next to the green, and I could see that it was a bitch of a hole.

The 16th was the last of the par 3s on the course and easily the most challenging. It was 200 yards long and ran alongside the shoreline all the way on the left. If that weren't enough to shorten my backswing, the hole also featured deep bunkers on both sides of the green from which escape appeared to be difficult at best.

I had learned a few things from Moonlight, however. I looked to the area in front of the green. Maxwell had again left the approach open in front, inviting the player to land the ball short and let it run on.

"What about bouncing one on with a five?"

Moonlight grinned his approval. With a deliberately thickened accent, he said, "Ya'r startin' ta sound like you're from Dornoch, what with ya'r talk 'bout runnin' the ball onto the green. Are ya' sure ya' don' have a bit a' Scot in ya', lad?"

He held my 5-iron out to me. If I hit it where I wanted, it would either bounce right on or leave me with a chip that was straight and flat all the way to the hole.

I caught the ball slightly in the heel of the club, so it started left of my line before drifting back toward the middle as it began to fall. It landed about five yards short of the green, bounced twice, and rolled to within 15 feet of the hole.

Because of the gentle downslope, we almost trotted down to the green. Once again, I took full advantage of an opportunity to take in the magnificent ocean view.

I turned toward Moonlight. "Did you ever get used to this?"

He shook his head. "Now that'd be a sin, wouldn't it?"

I understood. And agreed.

The flagstick was on the right side of the green. Moonlight frowned ever so slightly as he read the putt from the other side of the hole.

"I had to look at it from over here to be sure. This'll be a little tricky. The green falls away to the water, so we'll have to play it to go to your left. It'll be a little quick, too."

Walking back behind my ball, he took one last look and then said reassuringly, "That's it. Half a cup on the right, an' it'll go. Just start it on line."

I didn't even bother to read it myself.

I liked the putt the minute I hit it. It started right on the intended line and then slowly began to turn to the left. I had hit it a little too hard, however, and the ball slid just by the cup on the high side, finishing a little over two feet past the hole.

Moonlight showed his first sign of disappointment all day. "Damn! That was a good roll, Charley. We deserved better."

After I tapped in for par, Moonlight replaced the flag, took my putter, and clapped me on the back. Under the circumstances, it was hard to feel much regret.

Chapter 24

THE 17TH TEE was a hike of over 50 yards back up the slope from the 16th green. The hole itself normally called for three shots, measuring 497 yards, and ran north and away from the ocean. It featured an ever-so-slight shift to the right about halfway to the green.

As Moonlight gave me the driver, he offered his appraisal of the way to play the hole. "The green here can be reached in two, so it's a good chance for a four. Ya' want to be down the right center with your drive. Ya' can afford to miss to the right, but if ya' go left, you're likely to catch the bunker over there an' be cut off from the green on your second shot."

As he talked, I looked down the fairway. Scattered cypress trees and brush lined both sides from the tee, but the fairway was generous. Since the hole ran downhill, I could tell that a good drive would place me within reach of the green in two.

Pointing out toward a tall cypress, Moonlight said, "Ya' see the tree? Take that line. It'll keep ya' on where ya' need to be."

I could see the tree moving ever so slightly in the ocean breeze. It was situated on a line that extended from the 17th tee down the right edge of the fairway on the hole. Moonlight had given me a good target.

The ball appeared to bounce high when it landed, and I could see the effects of the land sloping away from us as it ran much farther than expected. Moonlight was pleased. "That's just 'bout perfect."

It was now getting close to five o'clock, and the air was becoming cooler. Walking the course was keeping us warm, however, and the drop in temperature was not uncomfortable. If anything, it felt crisp and clean and refreshing. As we walked along, I couldn't imagine ever being uninspired by the setting. The whole scene brought to mind the tag line of an old beer commercial. I turned to Moonlight and said, "It doesn't get any better than this."

He either didn't recognize the line or didn't think it was funny. Instead, he pointed to the green and said, "A lot a' great things happened on this hole. For some reason, more matches seemed to be decided here than on any other hole."

From the look on his face, I knew I was going to hear about one of them. He didn't disappoint.

"I haven't told ya' that Jack Nicklaus played here, have I?" Without waiting for an answer, he said, "He had just won the Amateur for the second time. Must've been 'round '61...yeah, he'd just won at Pebble Beach, when he beat the tar out a' some poor fella in the final. Anyway, everyone heard these incredible stories 'bout him, an' Mr. Jones had him out here."

I certainly didn't want him to stop there. "So what happened?"

He pointed up the fairway again. "Mr. Jones brought Arnold

Palmer out here, too. They'd never played head-to-head, an' he wanted to see it. Ya' know, Mr. Nicklaus had already played in a couple of Masters'. That's when Mr. Jones supposedly said Mr. Nicklaus had a game with which he wasn't familiar. Anyway, I got Mr. Nicklaus's bag."

I marveled again at what extraordinary events the little man next to me had witnessed and experienced. "You carried for Nicklaus?"

He just nodded. "Yeah, an' let me tell you, he was somethin' else. Had a game like nobody I'd ever seen—just like that young man they call Tiger does now."

"So what happened here?"

He pointed to a spot about 50 yards ahead. "They were all even comin' to this hole. We had our drive out past Mr. Palmer by a good 30 yards—like we had all day. God, that man was long. Anyway, Mr. Palmer ain't exactly rollin' over for us, if ya' know what I mean. He smokes this 2-iron that runs forever—clear to the green. Finishes no more'n 20 feet away. Then he just looks over at us an' smiles. You know, kinda like, 'Take that, fat boy.' So Mr. Nicklaus asks me for his 4-iron. Hell, I'd given up tryin' to club him. He hits this high cut. I'd never seen anybody hit the ball so high. It just hung in the air, like it wasn't *ever* comin' down. Finally, it does—three feet from the hole."

Moonlight stopped to catch his breath. "Mr. Palmer misses, we make. We end up winnin' one-up."

Moonlight smiled at the memory. "An' ya' know what the best part was? Mr. Jones watched the whole thing. Had to use a golf cart, but he got to see it all. Never stopped grinnin' the whole time."

I could only imagine how that first match between the two must have jump-started one of the greatest rivalries in the history of sport. Palmer, the unquestioned king of the game, had been beaten by the pudgy amateur from Ohio for the first time. And yet as far as I knew, neither of them had ever publicly acknowledged the match or otherwise betrayed Jones's secret.

We were now close to my ball. It was sitting up nicely, and the view of the 17th green from where we were on the right side of the fairway was unobstructed.

As I stood there taking it in, Moonlight pulled up alongside me. "This won't play as long as it looks, 'cause the green's below us. Ya' might be able to get there with the 3-wood. Just land it down in front an' let it run on."

He pointed toward the left of the green. "Ya' see how the slope a' the land runs down to the left? Everythin' goes to the water, ya' know. So aim to the right."

I picked out a line about ten yards on the high side of the green. If the ball landed anywhere near where I hoped it would, it would bound down and to the left and should finish on or near the putting surface.

Some wag once said that a well-struck golf shot was the "second best feeling in the world." This one certainly felt good to me. I had read once that Ben Hogan had such a refined sense of feel that he would complain if he struck the ball "a groove high" in the clubface. My standards were never quite so exacting; I've always been satisfied if the shot didn't sting my hands.

At any rate, the ball flew straight toward the target area on the high side of the green. When it landed in front of the green, it bounced toward the left and started hunting the hole.

The 17th green didn't look very large from where we stood, more or less typical of the par-5 greens on the course. They were designed to receive a short third shot, at most a pitching wedge. The player who wanted to cheat par by reaching the green in two for an easy birdie had a very small target.

As I watched the ball scoot along the slope, I just hoped it would reach—and then stay on—the green. Anywhere on such a small green would leave me with an easy two-putt. But the ball headed directly for the hole, and I watched in amazement as it struck the flagstick and bounced away. When it stopped rolling, it appeared to be no more than eight to ten feet to the right of the hole.

From behind me I heard Moonlight. "Second time today we were robbed."

I was probably feeling a lot of different emotions at the moment, but cheated certainly wasn't among them.

As we began the long walk toward the green, I thought about how enjoyable it was to walk the course with a caddie. Golf is unique among games in that it can be equally pleasurable played alone, with friends, or even in the company of strangers. But playing the game with a caddie is a special pleasure.

I was no expert on caddies, but I could tell that Moonlight was a damned good one. He had obviously mastered the critical skills of his trade, from reading the line of a putt to figuring how the wind affected the shot to be played.

I figured he had probably saved me five or six strokes already in the round, and I saw no reason why he couldn't do the same for the best of players. I wondered whether he had ever worked on the tour.

He shook his head. "Nah. Except for the few really great ones, most a' the tourin' pros were a pain in the ass. When it came to caddies, all they knew was that we carried the bag."

When I laughed, he said, "Nah, lad, I'm serious. Most of 'em didn't know how to use a caddie. Why work for someone like that when ya' can carry Mr. Jones's bag? An' why go live out of a suitcase? I've seen enough a' the world, thank ya'."

It occurred to me that Moonlight's affection for this place and for Augusta National had as much to do with his need to belong and his sense of place as it did with his love of golf. Moonlight seemed to be the kind of person who put down roots. He took great delight in walking the same course day after day and discovering something new each time. For him, every game was different, and every day was an opportunity to discover something new. He didn't need a change of scenery to find fresh meaning in the game or the people who played it. It came down to this: the tour may have needed Moonlight, but he had never needed the tour.

As we reached the green, a large wave crashed in the cove at the nearby 11th hole, producing a fine mist into the air that refreshed us. The 17th hole terminated about midway between the 10th and 11th greens but was elevated slightly higher because it was back from the water's edge on a small bluff. Once again, I found it difficult not to be distracted by the majestic scenery.

Moonlight allowed me a minute or two to take it all in. He obviously wanted me to commit as much of the place to memory as I could. When I turned back to look at my eagle putt, he told me it was a ball out on the left.

In a perfect world, I would've made it to match Nicklaus's eagle so many years before. But I wasn't Nicklaus, and so I pulled the putt. I consoled myself, however, with a tap-in for birdie.

It was apparent that the 18th was a great finishing hole. It was a mere 354 yards, short for a two-shot hole, but its measured length was deceptive because the hole climbed uphill all the way to a green that sat just below the clubhouse. It featured a slight dogleg left that hugged the shoreline and kept the ocean in play along the length of the entire hole. I was a little sad that our round of golf in this paradise was coming to an end, but I made up my mind to enjoy every last second until it was over.

"Ya' need to favor the right side so ya' can take advantage a' the angle. The green'll look a whole lot better from over there." As Moonlight spoke, he pointed with my 3-wood down the line he wanted me to take. "That chimney on the right side a' the clubhouse is your target."

I saw the clubhouse above us on the slight rise above the beach. I hadn't noticed the chimney before, but I recalled the fireplace in the locker room just off to the side of the small bar.

As Moonlight handed me the club, he said, "Just try to hit the top a' that chimney."

I teed the ball on the left side and stood behind it so that I could pick out the line. This swing was much like the others on this remarkable day. The ball started down the line toward the chimney just as planned. Then a strange thing happened. As it lost power, the ball appeared to change direction. It made a sudden turn to the right, as if something above had caught the ball in midair and tossed it aside. I watched in disbelief as my tee shot disappeared into one of the trees that guarded the right side of the fairway.

I looked at Moonlight. "What do you make of that?"

He had his eyes trained on the spot where we had last seen my tee shot. "The wind can ricochet off the trees out here. It's one a' the things that makes this course so hard. It was bound to happen sooner or later."

He sheathed my 3-wood and began walking in earnest toward where he had last seen my ball. He was moving fast, and I had to hustle to keep up. For the first time, the diminutive Scotsman appeared uncertain about locating my ball.

As we rambled along, I also remembered that this was the only ball we had. The stroke-and-distance penalty for a lost ball wouldn't matter if we couldn't finish the round.

It struck me that perhaps there was a reason for the strange detour my ball had taken. Perhaps the spirit of Bragg's Point had asserted itself to warn us against finishing the round. Maybe we weren't supposed to break the spell or otherwise disturb the long state of repose that the place had enjoyed.

I didn't broach any of this with Moonlight, as he was bearing down on the point where he last saw the ball enter the trees. The last thing I wanted to do was distract him. I remembered how he got his nickname. This was going to test his reputation.

He dropped my bag in the fairway next to the tree that he had marked as closest to our most likely landing spot and began looking for the ball. Although he didn't invite my assistance, I started walking through the tall grass.

When he heard me rooting around, he never looked up as he warned me. "Be careful, now, lad. If ya' move your ball, ya' take a penalty stroke."

After a minute or so, I began to fear that the ball really was lost. Moonlight had been on the money all day long, but he appeared unsure of himself now.

I found myself retracing my steps to see if perhaps I had simply missed seeing the ball the first time I looked. Moonlight was some 30 yards away, expanding his search in a widening circle. I had my eyes fixed on the ground, but I could hear him off in the distance as he shuffled through the tall grass.

"Over here."

I looked up in the direction of an unfamiliar voice and saw only a ball sitting up in grass about 20 yards beyond the tree line. I knew the voice hadn't been Moonlight's. I looked all around but saw nothing more. Moonlight was still looking down. I called over to him excitedly. "There it is!"

He saw where I was pointing, and the look of relief on his face was evident. He literally ran over to grab my bag as I moved toward the ball. As we met, I grabbed his sleeve. "Did you hear that?"

"I heard ya', lad."

"No, not me. Did you hear the voice that told us where the ball was?"

He gave me a queer look. "What are ya' talkin' about?"

"A voice," I said, pointing to a spot behind the trees. "There. It said, 'Over here.' That's how I found the ball."

He shook his head. "Nah. I didn't hear nothin'."

For a second, I didn't believe him. "Are you sure?"

His face took on a grave expression. "I *told* ya' I didn't hear anythin'." The tone of his voice made it clear that he would entertain no further discussion of the subject. He then turned his attention to figuring our next play.

Finding the ball was a mixed blessing. We didn't appear to have a shot. The trees blocked our line of flight to the green.

Moonlight was apparently making an inventory of our options. I noticed that he was looking down the other side of the trees. He called to me, and I walked over to where he was standing. He pointed up the hill. "Can ya' hook the ball?"

"I believe so."

"Good. Ya' see the eighth tee over there in front a' the clubhouse?" Moonlight was pointing to the small mowed area that was no more than 30 yards from the front porch of the clubhouse.

"Yeah."

"Alright. Do ya' think ya' can start it there an' hook it 'round to the green?"

I looked at where he was pointing and then beneath the tree limbs to the 18th green. It looked to be about 50 yards apart.

"That'll take one helluva hook."

Moonlight nodded. "It's the best play, though. We can avoid the big bunker that crosses the front a' the green. Even if ya' don't make it, we've got a decent chance to get up an' down from those mounds on the right side a' the green."

The more I looked, the more I understood what he was saying.

"How did you ever figure that out?"

He laughed. "Bootsie had Mr. Snead play it that way once. He was playin' Mr. Demaret. They were two down but had presses on that were worth more'n they'd bet on the 18. Mr. Snead hooked it all the way 'round an' made birdie. He gave Bootsie half a' what he won."

Given Snead's reputation for parsimony, I knew that was extraordinarily generous.

Moonlight pulled out a club and offered it to me. "This oughta be perfect."

I saw that it was a 5-iron. As I held it, he offered, "It's okay to miss right. Stay away from the trees. Make sure ya' swing toward eight an' trust the closed face to bring it back."

Despite my best efforts, the ball still started left of my target, although not by much. Even as it started its curve to the left, I was fairly certain it would get past the trees without interference.

It did, and landed just below the top of the rise where the eighth tee was situated in front of the clubhouse. The overspin guaranteed that the ball would run pretty hot to the left. Since it landed about 30 yards right of the 18th green, I would need a lot of help to make the putting surface.

My now well-beaten ball was working hard to reach that destination, but I didn't know if it had enough energy to get there. As the ball neared the right side of the green, it became obvious that it was running out of steam. The mounds there killed the last of its roll.

Nonetheless, Moonlight appeared to be happy with the result. "We have a play from there, lad. It's a chance for four. That's all we could've hoped for." Gesturing at the trees as we walked along, he added, "The main thing is to get outta jail. We could've gotten hung up in there an' had real problems."

For the third time that day, something flashed in the corner of my eye. But once again, I reacted too slowly to see anything. I thought it was white in color, but couldn't tell anything more about it. I wasn't about to say anything to Moonlight. He already thought I was seeing and hearing things that weren't there.

When we reached my ball, I saw that it was sitting down in the grass. Not a bad lie, but certainly not a good one, either. It didn't make the next shot impossible, but it definitely raised its degree of difficulty.

The hole was located toward the front of the green, which was below us. The ball would run away from where we stood, making the shot even more difficult.

Moonlight didn't appear to be certain about what to do. He walked halfway to the hole, inspecting possible landing areas and apparently trying to picture how the ball would behave on the ground in each instance.

As he walked back to me, he said, "Ya' don't want to leave it short. You'll still have a downhill putt or, worse, a downhill chip if ya' leave it in the grass on these mounds. If ya' run past, you'll at least have it uphill back to the hole. Let's open that sand wedge an' try to drop it just on the other side a' the mounds."

The ball came off the club cleanly and landed just beyond the mounds. It bounced twice and then settled into a slow roll down the slope toward the hole.

I could tell the ball would miss the hole on the left. But the right-handed spin of the flop shot was pulling it back toward the hole, and my hopes rose as it drifted closer and closer.

In the end, it just didn't get close enough to catch the left edge of the cup, and the ball rolled on by the hole by several feet. It was farther from the hole than I wanted, but I reminded myself that I never expected to have *any* putt for par when we were back in the trees searching for my ball.

Moonlight pulled the flagstick from the hole and walked over behind my ball. He bent down, holding the flagstick across his knees, and surveyed the three feet or so remaining in my maiden voyage around the lost course he had brought me to just a day before.

"I say it's straight. A little uphill, too. Couldn't ask for a better putt to finish the round."

Glancing down the line to make sure I was square to the hole, I made my best shoulder stroke. The ball went straight in the center of the cup.

Chapter 25

MOONLIGHT REPLACED THE flagstick and handed me my ball. It had so many contusions that it looked like a driving range reject, but it was certainly precious to me. As he curled my fingers around it, he said, "I'd hang onto that if I were you. You'll wanna remember this day, lad."

I just stood there, not knowing what to say. Every golfer knows the intense pleasure that even the smallest triumph over the game's challenges can bring. You can imagine how I felt when that last putt settled into the bottom of the cup and my magical round was complete.

Just as quickly, though, I was distracted by nagging questions about this surreal experience. We were not alone. At least, I didn't think we were.

Moonlight seemed to think I was imagining things. But someone had obviously prepared the course for our arrival. Flagsticks had been placed on the greens. Tees and greens had been mowed. Beyond that, the place just didn't look like it had been abandoned for over 30 years. Was it magic? Was I seeing things out of the corner of my eye that weren't there? Was that really a voice I heard telling me where my ball was or just the wind whistling through the trees?

I knew enough about the power of suggestion to realize that I could have imagined things that weren't really there. Hell, anyone who's ever been scared of the dark knows that. The mind can make you hear and see things that disappear with the flick of a light switch.

But the condition of the course wasn't the product of my imagination. Contrary to what Moonlight may have believed, he wasn't the only person left who knew about this place. There had to be others.

Who were they? What was their interest? Was it the same as ours? There was so much more to be learned before the story of Bragg's Point could be told.

As we sat on the front porch of the clubhouse taking in a spectacular sunset, Moonlight was still thinking about my golf rather than the possibility of gremlins hiding nearby among the trees.

"Ya' know, Charley, Mr. Jones once shot a 66 at Sunningdale, in Berkshire, England, that was said to be the greatest round a' golf ever played."

I had never heard that. "Of all the great golf played by Jones, why that round?"

Moonlight wrinkled his nose. "Because just 'bout every shot was played as it should've been." He looked off in the distance. "That's really what ya' did today, lad. Ya' took what the course gave ya'. Ya' played away from trouble. An' ya' made the shots ya' needed to make."

Of course, I hadn't shot 66 as Jones had (in fact, I didn't even know my score at the time), but I understood what Moonlight meant. All day long, he had shown me how to play the angles and the terrain to my advantage, keeping the ball in the best position to complete each hole in the fewest number of strokes.

"Ya' see, lad, it's not 'bout how ya' swing, but where ya' put the ball. That's what made Mr. Jones so great. Ya' never heard anyone say that a particular course favored Mr. Jones or was well-suited for his game. He studied every course he played to figure out the best way to play each hole. Mr. Hogan was the same way."

Moonlight shifted as he pulled his left foot up on the steps. "Ya' see, golf's 'bout you an' the course. That's the game. It's a competition between the two of ya' an' nobody else. The great ones never forget that."

He then gestured toward the course below us, which looked golden as it lay in repose under the setting sun. "Ya' see how it's restin' now, Charley? It knows that we won this round. We outsmarted it—today, at least. But it's gatherin' its strength now, an' it's waitin' for ya' the next time."

Moonlight was still looking out over the layout that had tested us for the past several hours. "That's what Mr. Jones loved so much 'bout this place. It challenged him every time out. Play the ball left, it said. Then play the ball right, it said. Keep the ball on this side a' the hole, or keep the ball below the hole. Never the same test, either. It made ya' bring your whole game, or ya' left with your tail 'tween your legs."

As I looked out at the beast that now lay so tranquil before us, I found it difficult to believe that it had been shut off from the world for these many years.

"Moonlight, why didn't they keep the course open after Jones died?"

"A good question, lad. All I can tell ya' is that Mr. Roberts shut it down right after Mr. Jones's death."

That raised another question. "Well, it doesn't look abandoned to me. Someone has been taking care of this place."

Moonlight shook his head. "I'm tellin' ya', Charley, I'm the last one connected with the place from Mr. Jones's days."

"What about the players? Byron Nelson is still alive. So are a few of the others. Not many, but a few."

He shook his head. "But they don't know the whole story. An' they haven't been back. Do ya' think some a' them been mowin' the grass?"

"But suppose they've been paying to keep the place up? You know, it's not entirely out of the question. After all that Bobby Jones did for the game and for the pros who played it back then, it would be a fitting way to repay the debt."

I could tell Moonlight thought my theory was a bit far-fetched. "I don't think so, Charley. As far as they're concerned, this place has gone to seed. They probably think the government took it back. It's nothin' but a distant memory that they've kept secret out a' respect for Mr. Jones."

Anyone not familiar with the virtual obsession for secrecy that to this day attaches to the private affairs of Jones and Roberts and the club they founded at Augusta might find it difficult to believe that the existence of Bragg's Point could be so effectively concealed. But I knew otherwise.

Part of the unique culture of Augusta National is the primacy it has always placed on tight lips. More than anything else, insiders are judged by their ability to maintain confidences. Although its redactors are long gone, this code of silence remains every bit as strong today as it was in Cliff Roberts's time.

Such things tend to have their own inertia and are remarkably resistant to change. Thus, to a certain extent, trying to understand why anyone would maintain the secret of Bragg's Point for nearly 30 years after the reason for doing so had died was pointless. Like many cultural values, it really came down to a matter of faith.

For these reasons, the idea of a band of survivors maintaining the property as a monument to Jones seemed very plausible to me, despite Moonlight's pessimism.

Chapter 26

I FELT LIKE I could have sat on that porch forever, but the light of the gloaming was rapidly fading. Too, Moonlight was clearly tired, so we gathered our things and headed for the car.

To my surprise, the car was only a short distance from the clubhouse. I was almost certain that we had parked it more than a hundred yards away, closer to the entrance to the property, when we had first arrived. I had left the keys in the car, thinking no one else could have gotten through the maze it took to find the place, much less have breached the locked gate. If our gremlins were indeed lurking around somewhere, they would have had no reason to move our car except to remind us that we were not alone.

As Moonlight replaced my clubs in the trunk, I pointed toward our original parking place and asked him, "Wasn't the car over there when we left it?"

He just shrugged. "I dunno." After he closed the trunk, he said, "Why? Ya' think it moved?"

His tone was playfully sarcastic. All day long, Moonlight had put down my suspicions about others on the property. I was beginning to wonder whether he was hiding something from me or just thought I was paranoid. Before the night was over, I hoped to find out which was true.

The drive back to the hotel was quiet. I could tell that the day had taken its toll on my caddie. He leaned back against the headrest as soon as we cleared the security gate and was asleep before we reached the highway.

As I drove along in silence, I again replayed in my mind the wondrous round that we had just completed. As I did, I smugly congratulated myself on the numerous shots that I had successfully executed, but I knew full well that I couldn't have done it without the man who was now asleep in the car next to me.

Moonlight had kept me on my game. Like many amateurs, I tended to be a golfing chameleon, taking on new swing thoughts at the first hint of unreliability in my game. Perhaps it was the result of an overactive imagination or, worse yet, a lawyer's irresistible temptation to overcome difficulties by sheer willpower.

Whatever the reason, I was all too eager to abandon the only golf swing I really knew the moment the first shot came off poorly. Moonlight kept me trusting my swing by making me focus on tacking my way around the course rather than the mechanics of striking the ball.

He woke up just as I turned off the ignition in the parking lot of our hotel. He squinted his eyes a couple of times and shook his head. The nap must have refreshed him, because his only comment as we got out of the car was that he was hungry.

After we both showered, we headed out to a place we had passed on the highway going to and from the course. The sign advertised seafood and steaks, and the parking lot had been full. My father had always said that that was the surest sign of good food.

The place was called Fontana's. It was covered with gray clapboard that had not recently been painted. There was a crowd standing around just inside the door as we entered. The blonde girl who greeted us at the door told us there was a half hour wait for a table.

I asked Moonlight if he minded. He looked over my shoulder and pointed. "If that's a bar behind ya', no."

We walked over to the lounge just off the main dining room, which was also crowded. I found two unoccupied stools at the far end of the bar. Moonlight sat down heavily. I remembered how tired he had been earlier.

"You okay?"

"Yeah. Just the excitement a' the day, I guess. It's been a long time since I was here. Brought back a lotta memories. Good ones, too. At my age, they're the most precious things I got."

I wondered if he had family.

"Nah. I was married once. Didn't work out. Got a sister in Nashville. She's my closest kin. She lost her husband a few years back. I spend holidays with her, an' her kids an' grandchildren. Had a brother, but he passed away more'n 20 years ago."

He looked up at the expectant bartender. "Ya' got Rolling Rock?"

I started to order a martini, but this didn't look like the place for it, so I had a beer, too. As we each savored the cold brews placed in front of us, I looked into the mirror behind the bar and began to study Moonlight's wizened features.

While he was certainly not a wealthy man by any of the standards typically used to measure such things, Moonlight had seen and experienced the kind of golf that money can't buy. It amused me to think what the people milling around in the bar would say if they had any inkling about the people and events the little man sitting next to me knew firsthand. Moonlight had spent virtually his entire adult life either at Augusta National or at Bragg's Point. On a routine basis, he had witnessed greatness on the golf course that most of us only get to read about. He had actually known Bobby Jones, not to mention Ben Hogan, Byron Nelson, and Sam Snead.

As I drained the last of my beer, the fact that Moonlight had been a part of all that impressed me more than my improbable round. In fact, the reality of my golf still hadn't sunk in. It probably sounds stupid, but I just didn't believe it yet. It was as if someone else had made those birdies, not me. That kind of mastery of the game simply didn't fit with the lifelong picture I had of myself.

Moonlight must have been reading my mind. I felt him nudge my elbow. He slid the scorecard from the day over to me. "I thought ya' might want this."

I looked down at it. He had filled in my scores for each hole. The total was 73.

"Thirty-three on the back nine, Charley." He pointed to a spot on the bottom of the card. "Ya' gotta attest the score or it don't count."

I saw that Moonlight had signed the card as my marker. I reached over and grabbed a small pencil laying in the bartender's trough and signed my name.

"There," I said, "it's official."

He said something about drinking a toast to the events of the day, so we ordered another round. Moonlight appeared to be relaxing a bit, and I decided it was an opportune time to take advantage of his softened edges and ask some questions.

"Do you know who owns the property?"

"Nah. Like I tol' ya', Mr. Roberts put the place in a trust a' some kind. I don't know who's got it now."

I figured we could determine the ownership at the local courthouse. If the people in the local clerk's office were helpful, we would have an answer in a matter of minutes. I had learned how to run conveyance records while I was clerking at Butler & Yates, so I could use the vendor-vendee indices to trace the entire chain of title if need be. That would tell me who Roberts bought the property from as well as who had owned it since Jones and Roberts died.

Like a lot of older people, Moonlight felt free to say whatever was on his mind without introducing his subject matter. I wasn't surprised, then, when he abruptly changed the subject to share another anecdote with me.

"Remember I tol' ya' that Mr. Jones had the only cart allowed at the club?"

"You mean here at Bragg's Point?"

"Yeah. I didn't tell ya' the story a' how that came 'bout, though, did I?"

"No, you didn't."

"Well, that cart was given to Mr. Jones at Augusta National. It was specially built to make him as comfortable as possible. As he got sicker, he got weaker an' weaker. It wasn't just that he had trouble walkin'. He couldn't use his hands real well, either."

He paused to pull down more of his beer.

"One a' the companies that made golf carts put one together with special equipment for him to use. He really liked it. Mr. Roberts had it shipped out here so Mr. Jones could use it while he stayed here. Anyway, Mr. Jones invited the man who owned the company to come out to Augusta for a round a' golf. While he played, Mr. Jones rode along to watch. At some point, he asked Mr. Jones if the club would buy its next fleet a' carts from him. Mr. Jones said nothin', but when he got in that day he had Mr. Roberts ship the cart back from California an' return it to the man."

I felt like I had missed something. "Why?"

"It was like the man was puttin' strings on the gift. Mr. Jones didn't wanna feel obligated. He hated to give that cart back, but the man shouldn't have said anythin'."

It was an interesting glimpse of Jones's rigid Southern code of etiquette, and it also explained the unyielding attitude held at Augusta National about even the slightest breach of manners by anyone associated with the club. Gentlemen just don't do certain things. It's one thing to hope that someone will reciprocate a good deed; it's quite another to ask for it.

I didn't know if Moonlight was deliberately trying to sidetrack me, but I wanted to talk more about some of the strange goings-on I had seen during the day.

"Those flagsticks weren't there when we first went to the course yesterday, right?"

He nodded in agreement.

"But they were there when we arrived today. Do you still believe that they just appeared there by magic?"

He drained his second Rolling Rock, put it down on the bar, and leaned back. I could tell he was carefully choosing his words before he spoke.

"Charley, when ya' get to be my age, ya' don't feel the urge to have an explanation for everythin' that goes on in the world. An' ya' begin to allow for the unexplainable."

I shook my head. "Moonlight, those flags didn't just appear from nowhere."

"Lad, ya' just shot 73 on the best course you'll ever set foot on. What do ya' care how the flags got there?"

"Do you really think it's magic?"

"Ya' mean, do I think there's some kind a' ghost out there?" He laughed. "Nah. But I do believe there's somethin' 'bout the place that's magical. Ya' can decide what to make a' that, okay? Whoever—or whatever—put those flags out wanted us to play the course. So it ain't evil spirits, is the way I look at it."

I had to admit that whoever (or, as Moonlight put it, *whatever*) was out there was not unfriendly or hostile. They wanted us there and wanted us to play the golf course. It occurred to me that we might have some unexpected allies in our quest to give Bragg's Point its rightful place in golf history.

I felt a tap on my shoulder. It was the blonde girl telling us that our table was ready.

Chapter 27

GOLF IS A game that inspires blind devotion, the kind some-times lavished by foolish men and women on unfaithful and abusive lovers. How else can you explain the way golfers feel about a game that disappoints them—even spurns them—far more often than it returns their affections?

Moonlight obviously had fallen hard for the game early in his life. He had chosen to forsake any prospect of material wealth for the opportunity to be close enough to caress his great love on a daily basis. As the two of us followed the blonde girl to our table, I found it hard to fault him for doing so. Even as Moonlight approached his own sunset, he could look back at his life with contentment because he had spent it doing what he loved to do.

It made me think. Would I find that kind of satisfaction arguing with people for a living? Those who play golf police themselves, and the integrity of the game is important to all who play it. Lawyers, on the other hand, spend their lives policing one another. Given the nature of law, I found that sadly ironic. As we sat looking at our menus, I had the disquieting realization that the life of a caddy was far less corrupting than the life of a lawyer. It wasn't a happy thought for someone who had just finished three difficult years at a demanding (not to mention expensive) law school like Tulane.

I considered ever so briefly whether I wanted to follow Moonlight's career path and carry a golf bag for a living. After all, I was single and had no dependents. Unfortunately, there were student loans to be repaid, so I rejected the notion of leaving Butler & Yates, at least for the time being.

My reverie about my career plans was interrupted by the appearance of our waitress. "Hi," she said sweetly, "my name is Michelle, and I'm your server this evening. What can I get for you?"

Moonlight ordered a filet, which the menu indicated was a specialty of the house. It sounded so appetizing that I abandoned my thoughts of eating healthy and ordered the same thing. We also called for our third round of beer.

As Michelle walked away from the table, Moonlight watched her in an admiring way. "Ya' know, I'm 84 years old, an' I've never met a girl named Michelle who wasn't pretty."

I laughed in admiration of his spunk. Moonlight reminded me of the pictures I had often seen of old Scottish caddies, still carrying a bag every day well into advanced age. I didn't know if it was his heritage or the daily exercise (or both, perhaps), but Moonlight obviously still had a lot of life left in him.

It seemed to me that it was time to figure out where we were going from here, so I asked Moonlight what he had in mind.

"I want the world to know 'bout this place. Like I tol' ya'

from the beginnin', I want ya' to do for Bragg's Point what ya' did for Beau Stedman."

"Moonlight, we've got to have more if we want the USGA to do something with this story. It's too bad we don't have pictures from the old days. That would help us prove your story."

He smiled in a mischievous sort of way. "Ah, who said we don't have pictures—an' more, for that matter?"

I arched an eyebrow at my caddie friend. It wasn't the first time he had hinted at having additional evidence. "Have you been holding out on me?"

His smile grew. "Ya' may have wondered why I never let ya' in the house. I wasn't sure I could show ya' what I had just yet. I've got stuff, Charley, all kinds a' stuff, all over the house. Ya' want pictures? I've got pictures. An' that ain't all. I've got scorecards, flags, old clubs, bags, gin rummy scorepads, ya' name it. I ended up with everythin'."

I nearly choked on my beer. It had never occurred to me that Moonlight might be the curator of the Bragg's Point Golf Links collection. He was describing a trove of physical evidence that would corroborate all of his stories—and maybe persuade the USGA to share them with the golfing world.

"You know, Moonlight, one of the major golf magazines might pay you a lot of money for this story."

He immediately gave me a look of ill humor. "Are ya' forgettin' the deal we made? I tol' ya', we won't be makin' any money on this." He threw his napkin on the table in disgust.

I held up my hands. "Hold on, Moonlight. I'm not forgetting anything. And I'm certainly not questioning your integrity. I'll do it just the way you want. I guess the lawyer in me just wanted you to be aware of your options."

He gradually calmed down. I continued to talk to him in a soothing tone. "The first thing I think we have to do is document who owns this property. We need to trace the chain of title back to when the course was being played so we can prove that it was under Jones's control."

Our food arrived, which put an end to conversation for a while. About halfway through our steaks, Moonlight muttered something about "Augusta West."

"Augusta West?"

"Yeah, that's what some of 'em called the course out here. Mr. Demaret was the first. He'd tell Mr. Jones, 'When are ya' gonna have the tournament at the West course?'"

Moonlight's anecdote made me think of something. "You know, Demaret was the first player to win the Masters three times. They've got bridges named after Sarazen, Hogan, and Nelson, and they've got markers for Palmer and Nicklaus, but they don't have a thing for Demaret. Do you know why?"

He shrugged. "I can't give ya' a reason. Mr. Jones liked him, I know that. If he didn't, he wouldn't have invited him out here to play the course as often as he did." He finished chewing on another bite of steak. "Everyone liked Mr. Demaret. Hell, he was the only one I ever saw who could make Mr. Hogan laugh."

I commented that it was hard to imagine anyone making jokes around the man that the Scots called the "Wee Ice Mon." Moonlight quickly disagreed.

"I remember we came in late one afternoon after getting caught in the rain at the Point. We were all shiverin' from the cold. Mr. Hogan was mad that we had to quit, mainly 'cause Mr. Demaret was three up on him. Mr. Hogan said somethin' 'bout the cold keepin' him from makin' any putts. Mr. Demaret wasn't havin' any a' that. He looked Mr. Hogan dead in the eye an' said, 'Ben, ya' wouldn't have beaten me today if your putter had been blessed by the Pope.' Mr. Hogan just fumed at that. Mr. Demaret then winked at us an' said 'Watch me warm Ben up.'"

He took another bite of his steak before continuing. "Anyway, while Mr. Hogan was in the shower, Mr. Demaret found some liniment an' put it in Mr. Hogan's shorts. When Mr. Hogan pulled those shorts on after his shower, his face turned four shades a' red. That stuff must've burned like hell. Mr. Hogan whipped those boxers right off an' yelled for Mr. Demaret, but the man was already sittin' at the card table like nothin' had happened."

Moonlight laughed again as he recalled the scene.

"I'm surprised Hogan didn't choke him."

Moonlight shook his head. "Aw, he ended up laughin' 'bout it. To tell ya' the truth, I think Mr. Hogan knew it was Mr. Demaret's way a' bein' his friend. Ya' know, Mr. Hogan didn't allow himself a lotta friends. I don't think he trusted many people. But he trusted Mr. Demaret."

We meandered through the remainder of our meal exchanging thoughts about golf, life, and Bobby Jones. Back at the hotel, we agreed to find the local courthouse the next morning so that I could research the title to the course at Bragg's Point. After that, Moonlight wanted to take one last look at the golf course he so dearly loved before we caught an early flight the following day.

The combination of red meat and alcohol proved to be lethal. Both of us fell asleep as soon as our heads hit our pillows. I never heard Moonlight's freight-train snoring this time, and, when I awoke the next morning, I felt like I had slept for a week.

Moonlight, of course, was already up and gone on his morning walk. His note told me to meet him for breakfast. I showered, dressed, and went down to the coffee shop, where I found him in a corner booth covered with orange Naugahyde.

He handed me a menu. "I already ordered."

I could still feel the remnants of the huge steak I had eaten the night before and told the waitress just to bring me coffee, juice, and toast. Moonlight had apparently worked up an appetite; he was having eggs, bacon, hash browns, and biscuits.

I couldn't resist teasing him a little. "Where do you put all that food?"

"I dunno. Family trait, I guess."

We each retreated into our own thoughts for the rest of the meal. Once we were done, we got directions to the local courthouse from the cashier and headed out to the parking lot.

The Mendocino County courthouse was located in Willits, a small town that was only eight miles away. We found it easily, and I made a mental note to thank the cashier later for her directions.

The courthouse was an old building, and the conveyance records were kept in the basement. The clerk there was cooperative and helpful and showed us where everything was located. I found the volume for the 1930s and began looking under the letter "J" to see if we could find anything purchased or sold in the county by Robert Tyre Jones. Nothing.

The results were different, however, when I looked under "R" for Roberts. On October 12, 1935, the United States Government issued a patent conveying a 124-acre tract of land to Charles de Clifford Roberts, Jr., for $5,200. I quickly did the math in my head, and it came to less than $50 an acre.

That seemed like an absurdly low amount of money for such a splendid piece of land, but I reminded myself that this was still the Depression. Besides, this part of California must have seemed like the middle of nowhere back then. I just didn't have enough information to tell whether the price represented the fair market value of the property.

I then ran the records to see what happened to the property after Roberts acquired it. He didn't hold onto it for long; there was a deed dated less than a year later in which Roberts conveyed the property to something called the Bragg's Point Charitable Trust.

I found the trust instrument in the records. Neither Jones nor Roberts was the trustee; instead, someone named P. Harvie Moore was placed in charge. I assumed that, for tax reasons, Roberts didn't want to appear on both sides of the transaction. I also figured that Jones didn't want his name attached because it would only attract unwanted attention.

I had no idea who P. Harvie Moore was, but I suspected that he was a close friend and confidante of Roberts, possibly a member of the close circle of New Yorkers who had figured so prominently in the formation of Augusta National. On reading further, however, I saw that the trustee's address was listed in Atlanta. Moore was apparently an insider who came from the Jones side of the equation rather than from Roberts's connections.

Roberts had donated the property to the trust for use as a golf course. The donation stated that the property could not be transferred again for the maximum period allowed by California law and that, if it was ever sold, the proceeds were to be used to benefit golf.

I asked Moonlight if he knew anything about P. Harvie Moore.

"Yeah, I knew him. He was a member at the National. He was a few years younger than Mr. Jones, but they knew one another from East Lake. He was a doctor—surgeon a' some kind, as I recall. Pretty good player, too, for an amateur."

"Did he ever play the course out here?"

"Oh, yeah, lots a' times."

"Do you think he might still be around?"

Moonlight shook his head. "I dunno. He'd be 'round my age, an' there ain't that many of us left."

I knew the records might tell us the answer, so I went back to the indices to see if there were any further conveyances affecting the property. Remarkably, there was nothing until 1988, when Harvie Moore's son Stephen applied for and obtained judicial appointment as the successor trustee. His application stated that Harvie had died a few months before, giving rise to the need to name a new trustee.

The records showed no further transactions. Thus, for all we knew, the present trustee of the Bragg's Point Charitable Trust was Stephen R. Moore, whose address was given as 48 Peachtree Cove, Atlanta.

I paid for copies of the documents pertaining to the trust and to Stephen Moore's appointment, and we left. Moonlight wanted to see the course again, and for that matter so did I. So we headed toward Fort Bragg.

Unlike the day before, the gate was locked this time. When we reached the clearing, I noticed that the flagsticks had been removed. I looked over at Moonlight. "I guess they figured one round was enough for us." He just shrugged.

When Moonlight had insisted on returning to the course again, I thought he might have had a specific purpose in mind. Perhaps he wanted to show me something else about the place.

Instead, it appeared that he just wanted to breathe the air there one more time. He said little. We walked together down toward the water's edge. I began to relive the previous day's round, recalling shots played on the holes where we were walking. From the far-off look in his eyes, I could tell that Moonlight was recalling much more memorable events in the distant past.

I should have understood better then, as I do now, that the events and people of Bragg's Point were the defining moments of his life. Moonlight wasn't just a caddie here at this secluded golf retreat; he was treated as a friend and intimate of the greatest golfers who ever lived. These were people he sat in the clubhouse with, playing cards, sharing beers, and telling stories, joined together by the common bond of their love of a great game.

There were so few people admitted to Bragg's Point that it was pointless to draw class lines between them. Everyone who was admitted through the gate was on equal footing. Moonlight may have been a caddie at Augusta National, but he was a member at Bragg's Point. And it was his crowning achievement in life.

We must have wandered all over the property for the better part of two hours. This wasn't a place either one of us wanted to leave. Because I was less absorbed this day with the challenges of playing the game, I was able to appreciate better the marvelous design of the course. The way that the fairways traversed the slopes and ridges that graced the terrain seemed so natural and only served to enhance its features.

I thought again of Alister MacKenzie's design philosophy of "finding" the course in the land. Perry Maxwell had learned well during his apprenticeship. Every green seemed to be set in the only possible location it could have had, as if God Himself had done the routing of the course.

This was a place that inspired thoughts of the Almighty. It was a place not only of great beauty, but of great peace. No wonder it meant so much to Jones.

Unlike most world-class athletes, Jones did not thrive in the spotlight. Even while winning the four major championships of golf all in one year, he found performing for the public at the height of his powers to be so difficult that he vomited before virtually every championship round. Faced with the prospect of never again being able to enjoy a casual round away from public scrutiny—even at Augusta National—this hallowed retreat must have been the answer to his prayers.

And it must have become even more important when he learned, in 1948, that he had syringomyelia, a slowly debilitating disease of the spinal cord with no known cause or cure. Like most great champions, Jones had enormous pride. The thought of putting himself on display playing the game as he became more and more crippled no doubt was repugnant to him. Too, Cliff Roberts and the other members of Jones's small circle of confidantes almost certainly were just as pained at the thought of their wonderful friend being embarrassed to play the game of which he was once the indisputable master.

Without Bragg's Point, Jones would have had to give up the game years before the disease finally forced him to do so. Even after he put away his clubs for good, the seclusion of the place allowed him to drink in its beauty without onlookers and to be alone in his thoughts of a life well lived.

For the first time, it also occurred to me that, in bringing the story of Bragg's Point to the world, we were risking its destruction. I knew enough about the strong economic forces in this country to think, ever so briefly, that Bragg's Point might be reduced to some garish amusement park for golf if it fell into the wrong hands. I resolved that, no matter what, I wouldn't betray Moonlight and allow that to happen.

Chapter 28

WE COULD HAVE lingered there forever, but Moonlight and I eventually forced ourselves to withdraw from Jones's idyllic refuge. Moonlight seemed especially reluctant to leave.

"It took me so long to get back. I may never see this place ag'in."

I put my hand on his shoulder. "We'll get back here soon. You can count on that." When he smiled, I added, "I've got the feeling this is the first of many trips out here."

I had come to feel real affection for Moonlight. After what I had heard at Phil's Bottle Shop and being greeted by a shotgun at his door, my first inclination had been to dismiss him as an eccentric old coot. But, as I got to know him, particularly over the past few days, I could see that there was much about Moonlight to admire. He had a passion for life and a unwavering sense of values that directed that passion.

Moonlight also understood the game of golf better than anyone I had ever known. Not just how to play the game, but what it meant and why it was such a noble sport. He understood its integrity, and that was driving his attitude about how we should bring the story of Bragg's Point to life.

Some of that was rubbing off on me, too. For one thing, I felt the same sadness about leaving the place as he did. My promise to Moonlight about returning was selfishly made; I expected to be with him on the return trip.

As we returned to the hotel, we talked about a plan of action. We agreed that our next step was to find Stephen Moore. Moonlight then asked me how I thought Moore might react to our proposal for Bragg's Point.

"Hard to say. I would think he'd be pleased. It's certainly consistent with the intent of the trust. The property's not doing him any good just sitting there."

We both slept contentedly that night, and I looked forward to meeting Stephen Moore upon our return to Georgia.

The flight back was far less eventful than the trip coming out. Moonlight still needed the assistance of a stiff drink to prepare him for time in the air, but we passed through security this time without incident.

I had bought a golf magazine in the airport to read on the plane. After we were airborne, I showed Moonlight an article about Tiger Woods. I asked him if he'd ever seen anyone hit it consistently as far.

"Distance just don't impress me much anymore, Charley. Just 'bout anyone can buy distance these days. I'd like to have seen what Mr. Snead, Mr. Palmer, an' Mr. Nicklaus would've done in their primes with all that hot equipment. Mr. Jones, too—he was really long back when he played." He was quiet for a moment. "What *does* impress me 'bout young Woods is what I hear 'bout his short game. They say he knows how to make the ball behave 'round the greens. *That's* somethin' the great ones all had in common." He paused before adding, "'Course, it's a little early to put him in the same league as Mr. Jones an' the others. Plenty a' time for that." He then turned away from me and went to sleep for the remainder of the flight.

After arriving at Hartsfield in Atlanta, I promised Moonlight that I would try to locate Stephen Moore as soon as possible and arrange a meeting. I asked him if he wanted to be present, but he declined. Now that he was back in Georgia, Moonlight reassumed his old persona. We weren't at Bragg's Point anymore, and I suspect he had reservations about how a retired Augusta National caddie would be received by a prominent Atlantan.

After Moonlight headed off to Augusta in his ancient Ford Falcon, I got in my almost-as-ancient Chevy and drove home to my apartment. It was a Sunday afternoon, and traffic was light. Once home, I quickly unpacked. At the bottom of my suitcase was the scorecard with my 73. I set it against the mirror on my dresser so that it would serve as a daily reminder of our mission. In my mind, I ticked off a list of things to do once we had secured Stephen Moore's approval for our plan.

First, I needed to inventory Moonlight's memorabilia. By then, I knew that, contrary to his reputation at Phil's, my friend wasn't prone to exaggeration. Based upon his description of the contents of his house, I was pretty sure we would have more than enough artifacts to authenticate everything we had to say about Bragg's Point.

Next, I would call my old friend Brett Sullivan at the USGA. Brett was the curator of the USGA's museum and was responsible for its exhibits. He had worked with me to put together the successful exhibit for Beau Stedman the year before. Brett was creative and energetic. Once I told him what we had, he could direct our efforts.

I called Moonlight's home early that evening to make certain that he had arrived safely. When I told him what I intended to do, he said he had already started going through his things from the course. He again asked me to call him with a report as soon as I spoke with Stephen Moore.

After we hung up, I pulled out the telephone directory to see if there was a listing for Stephen Moore. There wasn't. When we first discovered his name in the 1988 record, I was afraid we might have trouble locating him after so many years, and this confirmed my fears. Still, there hadn't been anything in the courthouse records in Willits to indicate any change of address or designation of a new trustee, so I had been hopeful that Stephen Moore was still living in Atlanta.

If that wasn't the case, I didn't have the money to conduct a nationwide search. I could use the Internet, of course, and we might turn up something there. Otherwise, there was a distinct possibility that we might not be able to find Stephen Moore.

It then occurred to me that medicine was the kind of career that sometimes ran in families. P. Harvie Moore had been a physician. Maybe his son was, too. If so, that might have explained the absence of a residential phone listing. Most medical doctors didn't publish their home telephone numbers.

I turned to the yellow pages under "Physicians and Surgeons." I blanched at the number of names. It seemed that Atlanta had over a thousand entries. The directory broke medicine down into its specialties, but that obviously wasn't helpful. I didn't know whether Stephen Moore was a doctor, much less what specialty he practiced if he was.

I stayed in the front section, which listed all physicians. I got lucky; under the "M's" was a listing for a Stephen R. Moore, M.D. I copied the number and resolved to call him the next morning.

I got to work early the next day. For one thing, I was anxious to read whatever mail had accumulated while I was gone. But I was just as eager to make contact with Dr. Stephen Moore.

Even though I arrived at the office before eight o'clock, Gloria had beaten me there. She certainly lived up to her reputation; when I saw her, she was already at her desk, organizing the mail and preparing her boss for the events of the day long before he arrived, which was typically around eight-thirty or nine.

I couldn't resist kidding her. "Do you sleep here?"

She laughed. "Sometimes it feels like it." She reached for her coffee. "How was your trip?"

I must have looked surprised by the question. She smiled and added, "Mr. Guidry said you went to California."

I then remembered that I had gotten Emile Guidry's permission to take the time off. I hadn't gone into great detail about the reason for the trip—mainly because he hadn't asked. I certainly didn't want to get into it with Gloria, either.

"Oh, it was fine. You know, you've seen one wedding…"

She laughed. "Typical male reaction."

I retreated into my office. Although I wanted to called Dr. Moore right away, I figured his office wouldn't be open just yet, so I kept myself busy reading the mail.

I had only been out of the office a couple of days, but I was surprised at the amount of mail that had arrived in my absence. I shouldn't have been. When Emile Guidry first congratulated me on choosing litigation as my specialty, he warned me that it was a booming area of law.

"Times have changed, Charley. When I was just a little kid in the third grade in parochial school, we were playing baseball during recess one day when Bobby Tolbert, one of my classmates, was hurt. He had been playing catcher without a face mask, and he caught a foul tip right on the nose. Broke it in four places."

I winced.

"Anyway, the school should never have let us play without protective gear. So Bobby's father went out and bought the school a complete set of catcher's equipment—face mask, chest protector, shin guards, the whole works—and donated it to the nuns so no one would get hurt again. Nowadays, most fathers would just sue the good sisters instead. Makes money for lawyers, but I'm not sure I like what it says about people."

After dictating replies to those letters that required them and checking my calendar to make sure that any hearings for which we received notices were correctly entered, I saw that it was nearly ten o'clock. Time to call Dr. Moore. I pulled out the scrap of paper with the telephone number and dialed it.

A businesslike female voice answered crisply, "Cardiology Associates."

I asked for Dr. Moore. With most medical offices, speaking directly with a doctor on your first request is out of the question. Thus, I wasn't surprised when, without hesitation, the receptionist said, "I'll connect you with his nurse."

When the second female voice answered, I explained that I wasn't a patient and wanted to speak to Dr. Moore about a personal matter. However, the nurse was well trained at screening deceptive sales calls and asked, "Are you a friend of Dr. Moore?"

"No," I said, "but I have something important to discuss with him."

She was undeterred. "Dr. Moore is with patients at the moment. May I tell him what this is about so that he can call you back?"

I hadn't wanted to declare the nature of my business, but I saw no other choice. If I refused, she would probably assume I was a stockbroker making a cold call, and Dr. Moore would never get my message or be inclined to return my call if he did.

"Tell him it's about the Bragg's Point Charitable Trust."

"I'll tell him."

I said thank you, left my number, and hung up.

I didn't have to wait long. Within 30 minutes, our receptionist announced over my intercom that Dr. Stephen Moore was on the line.

"Hello?"

A rather unfriendly voice said curtly, "This is Dr. Moore returning your call."

I tried to explain in a warm and courteous fashion who I was and what my interest in Bragg's Point was.

Dr. Moore was unimpressed. "How is this any of your business?"

I should have prepared myself for the possibility that the trustee might not share our enthusiasm for our project, but I was taken aback by his bluntness.

"Well," I said, trying not to stammer or sound uncertain, "we think it's a wonderful part of golf history that should be made known to the world. Mr. Jones is long gone now, and there is no need to keep the place secret to protect him from curious onlookers."

I was going to say more, but the good doctor cut me off. "The property belongs to the trust. It is not a public corporation. You have no right to interfere."

"Dr. Moore, we certainly are not trying to interfere. What we are proposing is entirely in keeping with the purposes for which the trust was formed."

His tone indicated that he was losing what little patience he had for the conversation. "Look, by the end of the year, we'll be able to sell the property, and that's what we intend to do. It's much too valuable just to sit there. We've already got a buyer who is very interested, so I'm afraid there's not much I can do."

"But I thought the trust prohibited you from selling the property."

"I've got an opinion from a lawyer in California that says we can."

I knew from law school that restraints on alienation of property were disfavored under the law. Most courts refused to enforce them because they violated the public policy of keeping property in commerce. So what Dr. Moore said didn't surprise me.

I also knew that the trust provided that any proceeds from the sale of the property had to be devoted to promoting golf.

"What do you plan to do with the money you get from selling Bragg's Point?"

"Mr.…Hunter, I think your name is?…I don't see how that is any of your business. But if you must know, we will invest the proceeds to promote access to golf for the handicapped. The money will go to a nonprofit company that will design handicap-friendly courses and equipment. We believe that this more than satisfies the intent of the trust."

I had to admit, it was a laudable goal, certainly beyond criticism. Something told me to get more information. This might be my last opportunity to speak with Dr. Moore.

"That sounds like a very worthwhile donation. What is the name of the company?"

I had asked one question too many. "Now, Mr. Hunter, I've tried to be as accommodating as I could, but I really think that's way beyond any possible interest you should have in our affairs. Good day, sir."

With that, he hung up the phone before I could say anything further.

If Dr. Moore meant to discourage me, he really didn't know much about lawyers, particularly those who have chosen trial work as their specialty. Perhaps I was being overly suspicious, but I took his arrogance to be a sign he was hiding something—and as an invitation to do a little investigating.

Chapter 29

MOST LAW FIRMS have frequent need for background information on people, whether they are witnesses, prospective jurors, or adverse parties in litigation. Some use their own resources to search public (and sometimes private) records to obtain vital information about an individual's job, marital status, criminal record, property holdings, and virtually anything else they want to know. And that's just what's available at the courthouse.

In this day and age, there's not much in the way of human activity that doesn't get recorded somewhere. Churches record their members, as do professional organizations. The government keeps close track of its citizens, too, and its records are available under the Freedom of Information Act.

And that's not all. Private investigators are remarkably resourceful. Since most people are creatures of habit, a few days' worth of surveillance reveals a great deal about them.

Investigators are especially useful in collections work, which was a large part of my caseload. They can track a debtor's assets and tell you whether a case is worth pursuing. Once a judgment is obtained, they can help find property to seize in satisfaction of the judgment.

In the course of working my collection files, I had gotten to know Frankie Johnson, an investigator and jack-of-all-trades whom Emile Guidry had told me about. Frankie knew his way around Atlanta. Like most private investigators, Frankie was also something of a character. He was only a few years older than me but acted and talked like he was 20 years my senior. Frankie had, as he liked to say, been around.

He was also the kind of guy who lived hand-to-mouth. He was always hungry because money burned a hole in his pocket. Frankie wasn't 30 years old, but was paying alimony to two exes and child support for a three-year-old daughter he adored.

Because of these financial pressures, Frankie was deeply grateful whenever I called him to do an assets check on a debtor. He needed all the work he could get and would often call me just to see if I "had anything working." Invariably, he would tell me he "owed" me "big-time" and that I should let him know if I ever needed a favor.

It struck me that Frankie might be able to help me learn more about Dr. Stephen R. Moore, so I called him. I told Frankie that I needed to know everything he could find about Dr. Moore's background and, in particular, about this new company for handicapped golf that he had referred to when we talked.

"You got it, babe," he said in the New Orleans accent he had never shaken despite having moved from the Ninth Ward to

Atlanta when he was in high school. Frankie acted as if my request was easily fulfilled and promised to get back to me within a week.

I dutifully reported both my tense conversation with Dr. Moore and my retention of Frankie Johnson to Moonlight. He seemed a little agitated that someone would stand in the way of his grand plan, but I assured him that I was doing all I could and that Frankie would have a lot to tell us soon.

I had to admit that I was as anxious as Moonlight to find out about Dr. Moore, but I forced myself to be patient. As I had told Moonlight, no amount of hand-wringing would make things go faster.

It must have been a slow week for Frankie, because he called me back that Friday, two days ahead of schedule.

"Boy, have I got some news for you. I ain't done, but I've learned some things already that I thought you should know."

"I can hardly wait to hear. Tell me what you have."

He laughed. "I got some stuff to show you. Can you see me today?"

"Sure," I told him. "Come in at two o' clock."

"You got it," he said, and hung up.

I was distracted for most of the day until Frankie arrived promptly at two o'clock for our appointment. He was grinning from ear to ear when he walked into my office. In typical fashion, he was wearing an old blue blazer that looked like something from Goodwill and a garish purple-and-orange tie twisted in a knot that even a sailor couldn't untangle.

As he sat down, he boasted, "Nobody delivers like Frankie

delivers. I done you some good, Charley. You knew I'd come through for you, didn't you?"

I ignored his rhetorical question. "Tell me what you got."

He pulled a small notepad from the inside pocket of his blazer. "For starters, your man went to Emory for medical school and then back to my neck of the woods for his residency in heart medicine at Tulane. He used to practice downtown with a large group but went with a new hospital over in Alpharetta about five years ago. He's added two doctors to his own group, and they're makin' big bucks."

"Where does he live?"

"He's still at the address you gave me on Peachtree Cove."

"Doesn't that give him a bit of a commute?"

Frankie nodded. "Yeah, but think about it. He's goin' against the flow both ways. He leaves downtown for the 'burbs in the morning and heads back into Atlanta in the afternoon. No real traffic to speak of; it's all headed in the opposite direction each way." He paused a second, then winked. "Believe me, Cap, he ain't gonna give up that Peachtree address."

I scratched my chin. "What else do you have?"

"He's a member at Peachtree Golf Club, you know, the one that your guy Jones founded."

I knew all about Peachtree. A couple of the lawyers in my firm belonged to it. It had a terrific course that had been designed mostly by Jones himself when he put the club together in 1948.

Frankie wasn't through. "He's there almost every day. Stops by after work. Sometimes goes there for lunch. The guy must really like the place—or he likes rubbin' elbows with people who've got more money than sense." He immediately looked a little sheepish. "No offense. You probably go there, too."

I laughed. "None taken. I'm not in that league just yet."

Frankie looked at his notes. "He's got a wife and two kids. Just your perfect little family. They go to some private school, I got the name here somewhere if you need it."

I waved my hand. "No, that's okay." I leaned forward in my chair. "Have you found out anything about that company I told you about—you know, the one he's gonna give a bunch of money to? It's supposed to do things for handicapped access to golf."

He shook his head. "Not yet. But don't worry, Cap, I'll get there." He threw some photographs on my desk. "There's some pictures of his house, his office, his Jag convertible, and some other good stuff." Pointing to one in particular, he added proudly, "There he is goin' into the club yesterday after work."

Frankie then pulled some documents from his briefcase. "I've got copies of a couple of malpractice suits filed against him, too. Apparently, your boy messed up a couple of times doing—what do you call them things?—oh, yeah, angiograms. My sources tell me he doesn't do any surgery anymore; the insurance got too expensive."

I was impressed and said so. That pleased Frankie.

"I told you, Cap, I'll take good care of you. I like the kind of work you have me do. Beats the hell outta that divorce stuff. I don't like hidin' in the bushes tryin' the catch people in the act. Makes me feel kinda dirty, you know what I mean? I don't mind looking up records on deadbeats." He sniffed. "It's a little more dignified."

He paused for a moment and winked at me. "'Course, I looked in the criminal records just in case your doctor friend had had a little problem, like a DWI or somethin', but there wasn't anything."

"You're always very thorough, Frankie."

He stood up to leave. "Yeah, well, I'm gonna get the lowdown on that handicapped golf company. If it's anywhere in the state of Georgia, I'm gonna find it."

I shook his hand. "Frankie, thanks a bunch. This is real helpful. I won't forget it."

Frankie clapped me on the shoulder. "I'll be back with the other stuff in a couple of days." As he headed out the door, he called out, "Have a great weekend."

After Frankie left, I sat down and looked over the pictures and papers he had left with me. While they were interesting, they really didn't tell me anything extraordinary. Of course, I couldn't tell Frankie that I was disappointed in any way. After all, he was doing me a favor, and besides, it wasn't his fault that he didn't find something juicy we could use.

The one thing I was really interested in was the details about this company that would supposedly get the proceeds from the sale of the property. It was probably a legitimate deal all the way, but I needed to be sure. I figured I had to find some way to derail any sale of Bragg's Point, or the course and all its stories might have been lost again.

At that point, I couldn't think about it anymore. I had an

important deposition in a product liability case coming up on Monday, and I needed to get ready.

I didn't hear from Frankie again until the following Thursday. He was almost breathless on the phone.

"You got a minute or two to see me this morning?"

I looked at my calendar. "Sure. I can visit with you right now, if you want."

"I'll be there in ten minutes."

As I hung up the phone, my mind raced with possibilities. Frankie sounded like he had found something interesting. But, I reminded myself, he had sounded pretty much the same way the last time. Frankie had a way of making whatever he was doing sound important.

He didn't disappoint me this time.

After sitting down heavily in the chair across from me, Frankie said, "Well, I got good news, and I got bad news. Which do you want first?"

I didn't want to play games. "Give it to me in any order you want."

He shrugged. "Okay. The bad news is that your buddy's sellin' that property in California to a bunch of Japanese investors. I think it's some of the same ones who bought Pebble Beach a few years back. You know, they were a shady group."

I recalled something controversial about how the Japanese investors who bought Pebble Beach obtained their financing and that they had problems back in Japan, but I couldn't recall any details.

Frankie took a deep breath. "Anyway, this is apparently part of the same group. They want to sell a bunch of memberships back in Japan and turn it into an exotic country club of some kind." He laughed. "Maybe they'll have those geisha girls or somethin'."

I let him know that I didn't think that was funny.

"How'd you find that out?"

"I can't tell you that just yet. I've gotta protect my sources. Let's just say that not everybody likes Dr. Moore."

It was an intriguing comment.

Frankie looked at me with a sarcastic smile. "But that's not the stinky part. The company that's gettin' the money—this so-called golf company that will promote access for handicapped golfers—your friendly heart doctor owns it. Turns out he incorporated the business himself just a couple of months ago."

He pushed some papers across my desk. "That's a copy of the articles of incorporation and the certificate from the state capitol showing the date it was formed. You see who's listed as the incorporator? Stephen R. Moore, M.D."

Frankie had hit the jackpot. Dr. Moore was going to sell Bragg's Point and pocket the money in violation of the trust.

"Besides the money, do you have any idea why he would do this?"

"Did you say *besides* the money?" Frankie raised his eyebrows and shook his head. "You said that property was over a hundred acres on the Pacific Ocean. You got any idea of what that's worth today? If the Tokyo crowd pays him a hundred million bucks, they'll make it back through memberships alone. I don't care how much money these heart doctors make, it's small potatoes compared to that."

After Frankie left, I called Moonlight. Given his attitude about the Japanese, I anticipated his reaction when I told him what Dr. Moore was planning to do.

"Sonuvabitch," he kept saying, over and over. Then he muttered something about Truman stopping too soon before asking me whether there was anything we could do.

"Honestly, Moonlight, I don't know. I'll have to check around here with some of our trusts and estates lawyers to see if we have standing to challenge this."

"What's that mean?"

I realized that I had lapsed into legal jargon. "I'm sorry, Moonlight. It just means I need to check and see if we have the legal right to stop it. We're not a party to the trust in any way, so the law may say that it's none of our business."

I had an idea.

"But there's more than one way to skin a cat, as the old saying goes. This amounts to fraud. Maybe the authorities can bring some heat on Dr. Moore. Plus, there may be restrictions against the sale of this kind of property to foreign citizens, I don't know. The federal government may be interested in this, too. And we may get some help from the USGA. Maybe they can get the word out about the course. The media attention will turn a spotlight on Dr. Moore. He might not like that."

Moonlight seemed relieved. "Sounds great, lad. But who can ya' call?"

"I have a friend who might be able to help. Let me make a couple of phone calls, and I'll get back with you."

I hung up and put in a call to Brett Sullivan.

Chapter 30

THE VOICE ON the other end of the line had a familiar friendly tone. "This is Brett Sullivan. May I help you?"

"Brett, it's Charley Hunter."

"Charley! The man responsible for discovering Beau Stedman. How are you, buddy?"

Good old Brett. Always upbeat, I thought. It was a trait I admired. After we exchanged pleasantries about the state of each other's health and golf games, I told the USGA's curator the story of Bragg's Point. I must have talked for nearly ten minutes nonstop. Brett never interrupted me.

When he finally spoke, he was clearly fighting incredulity. In slow and measured words, he said, "You know, Charley, if anyone but you told me that story…"

"Hey, I know, Brett," I said quickly, "but, if you think about it, it's no stranger than the story of Beau Stedman."

He laughed. "Well, anyone who says lightning doesn't strike twice never met you. Who'd have thought you'd be part of another story like this?"

I explained the connection between Stedman and Moonlight.

Sullivan admitted that it made sense, and he began to warm to the idea of bringing out the story through the USGA.

"You ought to know from last time, this is the kind of stuff that we devote ourselves to, preserving golf history. It's always been part of our mission statement."

Sullivan agreed with me that the site should be kept intact. "If it's sold, God only knows what'll be done with it."

We talked awhile about how best to stop the anticipated sale. Brett was wary of getting any kind of exhibit together on such short notice, but he thought we might be able to publish something in the USGA's *Golf Journal* and draw the public's attention to the situation that way.

I told him I was also investigating the possibility of legal action. He said that might not be necessary. As he put it, "Never underestimate the power of public opinion. Anyone who's about to put a hundred million into a piece of property will think twice if the public's up in arms about it. Besides, California's got the most stringent permitting requirements for land use in the country. If we get the folks over there fired up about this, they could delay the whole thing for years and make the developers give up altogether. It's happened before."

I was encouraged by everything my friend at Golf House was saying. Before we hung up, however, he warned me. "This is all subject to the approval of our Executive Director. And he'll probably take it to the Executive Committee. I don't have the authority to move on something like this on my own."

I was worried about any and all delays. "How long will that take?"

"Well, as luck would have it, they're meeting this weekend at the Senior Amateur in Portland. I don't believe David is scheduled to leave until day after tomorrow. Let me see if I can brief him on this. If I need more information, I'll call you. I think I have enough, though, to get the Executive Committee to authorize us to proceed if we're satisfied with the evidence you've got. I've got to convince David first, though."

I thanked him profusely.

He laughed again. "Don't thank me. If it were anyone but Charley Hunter behind this story, I'd need a lot more before I sent this up the line. But your name carries a lot of weight after the Stedman thing. They know you're not some crackpot."

After he hung up, I called Moonlight and gave him a report of our conversation. He was excited, but he didn't like the idea of waiting the better part of a week before doing something.

"Ain't there somethin' we can do *now*?"

I tried to placate him by promising to spend some time in the law library to see what legal recourse we might have. I warned him, though, that I was skeptical that a stranger to a trust could assert a breach of trust claim. Still, he liked the idea that we were at least weighing our options.

I stole odd moments here and there over the next few days to research every conceivable law that might help us. While I was pretty comfortable looking through federal laws, I didn't feel very confident trying to understand California property and trust law, even though I could do research in the Stanford Law Library through the Internet.

I visited with Paul Watkins, one of the rising stars in the

firm's trusts and estates section, to see if he had any books that might help me understand the issues. He was naturally curious about why I was working in his area.

I told him it was a family problem that my father had asked me to look into for an uncle out in California and that all I was trying to do was get some general background information. Watkins was one of the really nice guys in the firm and offered to help with my project. I begged off by promising to come back to him if I got confused.

What I learned was not encouraging. One of the leading reference books on trust law, *Bogart on Trusts*, confirmed my worst fears: without a personal stake in the trust, we weren't entitled to bring a court action to challenge the trustee's actions. While the treatise didn't make specific reference to California, that seemed to be the general rule, and I had no reason to believe California was any different.

That left me to consider our alternatives.

Unfortunately, I didn't like what I kept coming up with. For one thing, we had no proof that Dr. Moore did *not* actually intend to devote the new company to improving golf course access for disabled golfers. We had our suspicions that that was the case, but suspicions without proof don't carry much weight in a court of law.

In simple terms, no wrong had been committed—at least, not yet. For that reason, no criminal prosecutor was going to get excited about pursuing anything against a prominent cardiologist like Dr. Moore.

According to the law, the only remedy for Dr. Moore's anticipated diversion of trust assets was to sue him *after* he did it. Even then, there was the question of *who* was entitled to sue. I knew we couldn't, because we weren't beneficiaries under the trust.

That's when it hit me. The immediate beneficiary of the trust was the game of golf. But in legal terms, someone (i.e., an actual person) had to be the eventual—or what the law called residual—beneficiary.

I didn't recall reading anything about a residual beneficiary in the trust when I first saw it, but I wasn't reading for that. So I went and pulled my copy. There, in the next to last paragraph, the trust stated in clear and unequivocal terms: "At the cessation of this trust, its corpus shall be distributed to P. Harvie Moore for his eventual disposition in accordance with the purposes expressed herein."

It was another dead end. Under the law, P. Harvie Moore's heirs would be substituted for him upon his death. We were back to Dr. Stephen R. Moore. So the only interested person who could sue to prevent Dr. Moore from dissipating the trust's assets was—drum roll, please—Dr. Moore.

It then occurred to me that P. Harvie Moore might have had other children. Of course, it was highly doubtful that any of them would stand in their brother's way, particularly if he offered to share some of the wealth with them. Still, it was something I needed to investigate, no matter how pointless it may have seemed. I hadn't asked Frankie Johnson to check out Dr. Moore's extended family. I knew that Harvie Moore's heirs would all be listed in the probate of his estate, which presumably was filed in Atlanta.

I had learned that one of the privileges of being a member of the local practicing bar was that I was allowed to check out courthouse records. I sent one of our runners for the probate record pertaining to P. Harvie Moore at the county courthouse.

Upon reviewing the judgment from the elder Dr. Moore's succession, I discovered that Dr. Stephen R. Moore had only one sibling, a brother named Francis X. Moore. None of the pleadings gave an address, however.

I could only hope that Francis Moore lived in Atlanta. Pulling out my desk copy of the telephone directory, I kept my fingers crossed while digging through the alphabetical entries under the family name of Moore. There was nothing for Francis.

There was a listing, however, for an "F. Moore." I called that number, but the woman who answered was named Frieda and didn't know anything about a man named Francis Moore.

By now, it was close to quitting time. I decided to wait and call Frankie Johnson the next day to see if he had any ideas about how to locate Francis Moore. Dr. Stephen Moore's brother might be our only hope.

When I called Frankie the next morning, he was his typically confident self. "Charley, I'll find him if he moved to Mars."

When I pressed for details, he became evasive. "Hey, I don't ask you about *your* trade secrets now, do I?"

I let it go at that. "Just get me his address or something I can use to contact him, okay?"

Late that afternoon, he called back.

"I found your boy, but I don't want to say nothin' on the phone. You free?"

I had a mountain of paperwork on my desk, but none of it held the urgency of Bragg's Point. The paperwork could wait. "Sure," I said. "How soon can you get here?"

I pretended to work while waiting for Frankie, but my mind was completely preoccupied. Where had Frankie found Francis X. Moore? What kind of man was he? Was he as surly as his brother? Would he even care about Bragg's Point?

Frankie walked into my office less than 20 minutes later, wearing the same rumpled blazer and ugly tie. Forgoing the usual pleasantries, he said simply, "He's in Mobile."

I was impressed and said so. "How'd you find him so quick?"

Frankie was proud of his work. "Okay, I'll tell you how I did it, but just this once." He paused, as if for dramatic effect, and then giggled a manly giggle. "I played a hunch. I figured he grew up here, so I checked the suit records in the courthouse downtown to see if his name turned up anywhere. Turns out he went through a divorce about 15 years ago while he was still living here. Those things can drag on forever, you know? Once the court here gets it, it don't matter where you go."

I knew that the court granting the divorce usually had continuing jurisdiction to hear all incidental matters, like alimony, child custody, and child support. Once you were pulled into divorce court, you were usually stuck there until your children registered to vote.

Frankie went on. "About five years later, his former wife filed a motion to change child support, and he countered by asking for custody of the kids. Only this time, his address was listed in Mobile. I then went to Mobile directories and, even though his address had changed again a couple of years ago, he was still in the area."

He handed me a sheet of paper. "Here's his current address and phone number."

I took the paper eagerly. "Thanks, Frankie. As usual, you came through."

Frankie's chest puffed out. "There's more. Your man is a big-time businessman. Owns three beer distributors. We're talking some big bucks."

"How'd you find that out?"

He smiled. "I got a buddy in Mobile."

"You seem to have a buddy everywhere."

"Yeah, well, I'm a popular guy."

Frankie was always good for a laugh.

He headed for the door, then stopped. "Oh, yeah. There's one more thing. Your man in Mobile must have pretty good connections."

"What do you mean?"

Frankie smiled. "He's a member at Augusta National."

Before I could react, he was out the door and gone.

Chapter 31

BEFORE I CALLED Francis Moore, I sat down and scripted the conversation. I had learned that from Emile Guidry. He preached effective communication as the key to successful lawyering. As he put it, "You can do so much more for your clients by avoiding fights instead of picking them."

So I made notes in a rough outline form of what I wanted to say to Mr. Moore. I ran through them a couple of times to make sure I had the right phrases and tone for what I wanted to say, and then dialed the number on the paper that Frankie had given me.

Of course, Moore wasn't in. His secretary informed me that he was out of town and wouldn't be back for a couple of days. I left my name and number, thanked her, and hung up.

I was disappointed, but not nearly as much as Moonlight. He acted like a kid waiting for Christmas. "More delay," he grumbled when I told him. "That's what I get for dealin' with lawyers."

I probably should have been offended, but his tone was more frustrated than malicious. I tried to remind him of how lucky we were to have located the man.

"Yeah, that's true," he conceded. "But we gotta wait two days to see if he'll even consider helpin' us."

"Maybe so, Moonlight, but it's progress. You have to be patient."

I don't think he was fully satisfied by what I said, but I promised I would continue with my research in the library while we waited, just in case legal action became our last chance to save Bragg's Point.

I was able to occupy myself with a couple of depositions and a brief over the next couple of days, so the time passed quickly. I was midway through the morning mail on the third day when our receptionist told me that a "Mr. Moore" was on the line returning my call.

I grabbed my notes and picked up the phone.

Francis Moore had a very pleasant voice that was quite different from his brother's haughty tone. I thanked him immediately for returning my call so promptly.

He laughed. "Well, it's very interesting that you called while I was in Portland. At the same time you were on the phone with my office, I was listening to a presentation by David Fay about a project of yours that hits very close to home with me."

I dropped my prepared text. "You were at the USGA Executive Committee meeting?"

The combination of awe and surprise in my voice made him laugh. "Yeah, I've been a part of that group for about three years now."

The news that Francis Moore was a member of the USGA's Executive Committee was quite a surprise, and a welcome one at that, to say the least. I became more optimistic than ever that Francis Moore might have a very different take on this than his brother.

"Then you know all about what I was going to tell you."

His tone remained gracious and warm. "Yes, I do. It's something that was very dear to my Dad, and so it's very dear to me." He paused, and when he spoke again I heard the first trace of emotion from him. "I regret that my brother doesn't see things the same way."

Although the conversation was headed in the direction I had hoped for, it was moving much faster than I anticipated. The radical departure from my prepared script left me with nothing to say about the intimate family differences that apparently separated Francis Moore and his evil twin. As a result, his remark was followed by an awkward silence.

Without changing his pleasant tone or otherwise showing any sign of embarrassment, Francis Moore calmly explained his dysfunctional relationship with his brother. "No one likes to wash dirty linen in public, but I'm afraid there's no alternative now. You see, my brother always seemed to feel the need to compete with me for my father's affection, as if it were a zero sum game. I don't know why; maybe it's just the way he's built."

In my one conversation with Dr. Stephen Moore, I could well imagine the man he was describing.

"As you probably know by now, my father was one of the early members at Augusta. You see, our family also had a membership at East Lake and knew the Jones family well. So it wasn't that big a surprise when Bob Jones asked my Dad to join the club after he had returned to Atlanta to practice. Dad eventually joined Peachtree, too, when it got started."

There was another pause as Francis Moore considered what to say next. "Stephen and I went to Augusta with Dad on many occasions. As we got older, Stephen made it clear that he wanted to join the club, too. If anything, he made it too clear, if you know what I mean. Campaigning for something like that is considered to be poor form at Augusta, and it hardly ever works. Dad tried to get him to cool it, but Stephen is…well, Stephen is who he is."

I felt the need to ease things by finishing the story for him. "But you are a member at Augusta. So you got invited instead of Stephen?"

He sounded relieved that I appeared to understand. "Yes. Apparently there was only room for one of us, and I got the call." He gave out a short and awkward laugh, more to ease the tension than anything else. "I enjoy it, but it wasn't something I had given a lot of thought to. It would have meant so much more to Stephen, and I've often wondered whether I should have turned it down because of him. If I had known then what it would do to him, I might have."

"Stephen's a member at Peachtree," I interjected. "Was that his consolation prize?"

He sniffed. "I'm not sure I would call a club as good as Peachtree a consolation prize. It's a wonderful place. Quite a golf course, you know."

I felt embarrassed by his graciousness. "I didn't mean to slight Peachtree, but I take it that your brother might have felt it was a step down."

"He apparently did…or I guess I should say still does."

I wondered how long he had known about Bragg's Point.

"Oh, I've known about the place for a number of years. Dad told us both after swearing us to secrecy. He wanted us to know about the trust in case something happened to him. He always said it was the most special place on earth."

That brought me to an obvious question. "Why did he make Stephen the trustee instead of you?"

I heard him sigh over the telephone. "Dad always felt guilty about me getting into Augusta and how it disappointed Stephen so much. He was afraid that Stephen may have gone into medicine just to please him, so he felt obligated toward him. When he told me he wanted to appoint Stephen to replace him as trustee for Bragg's Point, I told him it was okay with me. I hated to see him tormented by something like that."

"Were you aware of your brother's plans to sell the property?"

"I suspected something was up, but I didn't know what it was. The last time I saw Stephen, he said something about finally hitting a home run." Another pause. "You see, Stephen has never been satisfied. He makes a fabulous income as a cardiologist, but even that kind of money's not enough when it's the only way you measure your self-esteem."

I could tell that Francis Moore had long ago resigned himself to the flaws in his brother's character. "So you figure selling the property was his chance to join the heavy hitters' league and be somebody?"

He sounded a little put off. "Well, that's kind of blunt, but, yeah, I'd say that's right."

I had now come to the crucial questions.

"How do you think your father would feel about selling the property?"

He responded quickly and without hesitation. "He wouldn't like it."

"What do you make of your brother's new company?"

His voice immediately sounded sad. "I hate to say it, but I don't think he's going to do much with it. He may have convinced himself he will, but I'm afraid it's just a convenient place to park the money."

"You may be the only person who can stop him," I said evenly.

"I already thought of that."

I was wondering just how much he had, in fact, thought about it. "If necessary, could you bring yourself to sue your brother?"

There was a long pause. "It would destroy what little semblance of family affection still exists between us, but I really think that's what Dad would want me to do."

To reassure him, I said quickly, "We're hoping it won't come to that, but it may be our last resort."

He apparently didn't want to leave any doubt about his commitment to honor his father's wishes. "I'm not looking for a fight, but I'll do whatever I have to do."

This was a perfect example of how the very thing that makes clubs like Augusta so attractive to many folks—their exclusivity—is also their curse. Admitting a select few necessarily means rejecting an unselected many. Stephen Moore was obviously embittered by his exclusion from Augusta, particularly in light of his brother's admission into its inner circle.

The irony, of course, was that the brother who was deemed not good enough for a coveted membership at Augusta now held the fate of its second course in his hands.

We talked for another ten minutes or so. Francis Moore agreed to arrange a meeting with his brother and try to dissuade him from selling the property. If his brother was unwilling to back off, Francis would threaten legal action. In Georgia, anyone on the opposite side of Bobby Jones in a lawsuit —even though Jones had been dead for 30 years or so—faced a rather steep hill to climb. We were hoping that Dr. Moore would feel the same way and relent without a court fight.

"If your brother backs off, what do you think should be done with the property?"

His answer surprised me. "I think it should be donated to the USGA. Don't you think it would make a great permanent site for the U.S. Open?"

That wasn't something I had ever considered, not even in my wildest dreams. The U.S. Open had always been rotated around the country's grandest and most historic venues, such as Winged Foot, Baltusrol, Oakmont, Oakland Hills, Pebble Beach, and Olympic.

But the idea, as incredible—and politically impossible—as it sounded, made sense. Each year, the USGA invested untold numbers of staff man-hours and hundreds of thousands of dollars in its future Open sites to convert them into the perfect test of golf for four days. Its staff actually moves on-site in

advance of the national championship, overseeing the trans-
formation of the course into a stadium for golf. Then, as soon
as the champion is crowned, the entire show packs its tent and
moves on, to be reassembled the following year at another venue.

In that respect, all three rotating majors are no doubt envi-
ous of the Masters. Its headquarters never moves. Television
towers, media amenities, and all the other necessities of stag-
ing such a grand event remain pretty much in place or are
stored on-site. No one has to find new accommodations year
after year, because everyone knows where they are staying in
Augusta during Masters week.

By making Bragg's Point a permanent site, the USGA could
achieve the same economy. More importantly, it would have
total control of the golf course on a year-round basis, which
would better assure that the course would be the perfect test
for our national championship.

Beyond that, playing the same course every year would
build the same kind of drama that the back nine at Augusta
has enjoyed over the years. Golf fans relish speculating each
year about what the Sunday afternoon leaders will do at Amen
Corner or at the two par 5s on the back nine as the Masters
winds down to its critical moments. They could do the same
thing as the Open approached each year at Bragg's Point.

It was also telling that Pebble Beach, a shoreside course very
similar to Bragg's Point, had produced some of the most
memorable Opens ever played. First, there was Nicklaus's
1972 win, punctuated by a 1-iron that struck the flag at the
17th hole to produce a clinching birdie. Then there was

Watson's miraculous chip-in at the same hole to vault him to the 1982 championship. Next to come was Kite's unbelievable final round under nightmarish weather conditions to gain his only major championship at the 1992 Open. Finally, of course, there was Tiger Woods's remarkable 2000 Open victory, when he played like Secretariat at the Belmont Stakes and literally ran away from the field by 15 strokes.

I could easily imagine that much and more at Bragg's Point as the surf pounded the players who challenged it. The only negative I could see—and it was a big one—was lack of space. There wasn't a lot of land there.

"Isn't it kind of small for an Open venue? I mean, where would you put the fans, or their cars, for that matter?"

"Not a problem," Francis Moore said easily. "The place will handle about 25 thousand. Recent Opens have gotten too big anyway. Some of the committee's older members, who have been doing this for years, really miss the intimacy they say we used to have with the smaller crowds. And the government's got 200 acres nearby that's available for parking and concessions."

"Sounds like you guys have known about this awhile."

He laughed. "No, no one besides me knew about the place. I wouldn't have ever thought of the idea, quite frankly. But once it was dropped in our laps, some of our USGA people in California made a few quick calls. Fort Bragg has been downsizing for over three years now. That land's available, but only for passive use. Our deal would be perfect, just parking and concessions for a week once a year. No large permanent structures, and definitely no industrial use. They don't want any industry anywhere near the coast."

"What would you do with the place the rest of the year?"

He had a ready answer. "We could use it for a number of things. Testing new turfgrass. Testing balls, clubs. Tweaking the course. Perhaps other events, such as the Amateur or the Women's or Senior Opens. Nothing's carved in stone just yet, but there are all kinds of possibilities."

I was impressed by his apparent sincerity in wanting to donate a hundred million dollar asset to the USGA and said so. He snorted, "What would you have me do? Steal it for myself? Isn't that what my brother is trying to do?"

His response reminded me of Jones's famous retort when he was congratulated for calling a penalty on himself that eventually cost him the 1925 U.S. Open championship at Worcester Country Club. In deflecting what he considered to be a stupid compliment, Jones supposedly said that "you might as well praise someone for not robbing a bank."

I should have realized that Francis Moore thought what he was doing was nothing more than honoring the trust that Jones and Roberts had placed in his father. Considered that way, it was unthinkable for him to profit from the management of the property. It was equally insulting to him and his father's memory that his brother was contemplating that very thing.

When we signed off, Francis told me he would be calling his brother later that day to set up a meeting, and he felt he would have something to report very soon.

Chapter 32

I HAD JUST returned to my office from a meeting down the hall with Emile Guidry when Gloria handed me a telephone message. The slip indicated that Francis Moore had called a half hour earlier.

It had been two days since we had spoken on the telephone. I was relieved that he had finally called me back; I was growing tired of fielding calls from Moonlight every couple of hours asking for status reports.

I had tried to keep Moonlight busy by telling him to catalogue his many treasures from Bragg's Point. He complained in his last call that he had organized and reorganized the stuff so often that he was dreaming about it at night.

When I reached Francis Moore, I knew instantly from the deflated tone of his voice that the news wasn't good.

"I'm afraid that my brother has lost sight of why our father was put in charge of this trust. He told me in no uncertain terms that the decision of what to do with the Bragg's Point property was his and his alone. To quote him, he said to 'Butt out.'"

Francis Moore sounded more sad than angry about his brother's arrogance.

"I assume that it won't do any good to talk to him any more about some kind of friendly solution to this."

Francis sighed. "I'm afraid not. In the end, he hung up on me when I tried to reason with him. Told me not to lecture him."

"Do you think it would do any good to meet with him in person?"

Stephen Moore's brother sounded embarrassed. "He wouldn't even consider it. He's got blinders on and sees only one way to go with this."

After a long pause, I said, "Brett Sullivan thought we might put some heat on him through the media."

That didn't seem to impress Francis Moore. "I don't think the USGA wants to take sides by mounting a media campaign. It doesn't really fit our image. Besides, I'm not sure my brother cares about what the media thinks. He only sees the money—and maybe the prospect of gaining some kind of revenge against me."

I knew what that meant. "It may come down to our last resort, then, and that's suing him to stop the sale." I braced myself for a negative response. It wasn't unusual for people to talk bravely of "suing the bastards" only to get cold feet when it came time to take action.

I could hear him take a deep breath and exhale on the other end of the line. "I can be in Atlanta tomorrow. Can you see me then?"

We made an appointment for the following afternoon.

I called Moonlight and gave him the news. He was disappointed that we didn't have a quick solution but pleased that Francis Moore was apparently a man of his word.

He surprised me by offering to drive over for the meeting. Although Moonlight had been reluctant to meet Dr. Stephen Moore, he seemed much more comfortable with the thought of meeting his brother, who was sympathetic to our cause. I suspected that their common link to Augusta National helped.

I thought it would be a good idea. If nothing else, Moonlight could be a cheerleader in case Francis needed motivating.

After we hung up, I went over to Paul Watkins's office. His head was buried in a disorganized pile of law books spread across his desk. While most of the lawyers in the firm did legal research on the computer, he preferred holding real books in his hands and turning their pages. I stood at his doorway for a moment, waiting to see if he looked up. I didn't want to disturb him otherwise.

Paul appeared to be deep in thought. I knew how important it was not to disrupt a lawyer's concentration as he wrestled with a legal problem, so I turned to leave, figuring I would check with him later or send him an interoffice E-mail that he could answer at his leisure.

My movement apparently caught his attention, and Paul quickly took off his reading glasses and stood up. "Don't leave, Charley. I need a break anyway."

He pointed to his messy desk. "Some of the new tax rules on my favorite generation-skipping trust provisions are impossible to understand, and the publishing services are no help. Everybody's got a theory about what the Service is gonna do, but no one knows for sure."

He suddenly smiled as he realized that I had no idea what he was talking about. Pointing to a chair in front of his desk, he said, "Sit down and tell me what I can do for you."

I explained the situation to Paul as best I could and asked him if he would work with me on this project. I warned him that it was pretty much a pro bono kind of deal.

Watkins waved his hand and said, "Bobby Jones was a member of this firm. That has meant a great deal to us over the years. Still brings us a lot of business. We owe his memory that much."

After we talked about the issues in the case a bit more, Paul gave me a copy of a petition that he had filed the previous year challenging a trustee's proposed disposition of trust assets. "Use this as a form. It's pretty current." He winked at me. "I won this case, so the form is good luck. Just change it to fit the facts of your case. I'll look it over after you finish the first draft."

I thanked him and left. As I walked back to my office, I was grateful for the sense of camaraderie that existed at Butler & Yates. It was a good feeling to work at a place where the lawyers so willingly assisted one another. I knew that wasn't the case everywhere, and I was beginning to like my new law firm more and more.

Paul Watkins was a perfect example of this unselfish work ethic. He had just made partner the year before and was no doubt pushing himself to log as many billable hours as he could to impress his new partners. Each year, his percentage of the profits (called "points") would be increased if he continued to show high levels of production.

Although most law firms paid lip service to the notion of "pro bono" work (short for "pro bono publico," which is Latin meaning "for the public good"), they really discouraged it by expecting all lawyers to bill large numbers of hours. That wasn't the case at Butler & Yates, at least not if Paul Watkins's attitude was any indication.

Paul's involvement immediately raised my confidence in our case several degrees. Paul graduated from Harvard Law School with top honors and then obtained his Master of Laws in Taxation from NYU Law School, which had the premier tax program in the country. He really knew his stuff and, unlike most tax lawyers, understood litigation and thought like a trial lawyer. It was a deadly combination.

I spent the remainder of the afternoon preparing a draft of a petition on behalf of Francis Moore against his brother seeking an injunction against the proposed sale of the property. My work would have been much more difficult were it not for the form Paul Watkins had given me. I had to make certain that our petition included allegations about Stephen Moore's status, why the court had jurisdiction, the specifics of how Moore was violating the trust, and why we were entitled to the court's intervention to stop the sale. By following Watkins's form, I was confident I wouldn't leave anything out; it was a ready-made checklist. The last thing we wanted was for Stephen Moore to delay a hearing by filing technical objections to our petition.

I had what I felt was a polished draft by early evening. I printed a copy and left it in Paul Watkins's chair so that he would see it first thing in the morning.

By the time I left the office, it was nearly eight o'clock. At that hour, traffic was minimal, and it took only 15 minutes instead of the usual 30 to get home to my apartment, where I popped one of those delectable frozen dinners in the microwave as soon as I walked in the door. The great thing about eating so late was that your hunger made even the worst kind of food taste good.

While I waited, I noticed that the light on my answering machine was flashing. That was unusual; most people who wanted to reach me called at the office or sent an E-mail. I rarely had any messages on the answering machine.

I punched the button and soon heard a familiar voice.

"Hello, buddy, it's Ken Cheatwood. I'm sorry I haven't returned your calls. It's been a month since I started here, but you wouldn't believe the amount of work they've given me." He laughed, mainly because he knew I wasn't going to buy that excuse. Most judicial clerkships were pretty leisurely experiences.

"Okay, that may not be true. Actually, I've been taking advantage of late daylight to play a lot of golf after work. By the time I get home, it's usually too late to do anything but eat and go to bed."

It was my turn to laugh. What my buddy really meant was that, after drinking beer and chasing the ladies, it was too late to think about calling me or anyone else.

"Anyway, call me so we can catch up. I want to know about life as a lawyer at Butler & Yates. Do they treat their associates as well as their law clerks?"

The beep on the machine signaling the end of the message coincided with the one on the microwave telling me that my food was ready. The excitement from hearing from my good friend displaced my hunger at the moment, so I dialed the number he had left.

No answer. That figured. This time it was my turn to leave a message. I gave him my work number and E-mail address and told him to contact me the next day.

Cheatwood and I had become fast friends during the two summers we clerked together at Butler & Yates. He liked the place as much as I did, and I was fairly sure that he was going to join the firm when he finished his clerkship with the Eleventh Circuit.

Ken Cheatwood was an unusual guy. A scratch player, he had attended Oklahoma State on a golf scholarship, where he had played for Coach Mike Holder on a national championship team.

By his own admission, my friend had been a fairly indifferent student, majoring in political science in name only. His academic performance belied his considerable intellectual acumen, however. He was really a student of golf and had collected a remarkable library of golf literature and reference works. I had learned a great deal about the game and its traditions from Cheatwood, and he had been instrumental in helping me bring out the Beau Stedman story. Ken possessed great people skills and instincts that had helped persuade some of the powers that be at the firm to let me pursue the story that I had first discovered in some of Jones's old discarded and forgotten files.

According to Cheatwood, he came to law after shooting 80 on the final day of Q-School and missing his Tour card for the fourth straight year. He couldn't stand the thought of another year bouncing around the minitours, so he signed up for the LSAT the next day. He scored in the top 3% of all test takers and was accepted at Emory Law School—not coincidentally, he was fond of pointing out, the same law school that Bobby Jones had attended before leaving early to take (and pass) the Georgia bar exam.

I had missed my good friend. Ironically, he was my closest connection with my new law firm and a good part of the reason I chose to accept its offer of permanent employment. I really liked the idea of our practicing together and was disappointed when he took the clerkship, even though it only meant a delay of a year before he would join me at the firm.

I was looking forward to visiting with him the next day.

I was up early and in the office before eight in the morning. Of course, Gloria was already there, and I could smell the coffee she had made. I helped myself to a cup even though the coffee in Georgia paled in comparison to the stuff I was used to in New Orleans. The joke was that they tarred the roads in Louisiana with leftover coffee. Some people didn't like it so strong, but I came to enjoy the taste of the chicory and the jolt it gave me from the very first cup.

As I waited for the mail to be distributed, I checked my computer and saw that I had an E-mail message waiting. I clicked it on, and there was a note from Cheatwood. It had been posted late last night, probably when he finally got home from a party somewhere. He just wanted to let me know that he got my message and would be calling today.

Marty, our young runner, brought me the mail, and I busied myself for the next half hour or so looking through it. Half was junk mail; the rest was routine stuff. There were no fires to put out.

I decided to check with Paul Watkins to see what he thought of my draft petition. The unwritten protocol was that senior lawyers buzzed junior lawyers on the intercom, but not vice versa; junior lawyers usually went to senior lawyers' offices when they wished to see them.

I headed down the hall past Emile Guidry's office to where Paul's was located. He was just coming out of his office. Seeing me, he smiled and said, "Oh, I was just coming to find you." Holding out the petition, he said, "This is good. I made a couple of suggestions. Take a look at them and see what you think. Then run it in final form."

I thanked him and started to head back to my office. Over my shoulder, I heard him say, "I put signature lines for both of our names. It lets them know we mean business."

There was no doubt that having a partner's signature on the petition would enhance our credibility. In lending his name to the lawsuit, Paul was also letting me know that his support for what we were doing was more than token. He was serious about participating, and I was pleased to no end to have him aboard.

Chapter 33

I ADOPTED ALL of the changes that Paul Watkins had proposed, and not simply out of deference to him. Each of his
suggestions definitely improved my work product, and I
marveled at how a gifted lawyer like Paul could raise the
quality of a pleading in such a dramatic fashion with the
mere stroke of a pen.

Everything was done by lunchtime. I wanted to have the
final version ready for Francis Moore when he arrived at two
o'clock. We made a copy for service on the defendant and an
extra one for our client.

Moonlight arrived in time to go to lunch with me. He was
wearing the old Hogan cap he had on the first day I met him,
and he seemed as pleased to see me as I was to see him. He
seemed a little nervous, but I expected as much under the
circumstances.

I knew Moonlight wouldn't go for any fancy food, so I took
him to a great sandwich place about a block from the office
called Scelfo's. The owners were from Louisiana, and it was
the only place I had found that had genuine New Orleans-
style po-boys.

During my three years at Tulane, I hadn't been fond of the humidity and mosquitoes in New Orleans, but the food was another matter. Whether it was the fancy cuisine at Antoine's in the Quarter or the po-boys at Ye Olde College Inn uptown on Carrollton, there wasn't another place on earth that could feed you as well as the Crescent City—or anywhere else in south Louisiana for that matter. Emile Guidry and I were the only two people in the firm who truly understood the delights of boudin, fried oysters, and boiled crawfish.

Of course, the food at Scelfo's was a little more exotic than Moonlight was used to. As a result, I couldn't talk him into having a fried soft shell crab po-boy like the one I had ordered. He stuck with the plain roast beef.

After I doctored my sandwich with Tabasco, we settled down to business. I explained to Moonlight that the petition had been prepared and would be filed as soon as Francis Moore approved it. Moore would be the plaintiff, or the person who was filing the lawsuit. His brother would be the defendant, or the person who was being sued.

He took it all in without saying much. After he finished the first half of his sandwich, he took a sip of soda and said, "Ya' think he'll do it?"

I assumed that he was referring to whether Francis Moore would approve the suit. "I think so. He doesn't seem to have any real reluctance about it."

He then started on the second half of his po-boy, retreating again into his own thoughts.

I was having trouble gauging Moonlight's mood. He hadn't

said much since he had arrived, as if he was either guarding against disappointment or was afraid of saying something that would jinx us.

We spent the rest of lunch talking more about his collection of Bragg's Point memorabilia than anything else. After we were done, we went back to the office, and I showed Moonlight the petition. I knew that he wouldn't understand much of it, but it was physical evidence that we were going forward with our plan.

Francis Moore arrived promptly at two o'clock. I had reserved a small conference room with nicer appointments than those hidden by the clutter in my still-disorganized office. After depositing Moonlight there, I went to the reception area to greet the client I had yet to meet in person.

When I entered our waiting room, I encountered a distinguished-looking man who appeared to be about 60 years of age. He was perhaps six feet tall, which was around my height, and had an attractive tan indicating that he was more than a weekend golfer. His hair was more gray than anything but was full, and he appeared to be energetic. His lightweight tan wool suit fit him well. Francis Moore stood and smiled easily as I approached and extended my hand.

"Mr. Moore, I'm Charley Hunter. It's a pleasure to meet you in person at last."

He shook my hand. "Charley, I feel the same way."

As we walked to the conference room, I told Moore that there was someone there I wanted him to meet. When we walked in, Moonlight stood up.

"Mr. Moore, this is Moonlight McIntyre. He was the caddie at Bragg's Point who brought all of this to me."

Moore extended his hand. "And he was a caddie at Augusta, too." He smiled warmly. "I know all about Seamus McIntyre. He's a legend at the club."

Moonlight beamed at the recognition. I was puzzled, though; if Moore had known about Moonlight, why hadn't Moonlight known about him?

"Do you guys know each other?"

Moore shook his head. "I've never had the pleasure of meeting Mr. McIntyre before, but I feel I know him by reputation." Looking at Moonlight, he said, "You must've retired before I ever got the chance to have you on my bag."

Moonlight nodded. "Once my Social Security started, I cut back. Some a' the old-timers at the club would call me out, but other than that I didn't work so much."

As we waited for a tray of coffee, Moonlight and I told Francis how we had gotten to that point. He listened attentively, but I got the sense that it was more out of politeness than anything else. He seemed more interested in getting to know us than the story.

I soon learned the reason. Francis Moore knew a whole lot more about the story than he had let on. After we had talked for 20 minutes or so, and I had explained some of the more mysterious aspects of our visit to Bragg's Point, he walked over to the tray that had been left in the corner of the conference room and poured himself a second cup of coffee. After taking his first sip, he walked back over, sat down, and said, "Maybe I can clear up some of the confusion for you."

Moore then proceeded to explain how his father had kept him involved in the Bragg's Point Charitable Trust for a number of years, in fact long before he passed the torch to Stephen. "After what happened at Augusta, Dad didn't want Stephen to feel passed over again, so he appointed him as the next trustee. But he wanted me to watch over things, too. Without saying so, I'm not sure he was completely confident that Stephen would handle things right."

Moonlight grunted something about selling to the Japs.

Moore continued. "Anyway, I've been looking over his shoulder for years without him knowing it." He laughed. "I doubt that Stephen's even been out there since the first time my Dad took him. He's not much into golf history or tradition. But I've been out there at least once a year, and I have people who look after the place."

It clicked immediately. So I *had* seen people out there after all.

"Did these people know we were coming?"

He smiled in a mischievous way. "Yes, they did."

"So you had them prepare the course for us to play?"

He nodded. "It's not hard to find people to do that. I just asked the superintendent at Augusta to locate some reputable people out there. They've been tending the property for years, basically keeping the grass under control and killing weeds. It was easy to get them to set the course up for you."

I still couldn't understand. "How'd you know we were coming?"

He took another drink of coffee and put the cup down. "Augusta's a small town. When you went there looking for Moonlight, you asked a lot of questions. On my next trip to the club, I heard a couple of the caddies talking about it. And I heard them mention your name and Moonlight's name. It was pretty easy to put two and two together. You were on to Bragg's Point."

He stood up and walked to the window. "I probably wouldn't have thought of it on my own, because I tend to avoid anything that brings me into conflict with my brother. I didn't want to be the one to make it public because my father wouldn't have wanted me to. But I figured, if you were going to bring the story to the USGA like you did with Stedman, there was nothing I could do—or wanted to do—to stop you."

That still didn't explain how he knew we were going to the course. He smiled again when I pressed him on it.

"Moonlight told a couple of his caddie friends he would be leaving for a few days. It got back to me."

He saw from my expression that I was surprised at how closely our movement had been followed. Explaining further, he said, "I told you, Augusta is a small place. Given what was going on, I figured I knew where he was headed. I had someone call to make an appointment to see you during that time, and he was told you would be out of town. That clinched it. I called out to California and told them to get things ready."

I looked over at Moonlight. "I *told* you there were people out there watching us." I turned back to my client. "But tell me this: Why'd they hide from us?"

Moore looked at Moonlight. "I didn't want any of them involved. How would we explain that? It would just complicate things. Plus, if you thought the secret was already out, I didn't know but that you might have dropped the whole thing." He spread his hands out, palms up. "And if they don't mow the tees and greens and get the course ready, you may not see what's there or why it was such a great track."

I turned and looked at Moonlight. "You kept saying it was magic. I knew someone else was out there."

He was unmoved. "If ya' think what you've just heard has nothin' to do with magic, then ya' don't understand magic. We've had a guardian angel here all along, an' you're lookin' at him." He pointed to Francis Moore to make certain I understood what he was saying.

We spent the next half hour reviewing the petition. Moore had a number of questions. He seemed intent on understanding everything we were doing. At the same time, he never expressed any hesitancy about the course of action we were taking. If anything, as he spent more time with us, he became every bit as resolute as Moonlight.

When we finished our meeting, I asked our new friend if he needed someone to take him back to the airport. "I'd take you myself, but I can't leave for another half hour, and I don't want to make you late for your flight."

He smiled. "I'm happy to wait, Charley. It would give us a chance to talk more on the ride out. Don't worry about making me late. I flew up here in our company Lear. It won't leave without me."

On the way to Hartsfield Airport, I asked Moore if he had ever played Bragg's Point. He said that he had never been allowed to.

"It was Bob Jones's retreat, a very personal escape from a terribly painful condition. My dad used to say that the least understood part of medicine was the powerful effect the mind had on diseases and the pain they caused. He said that Jones was almost like another person when he was at Bragg's Point. He was away from public view and could really let his hair down. I understand that he would ride out to the water's edge and sit and watch the surf for hours at a time. According to my father, his face would relax in a way that showed that he had escaped his pain, at least for the time being. He was truly happy in that setting, and that's the most powerful medicine there is. Letting anyone out there who he wasn't familiar and comfortable with would have defeated the purpose of the place."

As we parted, Moore made it clear that he wanted to be kept in the loop on every development now that he was on board. I promised our new comrade-in-arms that nothing would be done without his approval. He also reminded me again that he could get to Atlanta on virtually a moment's notice on the Lear.

We filed the lawsuit the next morning, and I soon learned why Francis Moore had so carefully avoided any confrontation with his brother all these years.

Chapter 34

IT SEEMED LIKE the phone started ringing within 20 minutes after we filed the petition. At first, it was one of the local television stations, whose courthouse reporter had picked up the petition during a routine review of the court filings. Then it was a reporter from the *Atlanta Constitution*, who wanted to know how an Atlanta doctor came to control land overlooking the Pacific Ocean in northern California.

I guess I should have expected the media to run with it. Our suit had lots of sex appeal: a dispute within a prominent and successful family, lots of money at stake, prime oceanfront property, and a controversial foreign buyer. And, of course, as if that were not enough, there was the name of Clifford Roberts in the trust papers. Anyone who discovered that immediately knew there was a connection to Bobby Jones and Augusta National. In these parts, that was instant newsworthiness.

Still, it took me by surprise when the local media calls were followed by CNN, TBS, CBS, and all the rest of the alphabet soup television networks. Apparently, one of the local media organizations had put the story on the AP wire, and it got picked up by the big boys. The numerous calls I received in succession reflected a kind of herd instinct at work among the competing news departments of the various networks. If CBS was interested in a story, then NBC became interested, mainly out of fear of being scooped.

Instead of independent evaluation, each network seemed just to imitate the others. I suppose it was much safer for them that way (when you're wrong—like telling the country on election night that "we now can give the state of Florida to Vice-President Gore" —misery loves company), just not terribly creative or informative.

At first, I preferred to say "No comment" and let it go at that. I actually began to enjoy the pleas from some of the news representatives as they tried to get me to abandon that position. One young reporter even told me she might get fired if she didn't get at least one quote. I laughed and told her to offer her pain up for the poor souls in purgatory. When she asked me what it meant, I told her it meant that she obviously hadn't attended parochial schools.

Before long, however, producers of the various news programs were calling me back to respond to quotes from Stephen Moore and his lawyer expressing total outrage at the suit and threatening us with everything from a countersuit to disbarment. Their spin was that Cliff Roberts had acquired the property for speculative purposes. According to his lawyer, Dr. Moore was simply planning to convert an asset that had been out of commerce for years into money that could be used to make golf more accessible to handicapped and disabled persons. How could we be opposed to that, they asked.

I went to Paul Watkins for advice about what we should do in the face of this rhetoric. He told me that it wasn't unusual for lawyers to try controversial cases in the media. If the judge assigned to the case was sensitive to public opinion and perceived that public sympathy favored one side, it could make a difference.

So he advised me that, when one side started pandering to the media, it was sometimes important to give them back a dose of their own medicine. As distasteful as it was, his view was that loyalty to the client demanded it when necessary.

And it appeared to be necessary that day.

I locked myself in a conference room and sketched out some notes for a response to the blustering put out by Stephen Moore and his lawyer. Words and phrases like "wildlife sanctuary" and "unqualified foreign investors" appeared on my legal pad. I also penciled in the words "personal enrichment at the expense of handicapped Americans." That ought to have broad appeal, especially among the media.

The best, though, was the phrase about Bobby Jones "turning over in his grave." It was a cliché, but I had learned that clichés were useful for lawyers. Their vice was also their virtue: the very overuse that rendered such expressions as clichés also meant that there would be no doubt about their meaning.

Before long, I was giving interviews to numerous reporters on the telephone and before cameras, and my spiel got better and better with repetition. I learned to change it up a little each time, too. CNN preferred not to run the same sound bite that NBC had just shown a half hour earlier.

I chose not to challenge the way Dr. Moore and his lawyer downplayed the use of the property. Our petition had not gone into that in any detail, and something told me they may not have been fully aware of everything that happened there. Based on what Francis Moore had told me, his father may not have told his brother much about the magical golf being played at Bragg's Point.

It was to our advantage if our opposition was truly unaware of the historical significance of the property, and it gave us a hole card to play in court at a more opportune time. Besides, we had enough, I figured, for an effective counterattack for the time being.

Not long after the reports aired, I got a call from our client. In a tactful voice, he suggested that we not let things "get out of hand." In particular, he asked me to drop references to Jones turning over in his grave, saying "I'm not sure that's the right tone for what we're trying to do."

I got the message and apologized for getting a little carried away. It was an embarrassing lesson from my first experience with the news media.

According to the media accounts, Stephen Moore's lawyer was a fellow named Stuart Bordelon. At least, that's the lawyer who was being quoted. From everything I had learned, Bordelon had a good reputation. One of the partners in our firm, Henry Hoskins, had tried a stock fraud case against him a couple of years before. Hoskins gave Bordelon high marks.

Although I was put off by the bloated rhetoric I was reading in the papers, I tried to give Bordelon the benefit of the doubt. I knew that he would call sooner or later so that we could discuss the case and get down to business.

When the call came, I was prepared for it. I knew that Bordelon would do his homework, find out that I was a young lawyer, and test me early to see if I would fold as easily as one of those old squeeze boxes played by Cajun bands back in Louisiana.

Paul Watkins had talked with me about it. I asked him if he should deal with Bordelon instead of me, but he thought it was important that I take the lead. "This is your baby," he said, "and you need to see it through."

The test came almost immediately after our phone conversation began. Even though we had never met, Bordelon tried to sound familiar and friendly by calling me by my first name. "Look, Charley, I have a lot of respect for your firm. And if they took you on, it means you're a pretty good hand. I don't want to see this get expensive for your client. Unless I'm missing something, there's no way he can win this thing, so why don't you talk to him about dismissing it?"

Suppressing a laugh, I said, "Well, I appreciate your concern, but my client's determined to see that the intent of the trust is enforced. What your client wants to do violates that intent. But we will certainly entertain your offer to dismiss the case—just as soon as your client agrees to cancel the sale of the property."

Bordelon's tone immediately turned harsh and unpleasant. "You've gotta be kiddin'. Do you understand this is a hundred-million-dollar deal we're talkin' about?"

I was determined not to respond in kind and so replied evenly, "I don't see how the amount of money is at all relevant."

He guffawed. "In this business, young man, it's *always* about the money. Don't ever let your clients tell you otherwise."

I didn't care to be patronized, but said nothing. It was an old trick to remain silent as a way of making your opponent uncomfortable, something else that Emile Guidry had shown me.

Bordelon eventually filled the vacuum I had created. In a more conciliatory tone, he said, "Okay, what does your client want?"

Interesting, I thought. The first sign of weakness: before even answering the lawsuit, they want to talk settlement.

I tried to sound uninterested. "I just told you what he wants. Cancel the transaction."

"That's not possible. Let's talk about other solutions."

I was enjoying this. "I don't have any authority to discuss other solutions. I'm afraid my client is adamant."

He gave out an audible sigh. "Well, there's gonna be lots of bloodshed on this one before we're done. Please do me a favor and talk to your client to see if there's any other way to settle this deal. You know, we're dealin' with family here, and no matter who wins the lawsuit, their relationship with one another will never be the same."

"I'm aware of that, and so is Mr. Moore. But he feels obligated to fulfill the responsibilities his father took on at the request of Mr. Roberts and Mr. Jones, and I don't think he feels he can turn his back on that."

I purposely mentioned Roberts and Jones to remind Bordelon that he was taking on a rather influential part of the Georgia establishment if he continued to fight us. But he obviously had already given that some thought.

"I wouldn't be much of a lawyer if I refused to represent somebody just because our side wasn't as popular as the other guy's. If I've got to deal with the ghosts of Augusta National, then that's what I'll do." He laughed. "Hell, I don't even play golf; what can they do to me?"

I was impressed by his loyalty to his client, and he was right— I wouldn't have respected him much if he was unwilling to fight for an unpopular cause. But the fact remained that his cause was not just unpopular, it was greedy. And I intended to expose Dr. Stephen Moore's greed if necessary.

I told him I would speak with my client about settlement but made it clear that I did not expect Francis Moore's position to change. Then, as per Paul Watkins's suggestion, I asked him for dates for his client's deposition.

"That's kinda quick, don't you think?"

I knew that I had caught him off guard. "Well, we don't have much time. Your client apparently wants to get this deal done by the end of the year."

He muttered something about checking on Dr. Moore's schedule and calling me back. I wanted to let him know that we would be aggressive, so I added, "We'll be sending you some interrogatories and requests for production in the next day or two. Do you want us to serve your client, or will you accept service on his behalf?"

If Stuart Bordelon was hoping to discover that we were less than resolute about the case, he now knew otherwise. I could hear the disappointment in his voice when he said, "No, that won't be necessary. Just send your stuff to me." He paused and then added, "I'll have some discovery of my own to send you."

"Of course," I said, as brightly as possible.

When we hung up, I was exhilarated. While I reminded myself that it was just a telephone conversation, I had learned that every encounter with an opponent in a lawsuit was an opportunity to gain ground. Sometimes an advantage was gained by lulling an opponent into a false sense of security, but on other occasions it was important to send a very different message.

Stuart Bordelon had really called to take my temperature and see how I was reacting to their initial bravado. If he had sensed any weakness on our part, it would only have encouraged him. From the outset, we wanted to avoid giving any aid or comfort to the enemy.

I felt confident that we had achieved our objective. There was no doubt in my mind that, before Stuart Bordelon had replaced his telephone receiver in its cradle, he knew his client was in for a fight.

Chapter 35

AFTER BOTH SIDES swapped interrogatories and requests for production, we settled on a date for the depositions of the two brothers. Francis Moore seemed surprised that he would have to submit to a deposition.

"Why do they want to ask me questions? I'm not the one who's trying to sell the course."

I had to assure him that it was routine for all parties to be deposed. "There's an old rule," I told him, "that a lawyer should never ask a question that he doesn't know the answer to. A lawyer learns the answers to his questions by asking them in a deposition. They know you're going to be a witness, and they want to know what they should ask you on cross-examination when you testify at the trial."

Then I explained to him that a deposition was nothing more than an out-of-court question-and-answer session. He would be under oath, and a court reporter would be there to take down Bordelon's questions and his answers. "That way, if you change your story at the trial, they can bring out what you said before. It's called 'impeachment with a prior inconsistent statement.'" He still looked a little ill at ease, so I added, "It's done all the time. We'll go over everything with you beforehand. Believe me, you'll do fine."

He shook his head. "It's not that. I just *hate* any confrontation with my brother. Is there any way around this?"

"I'm afraid not," I told him. "Besides, if we try to get out of it, they'll think we're hiding something. It's best to act as nonchalant about it as possible."

Once I explained that we would be there the entire time, he became less reticent about the whole thing. Still, it worried me. Why was Francis Moore so worried about a deposition? Was he hiding something? Would he crater under the first bit of pressure applied by Bordelon?

I didn't quite understand his reaction, so I talked with Paul Watkins about it.

"You've got to put yourself in your client's shoes," he advised me. "You know all about depositions. They're routine for most lawyers. But, to a guy like Francis Moore, they're a really big deal. They see witnesses getting beaten up by lawyers on TV and in the movies. Maybe it's good for dramatic effect, but people begin to believe that's the way the real world operates."

He shook his head sadly. "On top of that, now we've got all this 'reality' court TV with pompous little dictators for judges, who are rude and abusive to the people who come before them—all in the name of entertainment. That really adds to people's fears about lawyers and the whole legal process." After a short pause, he added, "Isn't it amazing what happens to some people when they get in front of a camera?"

Without waiting for an answer, he then handed me a memorandum the firm had prepared. It was entitled "How to Prepare for Your Deposition."

"Sit down and go over this with Mr. Moore. It covers all of the situations and lawyers' tactics he's going to experience when he's deposed. Once you walk him through this, he'll be a lot more comfortable."

I sent a copy of the memo to Francis Moore and invited him to review it. I also promised him that we would go over it again when we met to prepare for his deposition.

In the meantime, I began preparing questions to ask Dr. Stephen Moore. Paul Watkins and I met several times over the next week to discuss our tactics. I also got some input from Emile Guidry over coffee one morning. This was the most important deposition I had ever taken, and I wanted to be prepared.

When the fateful day arrived, we went to the court reporter's office, which was a neutral site. There was a comfortable conference room there that accommodated us nicely.

Because we were the first to request a deposition, it was agreed that we would take Dr. Moore's deposition first. He arrived wearing his white lab coat. "The doctor's security blanket," Francis whispered in my ear.

As we were introduced, I noticed that Stephen Moore rejected his brother's extended hand, preferring to maintain a grave expression. Tension showed in his every movement. This guy is wound tight, I thought to myself. It was a good sign.

The deposition began rather uneventfully. Stephen Moore

woodenly answered my questions about his background and work history and showed little emotion. He arched his back immediately, however, when I asked if he had ever been sued for malpractice.

Sensing his client's difficulty with the question, Stuart Bordelon voiced an objection.

"On what ground?" I asked.

"It's irrelevant."

"It may or may not be. Are you instructing him not to answer?"

Bordelon knew that such an instruction risked sanctions if a judge later determined that the refusal to answer was unwarranted. He looked at his client, obviously hoping to find in his expression something that would inspire him. Stephen Moore only looked confused.

Bordelon backed down. I repeated the question to Dr. Moore. Reluctantly, he admitted that he had, in fact, been the subject of medical malpractice claims. Of course, I already knew that from Frankie Johnson, but I wanted to make the good doctor aware that we knew more about him than perhaps he wanted us to know.

With insistent questions, I forced Dr. Moore to divulge all of the details of the three claims that had been made against him, including the amounts of the settlements that had been reached with his malpractice insurers. He was clearly unhappy with the discussion.

Having set him back on his heels, I then showed our physician opponent a copy of the trust document. As I went through pertinent provisions, I read them into the record and asked if he understood what they meant. He said he did.

I asked him if he agreed that the trustee was not supposed to profit personally from the use of any trust assets. Speaking in a hesitant voice, he said he understood that. I then asked him if he knew that "self-dealing" was a legal term that described a trustee's prohibited dealing with trust assets for personal gain. Still talking slowly, he said that he knew that, too. I next asked him if he agreed with me that this trust did not permit him to make a personal profit from dealing with trust property and that it breached the trust to do so.

These questions were making Dr. Moore more and more uncomfortable. He began looking over at his lawyer, his eyes pleading for assistance. Bordelon knew better than to coach the witness; the local judges in Atlanta were quick to sanction lawyers for influencing sworn testimony.

The silence became increasingly awkward. Finally, Bordelon looked at his client and said quietly, "Answer if you can."

After what seemed like another long delay, Dr. Moore said with considerably less confidence than he had showed 20 minutes earlier, "I don't know how to answer that question."

I looked at him evenly and said, "Is it your testimony that you don't know whether making a personal profit from dealing in trust property breaches this trust?"

Stephen Moore shifted in his chair. He stared hard at a legal pad that had been put in front of him in case he wanted to make notes, as if he was looking for answers on its blank pages. Finally, he said, uncertainly, "No, no, I understand that."

"Understand what?" I demanded.

He cleared this throat. "Well...I guess I understand that I'm supposed to keep the trust's business and my business separate." He paused before adding, "Does that answer your question?"

"No, it does not," I said firmly. I sensed an opening, and I wasn't about to give up so easily or let him off the hook. One of the first things Emile Guidry taught me about taking depositions was to get an answer to every question, no matter how many times I had to repeat it. Leaning forward, I said evenly, "What I asked is whether you understood that a trustee who makes a personal profit from dealing with trust property breaches this trust. That's the question you haven't answered."

The beleaguered doctor didn't even bother to look at his lawyer this time because he knew no help was forthcoming. Instead, he stalled for time by taking a sip of water from a nearby glass that had been provided to him at the beginning of the deposition.

I could almost hear his frantic thoughts as he searched for a way to avoid answering the question. Dr. Moore knew that, if he answered yes, he was admitting that forming a corporation to receive money from the trust, regardless of the purpose, was wrong. And if he answered no, he was admitting that he didn't know what his most fundamental legal duties were.

In either event, he would be admitting that he was unfit to continue as trustee, and it was obvious that he knew it. Emile Guidry referred to this as putting a witness "in a box."

While I waited for his answer, I pulled out copies of the articles of incorporation for Dr. Moore's "handicapped golf access" company, including the initial report listing Dr. Moore as the incorporator. As if to prepare him for my next question, I pushed a copy across the table to the witness.

I watched Dr. Moore's eyes dart nervously across the pages I had placed before him. Unconsciously, his fingers traced the outlines of the seal from the Secretary of State's office certifying the document. Soon his shoulders began to sag, and his head dropped forward. The swagger he had shown when he first entered the room was now completely gone.

After a few moments, he looked at his lawyer and then at me before asking in a small and almost pathetic voice, "May I speak with my attorney before answering any more questions?"

I felt too sorry for him to refuse his request. Besides, there was nothing he could do at this point to get off the hook, and a witness's request to confer privately with his lawyer in the middle of a deposition under these circumstances amounted to a confession (and read like one in the transcript).

Bordelon and his client stood up and left the room. If body language meant anything, they were clearly back on their heels. Nonetheless, I expected that they would return shortly and that Dr. Moore would then provide well-rehearsed glib answers to my questions. Since the transcript would show that these answers came after an off-the-record conference with his lawyer, they wouldn't help Dr. Moore's cause much at all.

A few minutes passed, but no one returned. A few minutes turned into nearly a half hour. The court reporter became fidgety, and so did Francis Moore. We had left Moonlight back at the office waiting for us, and I began to imagine him pacing the halls as he drove himself—and everyone around him—crazy.

I finally excused myself to check on our two missing opponents. They were nowhere to be found. The receptionist indicated that they had had a loud and heated discussion in one of the other offices, whereupon Dr. Moore had stalked out with Bordelon following closely behind. She seemed reluctant to say more.

Leaving a deposition before it concluded wasn't just poor form; it was against the law unless whoever left had a damned good reason to do so. Disappearing without telling anyone only made it worse, especially in the eyes of the court.

I couldn't imagine Bordelon would do something so stupid, but I couldn't help but be secretly delighted that he had. Not too many judges would let that kind of behavior go unpunished. It might even constitute grounds for a default judgment against the defendant doctor.

I was just about to go back into the conference room and explain this bizarre situation to Francis Moore when the elevator doors outside the reception area opened. An obviously embarrassed Stuart Bordelon came walking out of the elevator and said, "Can we talk for just a minute?"

We went into an empty office. He closed the door behind us, turned to me, and said, "I'll get directly to the point. My client no longer wishes to contest the suit. He will cancel the sale."

He then turned as if to leave. But I knew we had them on the run and that there would never be a better time to press our advantage. I couldn't afford to indulge in self-congratulations just yet. Canceling the sale was only half the loaf; if Dr. Moore stayed on as trustee, he would still have control of the property and might decide to try the same thing later. I didn't want to fight this battle again anytime soon.

Shaking my head, I said, "That's not enough."

Bordelon spun back around. "What do you mean, it's not enough? It's what you said you wanted all along." He was becoming angry. "What are you trying to pull?"

I remained unemotional. "We want him out as trustee. Don't you see, that's the only way we can avoid being right back in another lawsuit if Dr. Moore tries this again."

Bordelon abruptly changed his tone into a kind of soft whine. "C'mon, Charley, you've got what you want."

I shook my head. "If we just drop this now, we won't have accomplished anything. This has been difficult for my client, too, but he doesn't want to come this far without seeing it through. If Dr. Moore won't agree to resign as trustee, I'll have to move for sanctions and ask that he be ordered to answer my questions."

I let that sink in before adding, "And remind him that he still hasn't produced the contract between the trust and his company or the income tax returns we subpoenaed."

He looked out of the only window in the office for what seemed like a long time. Then he took a deep breath and said, "Okay. He'll resign if you insist."

I still wasn't done. "And will he sign a document appointing his brother as successor trustee?"

Bordelon gave me an ugly look. He obviously wasn't used to

being on the losing side of a lawsuit, and he didn't like it. "Yeah, yeah. He'll sign it."

I went back into the conference room and informed a confused Francis Moore that he was now the trustee for the Bragg's Point Charitable Trust. He still seemed incredulous. "You mean, he's out, and I'm in? Just like that?"

I nodded and laughed, partly at the absurdity of the day's events and partly from the delicious thrill of winning that drives every lawyer who fancies a career in litigation.

In an uncharacteristic display of emotion, he put his arm around me and said, "Young man, if this is any indication, you've got quite a career ahead of you."

Chapter 36

AS WE SORTED it all out, Dr. Moore's bizarre behavior and hasty departure began to make sense. One of my law professors had warned me that, for all their brilliance in their chosen field of endeavor, many physicians are notoriously bad business people—as, he added, were most lawyers.

Dr. Stephen Moore typified that observation. His greedy little scheme, as simple as it was, did more than expose him to civil liability. If carried off, it would have violated a significant number of state and federal laws.

We speculated that Stuart Bordelon had given his client this unhappy news, probably well in advance of the deposition, but that Dr. Moore had stubbornly chosen to ignore the message and instead blame the messenger. When he found himself confronted again in his deposition with the reality of what he had done, however, he chose to bolt rather than to admit the error of his ways.

That left his lawyer to clean up the mess. Small wonder Bordelon was so agitated. I couldn't blame him.

My opposing counsel did have the presence of mind to require that the settlement agreement be confidential. His intent, of course, was to spare his client any further embarrassment, not to mention additional legal problems with authorities who might become interested in the seedier aspects of what the good doctor had attempted to do.

We were only too happy to oblige; our side agreed that we weren't quite ready to reveal the story of Bragg's Point to the media.

I probably shouldn't have worried. After the initial wave of calls, media interest had fallen off in the weeks that followed. Emile Guidry told me I should have expected it. He said the only two times the media paid much attention to lawsuits was when they were filed and when they went to trial. Nothing else was sensational enough to compete with the other news of the day.

Back in the office, I got more credit for all of this than I deserved. Paul Watkins and Emile Guidry sent out memos extolling my "victory" to the other members in the firm, and several partners took me to lunch so that I could give them a firsthand account of my epic struggle with the forces of evil. I have to admit, I liked my first taste of battle, especially the part about winning.

Francis Moore was apparently impressed, too. He called less than a week later to tell me that he was retaining our firm to handle his business and that he wanted me personally involved in anything he sent over. The partners in the firm were impressed. As Emile Guidry told me, "We don't expect first-year associates to be rainmakers, Charley. That's quite a feather in your cap."

My new client also let me know that he wanted to get moving on Bragg's Point. He asked me to prepare whatever documents were necessary to donate the property to the USGA, and he suggested that we meet to put together a presentation for the Executive Committee to make the Bragg's Point Golf Links the permanent site for the U.S. Open. He was collecting materials, he said, from the Northern California Golf Association and other regional and state groups that owned their own golf courses and would send a packet to me in the next few days.

Toward the end of the conversation, my new client offered a strange comment. He said that there was something about Bragg's Point that neither Moonlight nor I knew. I asked him what it was, but he said he wanted to tell us in person. He said we would talk about it when we met the following week.

In the meantime, Moonlight was clearly overjoyed at what had happened and particularly at the prospect of Bragg's Point becoming USGA property. He said it was what he had hoped for when he originally contacted me. As evidence of his pleasure at what I had done, he finally permitted me to enter his inner sanctum and review his Bragg's Point memorabilia.

Once I stepped inside, I quickly understood why Moonlight was reluctant to have visitors. The place was a virtual museum of golf history. Each wall seemed to be a chapter of the pictorial history of Jones's golf haven. It was all very neatly arranged—so neatly, in fact, that I was surprised. I hadn't figured Moonlight to be much of a housekeeper or to have an eye for such things, but everything in his modest home was surprisingly clean and orderly. He had obviously devoted considerable time and attention to the presentation of his memorabilia. It signified that he really treasured this stuff for the memories it represented.

At the same time, anyone who saw this incredible historical display wasn't likely to keep quiet about it for very long. As word inevitably spread, Moonlight's home would gain a lot of unwanted attention—not only from well-meaning golf historians and fans, but also from less desirable elements who might try to relieve him of his prized possessions. It had happened before.

So Moonlight had wisely kept his treasure trove to himself. Until now, when he was finally satisfied that it could be passed on to Francis Moore and me.

I was stunned by the collection.

First, there were the photographs—almost all in black and white, of course. Virtually all of golf's greats were pictured: Jones, Hogan, Nelson, Snead, even Walter Hagen. Some were taken in and around the clubhouse; others out on the course. I recognized one of Francis Ouimet on the 18th green. Some were posed and apparently taken by an experienced photographer, while others were snapshots obviously taken by an amateur (perhaps some of the caddies themselves) with an inexpensive personal camera.

"Where'd you get these?" I asked him.

Moonlight just shrugged. "They were in boxes that were given to me by some a' the guys...Eddie Eumont, mainly. I think Clarence Henderson, Henry Bradford, an' Slats Reinauer gave me some, too." Sensing my slight disappointment at his imprecise account, he said, "Ya' gotta remember, I got all a' this stuff in bits an' pieces over the years. I don't know who decided that I should be the one to keep it all, but somehow I got appointed. Somebody cleans out a garage, they say 'give the stuff to Moonlight.' It starts addin' up."

"Well, it's great stuff," I told him.

On one wall, he had mounted perhaps a dozen or more old scorecards from the course. I walked over to a couple of them and read the signatures. What I saw nearly took my breath away. Pointing to them, I said, "Are these the real McCoy?"

He grunted at me and said sarcastically, "What d'ya think, I forged 'em?"

I felt a little sheepish. "No, of course not. But you've got cards signed by every great golf champion of that time. This stuff is priceless." I started reading through the scorecards like a kid finding a cache of priceless baseball trading cards. "Look, here's one signed by Lord Byron *and* Ben Hogan." Seeing another, I said excitedly, "And here's one signed by The Haig and Bobby Jones!"

Moonlight just laughed. As excited as I was to see the signatures of these historic golf figures on old scorecards, I had forgotten that he had actually *known* these guys.

I looked at one card and whistled. "Look, here's one where Ralph Guldahl shot 67."

Moonlight nodded. "Yeah, Mr. Guldahl could play. Ya' know, he won the U.S. Open two years in a row an' then the Masters the year after that. Back then, he was as good as Mr. Hogan,

Mr. Nelson, Mr. Sarazen, or Mr. Snead. I carried for him twice at the Point. Nice fella."

Moonlight's collection also included napkins and coasters with the distinctive "B P" crest on them. He had even hung up a couple of old flags with "B P" in block letters and the number of the hole printed on both sides.

Down a hall were still more old photographs. These appeared to have been done professionally. They featured scenes of the clubhouse and course and had apparently been taken during the heyday of the place. Even in black and white, the elegance of the small clubhouse shone through, as did the majestic beauty of the property.

I looked over at Moonlight. He had been enjoying himself, sipping on a Rolling Rock and watching me act like a kid in a candy store.

"We need to call Brett Sullivan at Golf House. This will make a terrific exhibition, and we can reproduce these pictures for a *Golf Journal* article." I winked at my friend. "I bet they'll want to take your picture and put it in there, too."

He winced.

"You deserve the recognition," I hastened to assure him. "Besides, they'll have to interview you about how you acquired all this stuff."

Moonlight started to protest, but I waved my hand at him. "Don't give me that. There's no way around it. Look, you wanted me to help you get the story out, and this is part of it. We can't tell the story without you."

I could tell that it still hadn't dawned on Moonlight that his own story was inextricably bound together with the story of Bragg's Point. It would have to be told as well. I started to say as much, but thought better of it. If he was spooked at the thought of explaining how he acquired this stuff, there was not telling how he might react to that. When he gave me a resigned look as if he understood that further protest was futile, I let it go at that. There was plenty of time later to break the rest of it to him gently.

I don't recall how we got on the subject, but at one point we talked about the prospect of the golf course becoming a permanent site for the U.S. Open. Moonlight cackled at the thought of the best golfers in the world vying for our national championship at "the Point," as he often called it. "When the wind starts blowin', especially on all the shoreside holes, you're gonna see some strange goin's on."

I remembered how the scores had ballooned in the '92 Open at Pebble Beach under similar conditions. "If it's anything like it gets at Pebble Beach, it'll be a real test."

Moonlight finished his beer. "Ya' just don't know, lad. We caught the old girl on a good day. Ya' remember that little threat of a cloud ya' got so worked up about? I've seen a few a' those blow through so hard ya' can't do anythin' but grab the grass an' hold on."

He laughed and continued. "You'll see some funny things on the greens. I remember one day, we were on 8, an' Mr. Roberts made his caddie lean against him so he could stay still enough to putt. Mr. Jones let him do it an' then put two strokes on him. Mr. Roberts squealed 'bout it the rest a' the round, but

Mr. Jones stuck by it. Said there was no special exception in the Rules a' Golf, not even for Cliff Roberts."

As we talked more, Moonlight seemed more and more content with the notion of the USGA becoming the steward for Bragg's Point. As he put it, "Now I know it'll always be used in the right way."

I told Moonlight that Francis Moore said he had something to tell us about Bragg's Point that we didn't know. He cocked his head to the side. "Like what?"

"I honestly don't know. He didn't want to tell me anything on the telephone. He said he'd tell us when he's here next week."

Moonlight seemed a little disappointed that a small cloud had appeared on the horizon, especially as we were just now basking in our good fortune. "People usually deliver bad news in person. Ya' don't think he'd turn on us, do ya'?"

It was only a hunch, but I didn't think that was the case. "Now don't start worrying about it, okay? It won't do any good anyway. He didn't say anything about changing his mind, so let's just wait and see what it is."

I spent most of the next week barricaded in the library trying to complete a couple of briefs that unfortunately fell due within two days of each other. One case addressed the law governing an attempt to pierce the corporate veil of a subsidiary owned by a big company we represented. The other concerned the proper remedy for misrepresentations made to a client who sold his business to another corporation in return for stock that turned out to be worthless. Commercial litigation was pretty dry stuff for most people, but it was exciting enough for me. As a result, the time flew by.

Not so for Moonlight, who had nothing to do but obsess about the whole thing. I wasn't taking calls while I was down in the library, so my desk usually contained several messages from him when I returned at the end of the day. Moonlight seemed almost panicky at the thought of anything causing his dream to unravel when we were so close to the end.

When I returned his calls, our conversations mostly consisted of my repeatedly warning him against blowing things out of proportion. This hand-holding usually lasted no more than ten minutes, but it required several sessions over the week before Francis Moore's visit.

The day for our meeting finally arrived. I had come to feel that nothing Francis had to say could possibly be as bad as what I had been through over the past several days.

Our benefactor arrived punctually, and we met in the same conference room as before. I had told him earlier about Moonlight's impressive collection, and he was anxious to hear more about it from the curator himself. I could tell that the last thing Moonlight wanted to do at the moment was talk about his souvenirs, but he politely described everything he had.

Moore eventually sensed our anxiety over his announcement, however, and got to the reason for his visit. Looking at Moonlight, he said, "I guess Charley told you I had something to tell the two of you about Bragg's Point that I was certain you didn't know."

Moonlight looked grim. He appeared to have convinced himself that our friend was bringing bad news.

Moore turned to me and said, "Charley, do you remember when I told you not to comment anymore about Jones 'rolling over in his grave'?"

I nodded.

"Well, it was more than just a matter of good taste." He paused, and it appeared that he was deliberating carefully over what to say next. He then looked at each of us in turn and said evenly, "You see, one of the things that my father did for Bob Jones was to arrange for his secret burial at Bragg's Point."

It took a moment or two for that bit of news to register. Although my mind quickly raced through an endless list of questions, all I could do was stammer, "But, but, uh, I never saw a grave anywhere…" I then looked over at Moonlight, and he was shaking his head in agreement.

Our benefactor smiled patiently. "I knew it would be something of a shock. Most everyone thinks that Mr. Jones is buried here in Atlanta. But the marker here has nothing underneath it. His body is resting in his favorite place on earth, overlooking the Pacific Ocean."

I was still dumbstruck. "But where…"

"Right beyond the 11th green, almost at the edge of the property. In fact, if you had looked, you would have noticed special bulkheading there to make certain there was no erosion."

Moonlight and I sat there and looked at one another, still unable to say much of anything.

Moore continued to smile at our apparent confusion. "I know

it comes as a surprise, but it really makes sense when you think about it. As Moonlight surely knows, Mr. Jones wanted solitude more than anything. He worried about his gravesite becoming a curiosity or, worse still, being desecrated by souvenir seekers. I wouldn't go so far as to call it an obsession, but some of the people who knew him will tell you he had very strong feelings about it."

Our patron got up and walked to the window. Turning back to us, he said, "Let's face it, Bob Jones wouldn't have retired at the age of 28 if he really enjoyed public attention or being in the limelight. The fact is, he didn't. He just wanted to be with his friends at his own club. Unfortunately, you can't do that these days without being 'politically incorrect.'" With a trace of anger in his voice, he added, "You know, people can't just talk about his great golf or his other accomplishments any more. Now they have to criticize him for not single-handedly changing the world that existed back in his day. They can't leave the man alone even when he's been dead for 30 years."

I had finally regained control of my vocal cords. "Who knew about this?"

"His family, of course, my father, who used his medical connections to transport the body there...and Cliff Roberts." He paused. "That was about it."

"The people who take care of the property don't know?"

He shook his head. "Not really. There's a small marker but no real inscription. They know it's a grave and treat it respectfully as such, keeping it from being overgrown. But they don't know that it's where Bob Jones is buried."

Moonlight finally spoke. "Now I understand why ya' stayed so close to the property an' had people take care of it. It wasn't for the golf; it was for Mr. Jones."

Moore was slow to answer. Finally, he said, "Well, yes and no. I have to admit that preserving the grave was most important, but that old course meant a lot, too. It's all part of the same thing, you know?"

Moonlight nodded his understanding and said, "That must've been expensive over the years."

Moore smiled. "Not really. Mr. Roberts paid for it while he was alive, and then he left a lot of money for Dad to use when he died in 1977."

He gave us both a look that indicated he had more to say. With a slight hint of a smile, he said, "That's not all. There's more than one grave out there."

I leaned forward. "What do you mean?"

"Where do you think Cliff Roberts is buried?"

Moonlight exclaimed, "I should've known. No one 'round the club ever knew what happened to Mr. Roberts after he shot himself down at the pond on the par-three course. They said he was cremated, but no one ever saw the ashes."

Moore smiled at Moonlight and said gently, "Well, now you know. He wasn't cremated at all. He was placed to rest next to Jones, just as he requested in the note he left."

"Is the grave marked?" I asked.

He nodded. "Yes, but with nothing more than initials. Just something to let you know that there's a grave there."

So now we knew what Francis Moore had waited to tell us. Bobby Jones and Cliff Roberts were buried at the Point.

Chapter 37

FRANCIS MOORE WAS a decisive man. Now that he had wrested control of the Point from his brother, he wanted to move quickly with a plan to transfer the property to the USGA. But he knew that the USGA wouldn't take on an asset like this without careful study. Besides, the idea of having a permanent site for the national championship was pretty radical.

He also believed that we should all visit the place together. He described it as kind of a brainstorming session on-site. He wanted to talk through his ideas with us before putting together a proposal to submit to the Executive Committee.

When he brought it up in our meeting, I expressed my reluctance at leaving work again so soon. He reminded me, however, that he had the Lear at his disposal and proposed that we fly down on Friday after work and return on Sunday.

Moonlight was immediately apprehensive. "How big is this plane a' yours, Mr. Moore?"

I said quickly, "Moonlight's not real fond of air travel. Our trip to California was his first flight." Chuckling, I added, "I damned near had to sedate him to get him on the plane."

Moore laughed and turned to our frowning friend, who did not appear to enjoy my joke. "Moonlight, we have one of the most modern jets made. It has all the latest equipment, and our pilots are the best." He thought for a moment. "And I don't fly in bad weather. That's one of the advantages of owning a plane. It only leaves when I want it to leave."

Moonlight said nothing more, but he still seemed a little unhappy at the prospect of making another cross-country flight while the unpleasant memory of his first experience was still fresh in his mind. In the end, however, he agreed to leave with us that Friday.

In the meantime, I finally got to talk with my friend Cheatwood. I called him from the office and caught him at work. We had a lot of catching up to do. Because he was a golf history buff, he was especially intrigued by the story of Bragg's Point.

It was fun talking with him about it, because it helped remind me of what a special story it was. And if Cheatwood's reaction was any indication, the story would shake the golf world when it was finally told.

"How on earth did they keep this such a secret?"

I laughed. "You're gonna start asking all of the questions I've been asking Moonlight since we first met. And the answer, when you think about it, is pretty obvious. They kept this secret the same way they've always kept most things about Augusta National secret. People only know about Augusta National what the club wants them to know: the Masters and the golf course. The rest of it's a mystery."

He agreed.

I added, "And remember, they weren't playing a famous tournament every year at the Point. So it wasn't like Augusta. The media never descended on the place or had any reason to write about it."

My friend reminded me that there were a number of ultra-private golf clubs with terrific layouts that were relatively unknown. "Remember what I told you once about Garden City Golf Club?"

I said that I vaguely recalled hearing the name.

"It's a great course out on Long Island, rated in the top 100 all the time. Very old. I played an amateur tournament there during my college days. Hosted several U.S. Amateurs in the early part of the century. But it's one of the best kept secrets of the golf world."

He paused briefly. "If Garden City can be forgotten by the media—which by the way suits its members just fine—I guess it shouldn't seem so strange that places like Bragg's Point can go unnoticed."

After he let his point sink in, he added, "And that's not an isolated example. There are a lot of great courses that virtually no one has ever heard of."

What Cheatwood said certainly made the secrecy surrounding Bragg's Point less difficult to understand. Besides, there was no one in all of golf more respected than Bobby Jones. And as Moonlight has told me more than once, anyone who played the Point was carefully screened beforehand. Simply put, they were the people who wouldn't dream of ruining the great man's last refuge. Besides, as much as the players loved Jones, they feared Cliff Roberts. None of them wanted to jeopardize his annual invitation to Augusta. Frank Stranahan, a great amateur, was banished from Eden for violating Roberts's self-imposed rules about practice rounds. Everyone who played in the Masters understood from the outset that their participation was not a right, but a privilege—and a fragile one at that. It wouldn't have been hard to foresee how violating Jones's confidence about Bragg's Point would have meant immediate and permanent exile from Augusta.

For some reason, I didn't tell my friend about the graves. In retrospect, I suspect that I already had reservations about bringing the U.S. Open to Bobby Jones's gravesite. Whatever the reason, I wanted to be very careful with that last bit of information.

After hearing my description of its physical beauty, Cheatwood asked me a question I knew was coming. "Okay, I can't stand it—when do I get to see the place?"

"I honestly don't know, Ken. But I hope you get to see it soon. You're going to love it; it's one of a kind."

We continued to talk for more than an hour. For one thing, my buddy wanted me to replay my round at Bragg's Point shot by shot. While I could vividly recall all the holes in great detail—not to mention the stories that went with them—I was surprised to find that I didn't remember quite so much about the golf. Cheatwood then asked me a hundred questions about Moonlight, and I was happy to tell him all about him.

I had forgotten how much fun it had been to share the Beau Stedman story with him—and how valuable his instincts and insights had been as we pieced the whole thing together. I knew that my friend would instantly understand and appreciate Moonlight's passion for the game and for what Bragg's Point meant.

The best news from our conversation, though, was that Cheatwood had decided to limit his clerkship to one year (even though he had been offered a second year by the judge) and that he had informed Emile Guidry that he would be starting his career at Butler & Yates the following July. Until then, I hadn't been certain that he was really coming, but now it was official.

I talked with Moonlight again on the evening before we left. I had to reassure him again about the flight. I told him how Lear jets were well-known for their reliability and safety, but I'm not sure he was convinced. It was pretty clear he was going to need a drink or two before getting on the plane.

Just as we were signing off, he said, "Charley, what do ya' make a' the news 'bout the graves?"

I wasn't sure what to say, probably because I still didn't know what to make of it all just yet. "I don't know, my friend. Maybe that's why the place has such a spiritual feel to it, you know?"

"I was thinkin' the same thing. It's like they was walkin' the course with us." Before I could say anything more, he added a short postscript for emphasis. "I just knew there was magic there. An' I told ya' that, didn't I?"

I laughed. "Yeah, Moonlight, you told me. You certainly did." After a fashion, I added, "You also told me that Jones had never left the place. Sounds to me like you may have known about the graves all along."

He was quick to answer. "No, Charley, I swear I didn't. I was talkin' 'bout his spirit, ya' know? I just didn't know how right I was."

Neither of us said anything for a while. Then Moonlight spoke again. "Ya' know, I always had a funny feelin' 'bout that hole. At least now I know why."

After we hung up, I finished packing.

We had agreed to meet Francis Moore at a small FBO at the west end of Hartsfield Airport at four o'clock Friday afternoon. That was early enough to avoid the worst part of the afternoon traffic.

Moonlight was waiting for me when I got there. He was pacing around inside the small lobby and looked very nervous. As I walked up to him, he greeted me with a complaint. "Ya' didn't tell me there wouldn't be a bar here."

"Well," I said, turning my palms up, "it's not like the main terminal." I reached into my pocket and pulled out a small packet. "Here. It's Dramamine, the same stuff I gave you before the last trip. This'll take care of you."

He took it from me, but grumbled that he would have preferred to chase it with Scotch rather than the soft drinks that were sitting on the table against the wall. I explained to him that most of the people who frequented the FBO were pilots of private aircraft and that, thank goodness, most of them didn't drink and drive.

He looked at me sharply and said, "Whaddya mean, *most* of 'em?"

I was getting exasperated. "For Chrissake, Moonlight, calm down, will you? It was a joke, okay? These pilots are very serious about what they do. They do not, I repeat, do not drink before flying *anywhere*. They'd lose their license if they did, and they'd never get another job flying a plane."

At that point, I was rescued from any further participation in our ludicrous debate by the arrival of Francis Moore.

Smiling as he approached us, he said, "You guys all set?"

I grinned back at him. "One of us is."

He looked over at my forlorn friend and said, " Moonlight, you're not still worried about the flight, are you?"

Before Moonlight could start over again about the dangers of air flight, I interceded to spare Moore his diatribe. "I think he was hoping to have a drink before we took off to calm his nerves, and he's a little upset that there's no bar."

Moore turned again to the diminutive Scotsman. "Not to worry, Moonlight. We have a well-stocked bar on the plane. Believe me, you'll enjoy the flight—one way or the other."

He looked at his watch. "The flight plan we filed calls for us to leave in about ten minutes. You guys got your bags?"

I pointed over to a corner. He said, "Great. I've already given mine to one of the pilots. Grab yours and come with me."

We walked outside on the tarmac and saw the plane for the first time. It was a beauty and looked brand new. I whistled in appreciation. Francis turned to me and said, "Glad you like it.

We've had it for almost a year now. It'll spoil you real quick. With all the meetings I have to go to, I don't know what I'd do without it."

It was as plush inside as it was pretty outside. As we walked on, Moore introduced us to his chief pilot, David Boyer, and his co-pilot, Ed Gallaugher. It was comical to watch Moonlight look them over. I half expected him to try to smell their breath. They apparently passed inspection, however, because he continued on board and sat down next to me.

The plane had eight seats arranged in a way that allowed generous space for the passengers. Toward the rear was a table for eating, working, or playing cards. On the back wall was a refrigerator and bar.

Pointing to the back, Francis said to Moonlight, "There's everything you need back there. If you're hungry, we've even got some sandwiches in the fridge."

Moonlight wasn't looking for a meal. He opened the bar, pulled out a bottle of 15-year-old Macallan single-malt scotch, and poured himself three fingers' worth, "neat." Then he quickly slammed it against the back of his throat.

I looked at him. "I thought the Scots believed in savoring their favorite drink."

He gave me an almost scornful expression. "Most Scots are too smart to get on one a' these contraptions."

He quickly poured himself another drink, but took a little more time with this one. By that time, the pilots had completed their preflight checklist. Gallaugher turned back to us and said, "Everybody buckled in? We're ready to go."

We settled in as the plane began to taxi down the runway. The Lear was true to its reputation as a powerful and smooth-flying aircraft. The takeoff was hardly noticeable, and Moonlight was asleep within ten minutes of finishing his second drink.

That left Francis and me to talk. The conversation was as pleasant as the flight. He wanted to know how I got involved in the Stedman story and how it was connected to my joint venture with Moonlight. He also seemed genuinely interested in my career in law, as well as my golf game. After I had satisfied his curiosity, I said turnabout was fair play and asked him to tell me about himself.

Francis was apparently comfortable with himself. He explained in an easy manner how he had grown up as a child of privilege, with a father who was a successful physician, and that he was taught early in his life to appreciate his good fortune. It had made an impression on him, as had most of the lessons his parents tried to teach their sons.

In particular, he talked about one piece of advice his father gave him that he had never forgotten. "He said that a father should have a reputation his children will want to live up to…not one they'll have to live down." It was an interesting comment that made me think of my own father, who always believed he could teach me more by example than by sermonizing.

Francis became sad as he explained that, for some reason he never really understood, his brother reacted very differently to the same upbringing. He didn't know why, but Stephen Moore, who was two years younger, never seemed to have enough.

Looking down, Francis said sadly that he sometimes felt his brother entered medicine only because he thought it might give him an advantage over his sibling in attaining his father's favor. "A rather curious reason to pursue a career, don't you think?" he asked rhetorically.

Francis fell in love with golf at a young age and was inspired by Bobby Jones, who was a friend of the family and someone his father openly admired. He still remembered when his father was invited to join Augusta and how he wanted to play the course with him.

But his father had refused to bring him to Augusta at the time, telling him that he was too young to play the course. He told Francis he would have to wait until he was two years older, but the young boy negotiated a different deal that foreshadowed his later business success: would his father take him to Augusta when he was able to break 90 at East Lake three times in a row?

Francis laughed as he told the story. "At the time, I hadn't *ever* broken 90. Hell, I was all of 11 years old. Dad must have thought that was the safest bet he ever made."

"How long did it take you?"

He took a sip of the bourbon he had poured earlier. "I started practicing every day after school. I'd hit balls, chip and putt, and then play a few holes after the members were finished until it was too dark to see. On weekends, I'd stay out there all day. I shot an 89 within three months. When I brought him the scorecard, he said it didn't count because I had played part of the round alone. He said the score wasn't 'attested.'"

I chuckled at the thought of his father squirming over his son's rapid improvement. "So he pulled the old rulebook on you, huh?"

"Yeah, and it made quite an impression. I made him show me the rule. I remember it to this day. Then I asked him to give me a rulebook of my own, and I started reading it at night. I wasn't going to be trapped again."

He took another sip and continued. "Anyway, I was gettin' real confident, even cocky. You know, the way only a kid who doesn't know any better can get. I was convinced that I'd never shoot more'n 89 again. And damned if I didn't start gettin' better and better."

He looked out of the window briefly and turned back to me. "It just goes to show you what a mental game golf is. I *believed* I was good, so I *was* good. My next two rounds, with a couple of friends as witnesses, were 86 and 88. I showed my father the cards, all properly signed."

He laughed again at the pleasure of recalling his favorite childhood memory. "Anyway, he says to me, 'Those boys are liable to sign anything. I'll accept these scores, but you're gonna play the third round with me.' So he dropped out of his regular Saturday game that week, and we went off the first tee late in the afternoon after all the members had teed off."

I was leaning forward in my seat, like a child listening to a favorite bedtime story.

He continued. "Well, it unnerved me a little. It was my first real exposure to pressure on the golf course. I could play in front of my friends, but under the stern eye of my father, well, that was another thing. I made a double bogey on the first hole, a wobbly bogey on the second, another double on the third, and a triple on the fourth. I was hittin' it sideways, and I was so upset that I started to cry. So then my Dad said, 'That's okay, Francis, there's always tomorrow.' He was writing off the round, already assuming from my lack of composure that I didn't have a snowball's chance in hell of breaking 90."

He raised his glass again and took another drink.

"Well, for some reason, that really burned me up. I got mad; so mad, in fact, that I wasn't nervous anymore. I hit every shot with a determination that I had never had before. You know how they talk about Arnold Palmer just *willin'* the ball into the hole when he was in his prime? That's kinda the way it went the rest of the day. I started attacking the ball, and I parred the next three holes, made a bogey, and then parred four more. And the whole time, I wasn't talkin' to my Dad. 'Course, he'd laugh, and that would make me mad all over again. I made a stupid double bogey at the 13th hole when I hit it into a hazard and then parred 14 and 15 before making a bogey at 16. Then I made another bogey at the 17th when my ball landed in a divot."

He looked at me and suddenly seemed embarrassed. "I hope I'm not borin' you with this. You know, I can't remember much about my career best round—I once shot 68 at Augusta —but I can still remember every detail of that round with my Dad."

I assured him that I wasn't bored and wanted him to finish. The truth was, I couldn't wait to find out how it ended.

"We're on the 18th tee. I still hadn't spoken to my Dad. I guess he figured I had it made, so he tried to break the ice and make sure we walked off the course on friendly terms. 'Well, Francis,' he said, 'you can make a quadruple bogey on this last hole and still break 90. I don't think there's *any* way you can fail now, is there?' Now, here I am, an 11-year-old, and I think he's trash-talking with me—only they didn't call it that back then. Well, it disarmed me. I don't know why, but I stopped being mad. I got nervous again, and I topped my drive. It went all of 50 yards. Then I topped my 3-wood, another 50 yards. Now I'm getting into a panic, and my backswing is so fast you can't see it. It's the kind of self-inflicted disaster that can only happen on a golf course. I top my 3-wood again, another 50 yards or so."

Francis finished his drink and looked at me. He could tell I was hanging on his every word.

"I looked at the green, and it was still 200 yards away. Hell, it seemed like 200 *miles*. I had to squint to see it in the setting sun. I looked over at my Dad, and his face showed the pain. He really *didn't* think there was any way I could fail, but the way I was goin', it looked like I might not even finish the hole. I know now that he would've given anything at that moment to take back what he had said, but he couldn't, of course. He looked at me and said, 'Why don't you try another club?' I'm too stubborn even to consider such a thing, so I said, 'No, I'm gonna hit this damned thing if it kills me.' I'd never before uttered a single cuss word in front of my Dad. In fact, I don't even know where the word came from at the time.

He didn't say a word. So I hit the 3-wood again. Another cold top, about another 50 yards."

Francis was starting to enjoy my eagerness at hearing his story. He decided to drag it out a little for dramatic effect by getting up and pouring another glass of bourbon. I thought about telling him he was describing what Cheatwood called "pulling a Van de Velde," but said nothing.

As he stood at the bar in the back of the plane, he continued. "Now I'm lyin' four with about a 150 yards to the green. And I'm still tryin' to hit that damned 3-wood. I get up to my ball, and I take another big swing and, thank God, I connect on this one. The ball ends up in the back fringe of the green."

He smiled at the memory of the shot.

"Now I'm five. All I have to do is 3-putt. I'm about 30 feet away, so it's no cinch, not the way I was unraveling. But I gave it a rap, and it's on line. If I hadn't hit it so hard, it might've gone in. As it was, it hit the hole, popped up in the air and stopped four feet away."

He paused, forcing me to ask, "So, what happened?"

He looked at me hard, almost as if he was angry that I had asked. Then he broke into a big grin and said, "I made it for an 88."

We both laughed, he in glorious recollection of a wonderful day and I in relief at the story's happy ending.

Finally, I looked at him and said, "So the 3-wood came through for you on that last shot."

He grunted sarcastically. "Hell, the first thing I did when I got home was throw that damned thing away."

We both laughed again. Francis looked at his now-empty glass and said, "There's something about bourbon that has the worst effect on my language. I got kinda carried away tellin' that old story, didn't I?"

"No, not at all," I assured him. "I enjoyed every second of it—and it wouldn't have been as good without the punctuation you gave it."

He laughed appreciatively. "Anyway," he said, "that's how I was able to play Augusta before my 12th birthday."

Chapter 38

FRANCIS MOORE HAD taken care of everything for the entire trip. Our hotel accommodations were at a place called the Andover Inn. It was a small hotel, with not more than 30 rooms or so, which sat atop a high bluff overlooking the Pacific Ocean. The view, of course, was spectacular. From what we could figure, we weren't more than ten miles from the Point.

As we checked in, Moore said, "This place was recommended by a friend of mine. He told me it's owned by a couple who retired and bought the property several years ago." Looking around, he said, "From what I can see, it's everything he said it would be."

I didn't know what Moore had been told, but it was certainly a nice place—definitely a cut or two above our previous lodgings. I glanced over at Moonlight, and he was rubbernecking the place with a look that told me he hadn't stayed in many places like this, either.

After we settled into our rooms, our patron summoned us to the lobby for dinner. I had a feeling that, as long as we were in Francis Moore's company, we were also going to eat better than we were accustomed to.

He took the wheel of our rented Cadillac (again, his treat) and drove 30 minutes or so to the south, toward Santa Rosa. We eventually arrived at a white stone manor with a small sign that read "Maisie's."

Although dress was casual, the place had a somewhat formal atmosphere. It was quieter inside than the diners that Moonlight and I had frequented—another reminder that Francis Moore traveled in a different class from us. The lights were low, and the main source of illumination at the tables was candlelight. As we were ushered to our table, Moore told us that the place was particularly noted for its seafood, especially its lobster. I saw Moonlight wrinkle his nose slightly; he rarely ate anything but red meat.

After we were seated, we were asked for our drink orders. Francis requested a wine list. As the waiter handed it to him, Moonlight said, "I'll just have a Rolling…"

Before he could say more, I suggested we try whatever wine Francis recommended. Moonlight gave me a look of disappointment, but I suspected that our host was just as expert in wine selection as he seemed to be in most other things.

And I turned out to be right. He ordered a white wine from Sonoma County with a name I didn't recognize (hardly a surprise there) that was light and deliciously dry. Even Moonlight grudgingly admitted that it was good. I felt a small measure of satisfaction in having exposed my friend to something new and different. While teaching Moonlight about wine wasn't exactly a fair trade for what he had taught me, it was a start. When it came time to order our food, however, Moonlight was through with his adventurous ways for the night. He insisted on a rib eye despite several subtle suggestions by our waiter about the salmon.

I could tell that Francis Moore was quite comfortable in these surroundings. He never looked at the menu, preferring instead to ask the waiter for his recommendations. He ultimately chose prawns in a wine and butter sauce. I had the salmon, which came in a light barbecue and horseradish sauce that was misrepresented to be "Cajun style."

As we began to talk about our impending visit to the Point, Francis asked if we had any thoughts about what the USGA should do with the burial sites when it took over the property. "The first thing we have to decide," he said, "is whether we should reveal who's buried there."

I told him that I didn't know how we could expect it to remain a secret.

He pursed his lips. "I guess you're right. We've got to let the USGA know that there are two graves on the property. I can't withhold that information from the Executive Committee if I'm going to propose that they take title to the property. The obvious question they will ask is who's buried there. We'll have to tell them, and the USGA won't be in a position to keep that a secret, at least not for long."

I ventured a suggestion that perhaps we could just say that two unknown caddies were buried there and leave it at that.

Francis shook his head. "What if someone learns the truth?

Can you imagine the stink? There's no way we can justify lying about it. It would ruin the USGA's credibility."

In that event, it seemed to me that we would have to secure the area where the graves were located. "Well, we can't just leave the graves as they are now. Once people find out who's buried there, we'll run into all kinds of problems. There are crazy people everywhere, but California has always had more than its share. There'll have to be a fence and some kind of decent security."

Moore seemed confident that the property could be secured. "There's really only one way in or out. The fence around the property can be reinforced. And we'll put another fence around the grave sites. That's a small expense compared to the value of what the USGA will be getting. We can make that a condition of the donation."

I noticed that Moonlight hadn't said anything. I looked over at him and could see a hint of trouble in his otherwise impassive demeanor. I suspected that he was harboring feelings about this that he preferred not to share at the moment, so I didn't press him about it. Francis didn't know Moonlight as well and apparently took his silence to indicate agreement with what he was saying. I suspected otherwise but said nothing.

We entertained ourselves for the remainder of the evening by talking about how the course might defend itself against the world's greatest players if it became the site of the U.S. Open. The first question was whether the course had the length necessary to test players under today's conditions. Thanks to improved physical conditioning and rocket-science equipment, players routinely drove the ball over 300 yards and hit wedges into greens where Jones and company hit 5-irons. Thus, Francis wondered aloud whether the Point was long enough at present to be an Open site or perhaps required changes to make it more suitable for our national championship.

I reminded my table mates that Merion was considered a fair Open test as late as 1981, and it was only 6,500 yards. Moreover, I thought the great virtue of the Point as a test of golf was its demand for accuracy under difficult shoreside conditions. It was a course that didn't have to be long in order to expose the weaknesses in a player's game. That, it seemed to me, was just the thing that the USGA sought in its Open venues as the best way to identify our national champion.

We talked about the dramatic Opens at Pebble Beach and how the Point would provide much the same examination of golfing skills. Francis agreed that the most demanding holes at Pebble Beach under Open conditions weren't the lengthy holes but the ones that were open to the shifting winds that whipped up and down the California coast. Those conditions were duplicated, I said, at the Point.

Francis finally noticed that Moonlight had been quiet. He turned to him and said, "Moonlight, you're the expert on all this. What do you think?"

The old man stared at his wine glass for the longest time. Finally, he looked up at the new custodian of Bragg's Point and said quietly, "It was the most wonderful place for golf I'd ever known. An' I wanted to make certain that it wasn't lost forever. That's why I contacted Charley here. But I didn't know Mr. Jones was restin' there…" His voice trailed off. We waited for him to say more, but he didn't look up again.

I could tell that he had said something Moore didn't want to hear. He quickly tried to assure Moonlight that he felt Jones's grave would be well fortified and that the world's greatest player would continue to rest in peace. "Besides," he said, "I've got a feeling that Mr. Jones would be delighted to see others enjoy his favorite place."

Moonlight only shrugged his shoulders.

After an awkward moment, I tried to change the mood by talking about the holes that I thought would give today's top players the most trouble if the Open were contested at the Point. Francis had his own ideas about that, and we had a lively discussion about how Tiger Woods, David Duval, Ernie Els, or Vijay Singh might play this hole or that. We debated about whether Justin Leonard, Lee Janzen, or Mark O'Meara might have an advantage there over the longer hitters because of their control of the ball. Francis even speculated about whether the Executive Committee might award special exemptions to Arnold Palmer and Jack Nicklaus into the first Open played at the Point so that they could return to the scene of their first head-to-head match.

It was delicious, every bit of it, kind of like a fantasy tour. We continued to play our version of "Let's Pretend" on the ride home. At one point Moonlight's mood seemed to brighten, and he even interjected a thought or two about the best way to play certain holes.

When we reached the hotel, we said our goodnights and agreed to meet for breakfast the next morning. My room had a small balcony, and I opened the glass door leading out on it. The sound of the surf crashing below combined with the smell of the sea air immediately reminded me of what it felt like to be at the Point.

I pulled a chair from the room out onto the balcony and intended to sit for awhile and watch the shaft of white light that was cast by the moon's reflection upon the ocean, which was otherwise black because of the night. I had just sat down when I heard a knock at my door.

It was Moonlight.

"What a coincidence," I joked. "I was just getting ready to enjoy the very thing you were named after."

He gave me a curious look. I pointed outside, and he caught on. "Oh."

"You want to join me?" I could tell that he had something on his mind.

"Yeah, if ya' don't mind." He seemed a little uncertain of himself and added, almost apologetically, "I won't be long."

I stepped back and held the door open. "Nah, come on in. It's not every day we can sit and listen to the ocean pounding on the beach."

I grabbed the remaining chair in the room and set it beside mine on the balcony. Moonlight sat down uneasily.

He didn't take long to get to the point. "I feel kinda funny tellin' ya' this. Ya' know, I got ya' involved an' all. But I trust ya', an' I know ya' got a good heart."

He stopped and looked as if he were deciding whether to say more. I encouraged him by saying, "Moonlight, I trust you, too. So if you've got something on your mind…"

He nodded, indicating that he was going to continue.

"When this started, I felt pretty sure 'bout things. Some of us had talked a few years ago. We wanted the world to know 'bout this place. Ya' know, it just didn't seem right to let it die without tellin' the story." He was watching me, gauging my reaction.

"Anyway, then the story a' Beau Stedman came out. We thought we knew what to do, an' that was to give the story to you."

I bowed my head slightly to acknowledge the compliment he was paying me.

"We didn't think we would be doin' it so soon, but when I was the last one left, I knew it was time."

"And that's when you sent me the notes," I said gratuitously.

"Right. Well, I've been so sure 'bout this thing for so long. But now…" His voice trailed off again.

I thought I knew what he was trying to say. "It's about the graves, isn't it?"

He nodded his head quickly. "Yeah. It's been botherin' me. I had no idea that I'd be disturbin' Mr. Jones's final restin' place. I don't want to be doin' nothin' disrespectful, ya' know what I mean?"

I was touched by his sensitivity and gentle spirit. "Yeah, Moonlight, I think I do know what you mean. And I wouldn't want to do anything disrespectful, either."

I paused and looked at him closely. "But, tell me, why do you think bringing out the story of Bragg's Point will be disrespectful to Jones's grave? You heard Mr. Moore say they could provide security."

He pushed his lips out and frowned, in a thoughtful rather than dramatic way. Then he said slowly, "It's kinda hard to describe. I just don't think Mr. Jones would like it. Ya' know, people'll start makin'—whaddya' call 'em?—ya' know, where people have to visit someplace?"

"Pilgrimages?" I interjected.

"Yeah. Pilgrimages. Mr. Jones came to Bragg's Point just to get away from that kind a' thing. People'll start comin' to the Point just to see his grave. An' Mr. Roberts's, too."

I told Moonlight that I didn't see Jones's grave being treated like a snake farm along the side of the road, with a carload of gum-chewing, camera-toting tourists in Hawaiian shirts unloading every few minutes so that Junior could pose in front of the tombstone. To the contrary, I said, what I expected was that only Jones's genuine admirers would come to Bragg's Point and, when they did, they would find the perfect place to pay their respects to the great man.

He didn't seem convinced. After awhile, he just stopped talking and sat there staring out at the ocean. I decided that this was no time to make a closing argument on the subject and instead let him think it through on his own.

Not long thereafter, Moonlight stood up and bade me good night. I told him I'd see him at breakfast and let him out.

I had trouble sleeping after his visit. Moonlight had given me an awful lot to think about.

Chapter 39

THE ANDOVER INN did not provide room service, so all meals had to be taken in the dining room. It was a small inconvenience, however; the room had a number of large windows providing an ample view of the hotel's principal attraction.

Unfortunately, there was a generous amount of fog shrouding the place when we came down the next morning for breakfast. In fact, when I looked outside just as I was leaving my room, I could barely see the property's edge, much less the ocean.

Francis was waiting for us in the dining room and had already secured a nice table next to one of the windows. He was deep into the morning newspaper by the time Moonlight and I appeared and was pouring himself what appeared to be his second or third cup of coffee.

His face brightened when he saw us. "Ah, good morning. I hope you two slept as well as I did. Must be something in the air here."

I just smiled and commented that Moonlight had been up for his customary "mornin' constitutional" since 5:00 A.M. despite the fog.

Francis pointed at our server and said, "They tell me it's often like this around this time of year. But it's supposed to burn off before too long."

Moonlight nodded in agreement. "We used to see this all the time."

While Francis stuck with coffee and a Danish, I ordered a California-style omelet and Moonlight had his usual fare of eggs, hash browns, toast, and bacon. Although all three of us talked excitedly about seeing the Point again, no one broached the subject of the gravesites.

We took our time eating breakfast, and, as a result, the fog had dissipated considerably when it came time to leave. The ride out was quiet. Each of us had drifted into our own reverie. Francis was no doubt still fantasizing about what a U.S. Open would be like at the Point. I figured Moonlight was continuing to wrestle with his self-imposed moral dilemma of destroying Jones's postmortem privacy. And I was wondering if there was some way to accommodate them both.

When we arrived at the security gate, Francis produced a badge of some kind, and we were waved through. The Cadillac was larger than the car we had rented on our previous trip, making passage down the road leading onto the property more difficult. I wondered why Francis had never had the path trimmed back by his caretakers.

He shook his head and asked rhetorically, "Wouldn't that make the road look more inviting to the curious?"

I had to agree. By leaving the road barely passable, it suggested that there was nothing at its end of any use to anyone.

"Besides," he added, "with so little traffic, it would've grown back soon anyway."

We passed through the gate and drove around to the clubhouse. As soon as we got out of the car, I noticed the crispness of the air. Although I had worn a sweater, I shivered as a waft of moisture-laden sea air penetrated its meager protection.

Before anyone could say anything, Moonlight asked Francis to show him the gravesites. Francis didn't seem surprised at his request and gestured for us to follow him as he began to walk toward the sea.

We crossed the eighth tee and then turned down the 18th fairway, working back toward the tee. When we reached it, we continued past it and walked toward the cliff's edge around to the 11th green. According to what Moore had told us, Jones and Roberts were buried just on the other side of the 11th green.

The land here sloped down toward the ocean, and as we got closer the white noise of the surf grew progressively louder and more insistent. I wondered whether it was a warning of some kind.

We walked across the 11th green. At that point, the land began to rise again here to a bluff above the ocean. There was only a small stretch of land beyond the green, perhaps a half acre or so. I immediately saw why Francis Moore's father had chosen this spot to put Jones and then Roberts to rest.

This summit was perhaps the most majestic point along the boundary of the property at the water's edge and offered the most striking of all of the spectacular views at Bragg's

Point. There was an outcropping of rocks beneath us that had been polished smooth in places from the steady pounding of the surf. The water would crash against the crags and then withdraw, leaving a white foam swirling in its wake before renewing its assault with another resounding collision.

There was an amazing peace about the place in the midst of the fury being generated below. Perhaps it was a recognition by the human spirit inside us of how powerless we were in the face of nature's might. Maybe there was an inner voice telling us that resistance against a force of this magnitude was futile.

Francis walked ahead of us and stopped. He pointed to the ground and said, "Here they are."

We looked down. There were two small bronze plates in the ground. One read, "R.T.J." and "RIP"; the other read "C.d.R." and "RIP."

None of us said anything for the longest time. The three of us just stood there, pants flapping as the wind whipped us with the salty mist of the Pacific Ocean.

I hunched my shoulders and turned my back as if to protect myself from the cold air, but it appeared to shift and come from different directions no matter which way I turned. I shivered audibly, and the sound seemed to break the spell that had gotten hold of us. Francis looked up and said sympathetically, "I don't ever remember it feeling quite this raw out here."

Moonlight nodded solemnly. "I believe the elements are talkin' to us."

Francis Moore gave him a curious look. "What do you think they're saying, Moonlight?"

Moonlight fixed his eyes directly on our benefactor and said, "They're tellin' us the place is sacred."

Francis laughed, and Moonlight's reaction immediately told him it was a mistake. He rushed to apologize. "I'm sorry, Moonlight. I didn't mean to make light of what you said."

Moonlight appeared to be more sad than angry. "That's okay, Mr. Moore. I don't expect ya' to have the feelin's 'bout this place that I do." With that he turned and began walking back toward the clubhouse.

Moore looked at me. "I'm sorry. The last thing I wanted was to offend Moonlight."

I took it as an opening to share our reservations about opening Bragg's Point to the world. "I think everything changed for him when he learned that Jones and Roberts were buried here. Moonlight thought long and hard about revealing the story before, mainly because this was Jones's last place of refuge. And he decided, after a lot of soul-searching, that it was a story that shouldn't be lost forever. Too many great players came through here, and the golf was really special."

We started walking together, following the path Moonlight had taken. He was a hundred yards or so ahead of us. I noticed that it suddenly felt warmer.

Moonlight wasn't likely to say much more about how he felt, so I felt I had to speak on his behalf. "Moonlight takes this as a sign that it's wrong to do this. You know, he's been pretty insistent about what he calls the 'magic' of this place. And he believes that Jones brought the magic here."

I watched Moore closely for a reaction, but he said nothing.

After we walked a bit more, I said, "Moonlight believed in Jones and everything he stood for. Jones gave Moonlight his identity and treated him as a member of this club, on equal footing with everyone who came here. Heck, he even allowed him to live here."

I could tell by his silence that Francis was carefully considering everything I was saying. We continued to walk back toward the clubhouse and watched Moonlight cross the eighth tee and sit down on the porch of the clubhouse.

Finally, he spoke in a soft and thoughtful tone. "If we open this place up, Moonlight will feel that he's betrayed Jones, won't he?"

I nodded and said slowly, "Yes, he will."

Francis looked up at the clubhouse and saw Moonlight sitting on the edge of the porch with his head drooping down. He was quiet as we walked a few more steps and then said in a sensitive and sad voice, "I can understand that."

Chapter 40

DINNER THAT EVENING was quiet and subdued, as each of us sorted through a wide range of emotions.

In a way, our feelings about the Point were not altogether different. All three of us loved the place and embraced what it stood for. We might not have called it "magic," as Moonlight had, but the difference was more semantics than anything else.

Part of it was perhaps nostalgia. Bragg's Point symbolized the romantic past that we had convinced ourselves was more noble and less complicated. Historians have repeatedly tried to debunk the myth of the "good old days," reminding us that life has never been better than it is now. But human beings believe what they want to believe, and they want to remember the past as something grander and more glorious than it perhaps was.

There was more than nostalgia at work here, however. Bragg's Point was a monument to the greatest golfer who had ever lived, a place created by people who loved him, just so he could have peace. And the fact that it remained hidden away from the public for all these years was testimony that men of the past and present could maintain a code of honor based on nothing more than their respect for that man.

There were plenty of other reasons to celebrate Bragg's Point in a public way. The place had incredible physical beauty, easily on a par with Pebble Beach and Cypress Point. It would be a fantastic test of golf, one that was unquestionably worthy of the U.S. Open.

Too, transferring the Point to the USGA and making it the permanent site for the Open would give its owner total control of playing conditions. Under the present system, tension inevitably resulted as the USGA essentially took over a host club for several years leading up to the championship. During that time, the organization dictated everything from course design to agronomic practices. Every change was supposedly "negotiated," but it was always clear who had the final say, and the process took its toll on both sides. As a result, most insiders said that the host club and Golf House were usually glad to be rid of each other by the end of the event. That would no longer be the case, at least for the Open, if the USGA had its own site.

The weather in northern California was a real plus, too. The Open is traditionally held during the third week in June. Most of the country is uncomfortably warm at that time of year, but it's sweater weather on the northern California coast all year round. And unlike the early part of the year, what little rain occurs there during the summer months is rarely severe enough to warrant any halt in play.

There was only one negative to weigh against all those

positives, but it was a big one. The fact that Bobby Jones was secretly buried there and that it was done at his request to escape the public attention that dogged him during his lifetime was a ponderous consideration.

As a result, we kept dinner conversation on the light side. Francis engaged Moonlight with questions about his days at the National, and the two shared stories about various characters, both members and caddies, who had been a part of the place in years past. Moonlight's mood grew a little brighter as he shared his memories, and we had a pleasant meal.

We had agreed to leave for the airport right after breakfast the next morning. By all indications, Francis was moving forward with his plans. He had apparently persuaded himself that the course could be reopened while maintaining proper regard for Jones's and Roberts's graves. I took the fact that he hadn't discussed it anymore at dinner to mean that the issue was settled as far as he was concerned.

I felt squarely in the middle. The Point was a remarkable property, and it was painful to think of it wasting away instead of once again becoming a gathering place for golf's greatest players. I found it easy to rationalize that making the place a grand and glorious venue for the most important championship in golf was something that Jones would have wanted.

At the same time, I didn't know Jones personally. Moonlight did. And he knew firsthand Jones's need for seclusion. To him, that was what Bragg's Point stood for, more than anything else. It was Jones's place of repose, first in retirement and then in death. Disturbing it now, when Jones and Roberts (not to mention Dr. Harvie Moore) were powerless to defend it, was in Moonlight's view an act of betrayal.

Was Moonlight overreacting? That was a question I asked myself as we headed down to breakfast that Sunday morning.

Francis had beaten us there again, demonstrating that he was an early riser by habit. I was, as usual, the slacker in the group; Moonlight had to bang on my door to rouse me when he returned from his early morning walk.

There was no fog this time, and the beautiful vista of the ocean in the early morning sun elevated our mood as we gathered at our table. Our friend put down his newspaper and greeted us warmly. As the waitress poured coffee for us, he said, "I thought we'd make one last trip out to the course before we leave." He added pleasantly, "One of the luxuries of having our own transportation is that it makes our schedule very flexible."

Moonlight and I looked at each other. We hadn't anticipated going out to the property again. It was a pleasant surprise, however; neither of us would ever pass up an opportunity to walk the hallowed grounds at the Point.

After breakfast, we checked out of the inn and piled into the Cadillac for the ride to the lost course. If Francis had a specific purpose in mind for this surprise inspection, he wasn't letting on, at least not right away.

When we got to the security gate, Moore flashed his credentials again, and we were waved through. When we arrived at the locked gate at the narrow path to the clubhouse, Moonlight got out, unlocked it, and swung it open for us to pass.

After we got out of the car at the clubhouse, Francis gestured for us to follow him. He stopped in front of the porch overlooking the wonderful course and surveyed the land falling away from us to the ocean.

"I've been thinking about all of this. A lot." He made a sweeping gesture with his right arm as if presenting the property to us. "You know, I've been dreaming of the day we would be standing on the first tee over there as they announced the players teeing off at the Open championship. The idea of the world's greatest players walking these fairways…" He turned to Moonlight. "Maybe I've had the wrong priorities, believing that we can relive past glory. I understand now that there's a difference between recapturing the past and violating it."

Moonlight and I looked at each other. He had tears in his eyes. Francis laid his hand on Moonlight's shoulder and said, "There's enough money in the trust to maintain this place just like it is. If it's alright with you, let's leave things the way they are."

I was stunned and quickly looked back to Moonlight. He put his head down for a moment, shuddered, and turned away. It was clear that he was overcome. I reached over and put my arm around him. He remained still for a moment and, after collecting himself, turned back to face us.

"Mr. Moore," he said, as a single line of tears stained each of his cheeks, "that's more than alright with me." He took a deep breath. "God bless you."

We took one last walk down to the bluff where Jones was resting. As we reached the gravesites, the blustering wind suddenly relaxed. The three of us stood there quietly for a time, each occupied with his own thoughts in the peaceful setting. After paying our respects, Francis and I turned almost on cue and began to walk back up the hill to the clubhouse.

Moonlight stayed behind. Before we were out of earshot, I heard him say softly, "It'll be alright, now, Mr. Jones."

BRAGG'S POINT
GOLF LINKS

Designed by Perry Maxwell

HOLE	LENGTH		HOLE	LENGTH
1	471		10	379
2	381		11	147
3	174		12	421
4	404		13	354
5	417		14	571
6	519		15	413
7	131		16	201
8	486		17	497
9	447		18	354
OUT	3,430		OUT	3,337
			TOT	6,767

Enjoy reading

The Greatest Player Who Never Lived

also by J. Michael Veron